Te

MW01173910

Edeana Malcolm's *Tea at the Empress* is a delight. The character of Edith positively sparkles on the page — a young woman living a life of excitement at a time when women were only beginning to access hard-won human rights. It is this exploration that makes the book so timely and needed today as those rights are threatened anew in North America. While Edith's story provides plenty of humour, nostalgia and entertainment, it also serves as an important call to action for this and future generations. A necessary book for a complex world.

Carleigh Baker, author of Bad Endings,
winner of the City of Vancouver Book Award

Using real headlines from the *Daily Colonist* to suggest shifts in time, Edeana Malcolm recreates 1920s Victoria, BC through the experiences of Edith, a late-twenties young woman who is the family rebel in more ways than is immediately clear. Tensions are high at family dinners as her siblings' growing children disrupt the order her mother craves, and Edith's past enters the family home. Just as Iona Wishart's Lane Winslow Mysteries transport Nelson, BC back to the 1940s, Malcolm shifts Victoria, BC back in time through familiar locations, local events and Edith's rich and complex past. It's delightful to follow Edith on her many missteps.

Yvonne Blomer, author of The Last Show on Earth,
Victoria Poet Laureate (2015–2018)

How do you deal with painfully wrong choices forced on you? With people making decisions for you that should not have been theirs to make? A society structured to allow that to happen? How do you endure a lifetime with the shattering consequences of sexism? A heartfelt novel of healing long sadness, Edeana Malcolm's *Tea at the Empress* examines the hidden suffering in the real costs of inequity through the life of a young woman in Victoria, Canada through World War I, Spanish influenza and the twenties. In a youthful voice that engages readers, Malcolm's rhythms and mystery draw us in. Independent Edith is immediately appealing as she dons her flashy flapper dress, checking out how the "fringes shimmered and shimmied — the perfect dress to wear to a family dinner to which I hadn't been invited." Edith is a loveable narrator through and through, the grief of her stolen autonomy appeased only with her conviction that love is the truest part of ourselves, that it was never wrong to love, only painful to lose relationships and people, to have choice stolen by war myths and social norms. *Tea at the Empress* is a thought-provoking story about the gendered economic oppression endured by a suffragette, the hidden losses behind the flashy garments and dreams of fairness.

Cynthia Sharp, author of *Rainforest in Russet*

TEA at the EMPRESS

TEA at the EMPRESS

Edeana Malcolm

THREE OCEAN PRESS

Copyright © 2022 by Edeana Malcolm

All rights reserved. No part of this publication may be reproduced, stored in a retrieval system, or transmitted, in any form or by any means, electronic, mechanical, photocopying, recording, or otherwise, without prior written permission of the publisher.

All characters in this book are fictional. Any resemblance to persons living or dead is purely coincidental.

Library and Archives Canada Cataloguing in Publication
Title: Tea at the Empress / Edeana Malcolm.
Names: Malcolm, Edeana, 1951- author.
Identifiers: Canadiana (print) 20220401233 | Canadiana (ebook) 20220401276 | ISBN 9781988915401 (softcover) | ISBN 9781988915418 (EPUB)
Classification: LCC PS8626.A426 T43 2022 | DDC C813/.6—dc23

Editor: Kyle Hawke
Proofreader: Carol Hamshaw
Cover and Book Designers: PJ Perdue & Kyle Hawke
Author photo: David Bray

Front and Back Cover Art by James Picard © 2022 Picard Studios

Three Ocean Press
8168 Riel Place
Vancouver, BC, V5S 4B3
778.321.0636
info@threeoceanpress.com
www.threeoceanpress.com

First publication, October 2022

*Dedicated with love
to the memory of
Olive (Dean) Malcolm,
who taught me everything I know
about being a mother*

Acknowledgements

Writing historical fiction requires research, made easier these days by the wealth of material that can be found online. It was a pleasure for me to take advantage of the archives of the *Victoria Daily Colonist* and I am grateful to the newspaper for making its pages readily accessible online. When the COVID pandemic began during the writing of this novel, I paid special attention to the stories about the 1918 flu epidemic in Victoria. I appreciated that the unnamed reporters injected black humour into their news stories, some of which found its way into the novel.

I am also grateful to Linda Baker, who gave me access to the archives of Victoria High School, my alma mater and an important setting in *Tea at the Empress*. In the Vic High *Camosun* of April 1914, I found the information about the Portia Society debates. There, I learned that my great-aunt Mabel Malcolm was a member of the society and I took the very large liberty of making her Edith's best friend, though Edith herself is entirely fictitious.

Because of my interest in the archives, Linda Baker also put me to work helping to pack up the treasures of Vic High's past as the school building was about to be gutted and renovated. I appreciate that the Victoria School Board decided not to tear down the venerable building, constructed in 1914 by my great-great uncle's construction firm, Dinsdale and Malcolm.

Thank you to Diana Jones, who read the original short story and recognized that it had more of a 'novel' feel. I am also grateful to my number-one beta reader and husband, David Bray, a retired journalist himself. My thanks also to James Picard for the stunning cover, to PJ Perdue for her graphic artistry, and to my editor and publisher, Kyle Hawke at Three Ocean Press. Kyle provided me with his research into the Famous Five and held on to the manuscript of *Tea at the Empress* until we could see some light at the end of the COVID tunnel.

I'm indebted to so many others, living and dead, who have encouraged me in my writing journey. I hope you know I appreciate your support even if you're not named here.

Finally, I want to express my appreciation to those people in the last two centuries who have worked so hard for women's rights in Canada, not only the Famous Five (Emily Murphy, Henrietta Muir Edwards, Nellie McClung, Louise McKinney and Irene Parlby), but also the many, many women whose names have been forgotten in the continuing struggle for equality.

1

Armistice Day

The Daily Colonist   November 11, 1927

"This is the ninth anniversary of Armistice Day, the day which the peoples of this Empire have dedicated for all time to the everlasting memory of their dead in the Great War."

Reaching into my closet, I found my shortest flapper dress, deep green and covered with fringes. I gave the dress a shake on its hanger and the fringes shimmered and shimmied — the perfect dress to wear to a family dinner to which I hadn't been invited.

Grandma had come by yesterday and told me not to worry. "Your mum's just been so busy getting everything ready."

"I know Mum's a fussbudget," I'd said, "but to forget to invite her own daughter!"

"She's in a tizzy because some family from Vancouver will be there," Grandma had explained. "My great-nephew and his wife and daughter have just moved here. It'll be their first Thanksgiving away from home."

Mum hadn't mentioned that to me either. Maybe I embarrassed her so much that she'd rather I didn't come. Well, my flapper dress would give her something to be really embarrassed about. She'll say, "You're too old to wear such a thing!" She always loves to rub it in that I'm almost thirty and still not married. "Look at Lucinda!" she'll say. "Your sister's four years younger than you and married with three children already!"

Fine, Mum, but look at me! I have a job at The Daily Colonist. *How many women can say that?*

1

I thought she wanted me to be a teacher, but it seems she really wanted me to give her grandchildren and I let her down.

I'll show her, I told myself, slipping into my flapper dress and giving it a good shake.

I caught a glimpse of myself in my dresser mirror and walked over to finish getting ready. I pulled on my silk stockings and slipped a green band over my bobbed hair. Then I lined my eyes with kohl and put on some lip rouge. That'd annoy Mum for sure. My cat, Biddy, knowing by my actions that I was going out, wound herself between my legs.

"Out of the way!" I cried as I stepped over her. Then I went into the kitchen to pour myself three fingers of single malt. I needed some fortification before a family get-together like Thanksgiving dinner. Prohibition might be long over in British Columbia, but it'd still be dry at Mum's house. We wouldn't even have a glass of wine to toast the memory of the dead from the Great War.

I didn't get it anyway. How were we supposed to mourn the dead and celebrate Thanksgiving on the same day? It never made sense to me. To make matters worse, there was going to be some distant cousins there. Another happy family for me to be envious of.

I threw back the scotch. Then I grabbed my coat and called goodbye to Biddy over my shoulder as I walked out the door. In the hallway of my apartment building, I smelled fresh paint.

Out in the garage, my 1919 red Chandler roadster was waiting for me. Long and sleek, it had long running boards and tires with white spokes like spiders' webs. Being an American car, its steering wheel was on the left and, as we drove on the left side of the road in BC, it was sometimes difficult to see traffic on the right. I loved that car and paid extra for the garage space to keep it in tip-top condition.

If only I could put the top down. The clouds were high and it didn't look like rain, but the wind still cut through my coat like cold steel. I jumped in and turned the motor over. She roared to life, then gently purred. It filled my heart with happiness to hear that sound and feel the power beneath me.

I put her in gear, unleashed the beast, and drove up Quadra to Fairfield, then to Linden. The car nosed her way down the hill to my parents' house, two blocks from the sea.

As I jumped out and slammed the car door shut, I took a deep breath. I missed living so close to the salty scent of the ocean. Whenever I was sad or angry or grieving growing up, I used to walk those two blocks to the sea. I'd sit on a driftwood log and listen to the steady, perpetual swoosh of the tide. My heart would slow to that rhythm and all of my cares would drop away as if they'd never been.

I should visit the ocean more often, I thought as I walked up the garden path. Mum had planted rose bushes along this path before I was born, I paused to take a deep whiff of the dying roses before climbing up the steps.

Mum answered my knock. She looked surprised to see me, but quickly recovered and gave me a peck on the cheek. She squinted at me and I noticed that her frequent frowns were etching lines between her eyes.

"You've been drinking," she said. Then, "Come inside."

I entered, feeling like a child again.

"Let me take your coat."

I took it off and handed it to her. She looked me up and down, then shook her grey curls.

"Why do you even own such a dress?" she asked.

She didn't wait for an answer but walked the width of the vestibule and hung my coat in the closet. The only adornments in the hallway were a blue china umbrella stand beside the front door and a matching vase on a wooden table. Being November, there were no flowers in it. On either side of the vestibule were double glass doors that were usually closed. The doors to the dining room on the right were open and a card table had been set up in the doorway.

Mum caught me eyeing the anomaly in her usually pristine house.

"It's the children's table," she said, shaking her head. "In my day, children didn't eat with adults." She opened the door to the kitchen and called to the maid. "Could you set another place at the table for Edith?"

So, she *didn't* intend to invite me. That stung.

"You didn't say you were coming," Mum said, looking embarrassed.

"You," I replied, "didn't invite me."

"Come," Mum said. "Let me introduce you to my cousin and his family."

We went through the glass doors on the left that led into the parlour. All the seats were occupied. My young nieces and nephew were scattered on the carpet. The two little girls jumped up and ran to me.

"Auntie Edith!" they cried.

"Hello, Smelly. Hi, Weasel."

Lucinda glared at me. She disliked my nicknames for her girls. Melissa and Louisa gawked at my flapper dress. I gave it a shimmy so they could admire its full effect. They laughed and clapped their hands.

The adults tittered too, but I could feel the tension in their laughter. More of an embarrassed giggle.

"Behave yourself!" Mum said, pretending to smile. "Let me introduce you to our guests. This is my cousin, James."

A handsome, boring-looking man stood up and shook my hand.

"How do you do," he said flatly.

"And his wife, Margaret."

She was seated on the love seat beside him. She didn't stand and I could tell that she disapproved of me at least as much as my mother did.

"And this is their daughter, also Margaret."

Mum indicated a girl sitting on the edge of a straight-backed chair. She was at that awkward age somewhere between childhood and adulthood. Too old to go on the floor with the other kids and too young to feel comfortable sitting with the adults. She smiled at me, obviously amused by my childish antics and impressed with my flapper dress.

But that smile took my breath away! Where had I seen it before?

I went over and shook her hand. She seemed embarrassed by the gesture. I could feel her mother glaring at me. Clearly, she saw me as a bad influence on her child. Well, I'd only just met the girl.

"I like your dress," the young Margaret said.

Such an astute child! I smiled back at her. "And I like yours." Her mother had obviously dressed her. She wore a frilly dress similar to my nieces' and a matching white hair bow stood up on her head.

Poor young Margaret made a face and her mother glared at me. She too must have heard the sarcasm in my remark.

"Now that everyone is here," Papa said, "we can go in for dinner."

Oh, yes. Papa was here. I hadn't even said hello to him yet. I went over and gave him a kiss on the cheek. He blushed. Papa was English and very uncomfortable with any public show of affection. He went into the dining room.

My sweet grandmother was sitting in an armchair.

"Hello, Grandma," I said.

She stood up and I took her arm and escorted her into the dining room, following my father.

Mum had outdone herself, with the help of the maid, of course. A long time ago, she'd been a maid in an upper-crust house and she always aspired to the same classiness in her décor. The mahogany china cabinet and sideboard gleamed with lemon polish. The table was splendidly set in autumn colours. The china pattern was India Tree by Spode. There were crystal water glasses only. So, no wine then, as I'd expected. But the smells of turkey, gravy and cranberries were heavenly. In that moment, I was glad to have invited myself to this table. No matter how bad the company was, the food itself would be worth the agony.

Mum had kindly put place cards around her table. I sat Grandma in her chair near Mum, who was seated at the end of the table nearest the kitchen door. Of course, Papa was sitting at the other end. I went around the table, found the place setting without a place card and sat down. I was seated between my sister and her husband, confirming that I was an interloper. Lucinda gave me a dirty look as if I'd chosen to sit there. My cousin James was sitting directly across from me with his wife on one side and Grandma on the other.

Young Margaret was doing a circuit of the table but couldn't find her place card.

"I put you at the children's table," Mum said to her. "I hope you don't mind." She indicated the card table sticking halfway out into the hallway.

"Of course she doesn't mind," Margaret's mother said.

Young Margaret glared at her mother and went to the table where my nieces were already sitting and where my two-year-old nephew was struggling not to be deposited by Lucinda. He had his arms wrapped tightly around her neck and wouldn't let go.

Young Margaret seemed equally reluctant, but dutifully sat, looking longingly at the adults' table. I felt some sympathy for her. But where had I seen that look before? That shy sadness?

Lucinda gave up struggling with her two-year-old and looked at Mum. "Do you mind if Roland sits with me at the adult table?"

Mum looked disgusted by the whole idea of a two-year-old at her well-decorated table, but she nodded.

Lucinda carried her toddler over to her seat beside mine at the big people's table. She sat down with him on her lap.

Papa had intoned grace. He thanked God for food and family, then he mentioned our gallant soldiers who had fought in the Great War. I silently thanked my father for remembering. When he'd finished, my mother started circulating the bowls of food around the table.

I asked after my brother. "Where are Rob and his family?"

I spooned a few Brussels sprouts onto my plate. I didn't like them much, but I took two or three from habit. Best not to anger Mum.

"Robert," Mum responded, "is with Florence's family this year. You know very well they alternate and, last year, they were here for Thanksgiving."

"Oh," I said, passing the sprouts on and taking the mashed potatoes. They looked more appetizing. I took a large spoonful.

"What do you do for a living, James?" I asked my cousin.

"I've just got a job with the provincial government," he said, moving a large slice of turkey from the platter to his plate. "I'm an accountant."

That left me nowhere to go in our conversation. I had no knowledge nor interest in accounting. No, wait. There was one thing.

"What department do you work in?" I asked.

"Finance."

I should have known. I put some more vegetables on my plate.

Suddenly, peas were flying everywhere.

"No!" Lucinda cried, grabbing her son's wrist. "Stop throwing peas!"

Rollo — my nickname for him — squished the peas that he was holding. Green mush seeped between his fingers. He had such a happy and mischievous smile on his face. I smiled back at him.

"Don't encourage him, Edith!" Mum admonished me. "Does everyone have everything they need?" she asked, looking around.

We all nodded with our forks poised over our plates, ready to dig in.

"Well," she said, "if you need anything else, let me know."

Lucinda was wiping little Rollo's hand with a napkin. He smiled at me. I looked down at my plate. One thing was missing.

"Could you pass me the gravy, Margaret?"

"I understand," Cousin Margaret said, passing me the gravy boat, "that you're a career woman. What kind of work do you do?"

"I work at *The Daily Colonist*." To say I was a reporter would be a stretch.

"What do you do there?"

Apart from fetching coffee for the real reporters, you mean? "I write for the Society and Women's Affairs page," I said, making the stretch.

"Oh, how fascinating!" she said — disingenuously, I thought. "Does it make up for not having a family?"

What a catty and cruel question! She and my mother had a lot more than a first name in common.

"Women," I said, getting on my soapbox, "are so much more than a husband and children. Women are persons in their own right."

Cousin James snickered. "You're referring to the petition those five women made to the Supreme Court last summer, aren't you?"

He must read the paper from cover to cover. The story was usually buried in the back pages. "Yes," I said.

"What is that about?" his wife asked.

"Whether women," I said, "are considered to be 'persons' under the British North America Act of 1867. Which they are. So Emily Murphy should be our first woman senator. But certainly not our last."

Mum shook her head and tsked at me.

Papa shook his head. "Could we not talk about politics at the dinner table? It does nothing to aid my digestion."

A quick glance at little Rollo showed me that he was still having a wonderful time squishing peas. That didn't help my digestion either. Nor did watching Lucinda spoon mashed potatoes into his mouth. He saw me looking at him, smiled and half of the potatoes fell out of his mouth onto Lucinda's plate. I made a face, then saw that Mum was watching too.

"Next time you come," she said to Lucinda, "I hope you'll think to bring a high chair for Roland."

"Give him to me." Lucinda's husband, Larry, spoke for the first time.

Lucinda passed Rollo over my lap to her husband. Rollo spit some more mashed potato onto my flapper dress. It would be a bugger to clean, but I didn't dare say anything. It would just be pointed out that I shouldn't have worn such a dress to dinner.

"Now, young man," Larry said sternly. "You will behave yourself at the dinner table."

Rollo immediately burst into tears. He grabbed my dress and pulled at it, trying to clamber his way back to his mother. He managed to rip off a little handful of fringes. I stood up and backed away from the table.

"Perhaps we should exchange places, Lucinda."

She switched the plates and moved to my chair. I brushed off the peas and potatoes that had collected on her chair before sitting down.

"Sorry," she murmured to me under her breath as Rollo jumped back onto her lap.

I smiled across the table at Cousin Margaret. "Children are so delightful, aren't they?"

"They can be." Grandma was sitting directly opposite me now. Something in the way that she looked at me when she said it made me feel unutterably sad.

2

The Daily Colonist   April 19, 1914

Commence Classes in New High School

When I was fifteen, Arthur Brooke was a god. He walked down the hallowed halls of Victoria High School a head taller than all his friends. I would tremble at the sight of his mane of dusty blond hair, his big green eyes and his sensual, expressive mouth. I thought I was invisible to him because I was in Grade 10 and he was in Grade 12.

I remember the very first day that we moved into the beautiful brand-new building of our school. It was a fresh, windy day in April, a day when anything felt possible. That morning, I was at my locker — my very first locker, with a lock on it! I had just stashed my coat in it and closed the door, and there he was.

Arthur. Without his friends. I almost fainted.

His mouth moved into the suggestion of a smile. He looked down and a hank of his hair fell over his eyes. He tugged it, pulling it flat against his forehead. That gesture seemed to give him the confidence to speak.

"Someone told me your name is Edith," he said. "Is that right?"

Unable to find my voice, I nodded.

"My name is Arthur — Arthur Brooke."

I knew that, but I still couldn't find my voice to help him. I stared at him, waiting to find out why he'd deigned to notice me. Was he going to say he had seen me staring at him and to cut it out?

He cleared his throat. "Would you like to go out with me?"

The floor fell out from under my feet, but I held on to my locker door and didn't pass out. I nodded again. But this was ridiculous! I had to let him know I had a voice, that I wasn't mute.

"Yeah," I croaked. I cleared my throat. "Sure," I said, attempting nonchalance. "What did you have in mind?"

That seemed to stump him. "Let me walk you to your classroom."

So, we walked down the hall together.

"Would you like to go to a moving picture show?" he asked.

"Would I?" Did I say it out loud? I didn't mean to sound so excited.

"Okay," he said.

Then I gave him my address and he told me what time he'd call for me on Saturday.

We reached my classroom just as the bell rang and we awkwardly said goodbye.

I got to my desk. Across the aisle, my best friend Mabel was staring at me with her head cocked questioningly. She must have seen us together at the classroom door and, of course, she knew how much I liked Arthur. I shrugged my shoulders. She wrote me a note and passed it to me.

What's up?

I scribbled on the paper: *I'll tell you after class*. I passed it back.

She would have to wait for an explanation. This was not something I could commit to paper and risk having intercepted. Then it would be rumoured all around the school, before lunch even.

I didn't hear a word Mr. Andrews was saying about history. My mind was too full of Arthur Brooke. The bell finally rang and Mr. Andrews stopped yapping and dismissed us.

Mabel was right beside me. "All right, Edith. Time to tell."

"Arthur Brooke has invited me to a moving picture," I replied.

"Oh, Edith," she said, mock-horrified. "Have you forgotten our debate last week?"

Mabel and I belonged to the Portia Society, a girls' debating club. She and another girl had argued "that moving picture shows do more harm than good."

"Of course not," I said, "but I seem to remember that your side lost the debate."

Mabel blushed a pretty shade of pink. "Some friend."

I smiled as penance for reminding her of her defeat.

"Well," she said, "don't forget next week's debate."

I didn't need reminding. I was arguing "that women should be accorded the franchise under the same conditions as men enjoy it in

British Columbia." I thought it was amazing that we were able to find two members of the Portia Society to argue against it.

Mabel and I had joined the society because we were both avid future teachers and we wanted to practice speaking in front of a group. Other than that, we didn't have much in common. Mabel's father looked after the horses at the Victoria Transfer Company and both her parents had been farmhands back in Scotland. There were eight children in the family and they lived in a crowded house near the high school.

I lived in a big house on Linden Avenue in Fairfield with my parents, my younger sister and brother, and my grandmother. My father was a pilot — he guided ships through the treacherous Juan da Fuca Strait into Victoria Harbour.

Mum didn't think Mabel's family was quite up to our standards. But Dad told her not to be such a snob. He said, "You forget you were only a maid when I met you, Maggie."

Mum sniffed. She didn't like to be reminded. "Well, in those days, women didn't have much choice in their occupation." She turned to me. "But you are so much more fortunate, Edith. You have the opportunity to be a teacher. What I wouldn't have given for such a chance. I had to leave school when I was the same age as you are now."

I'd heard this story a million times before, but I smiled anyway. Grandma often told me how lucky I was too. She had left school even younger to be a seamstress.

So Mabel and I looked to the future where we women would have the right to vote. And then... who knew what we might achieve?

But then I fell in love with Arthur Brooke.

It was pretty ironic that I used this lovesickness as an excuse for why we lost the debate the next week. I didn't do a good enough job defending women's right to vote because my mind was too muddled with thoughts of a boy.

The day before the debate, I went to the picture show with Arthur Brooke and I scarcely even watched it. All I could think of was his hand holding mine in the dark. It was warm and dry. Mine was so clammy and cold I was afraid he'd drop it. But still he held on. Every so often, I'd glance over at him and study his face — how he laughed when the show was funny and frowned when it was serious. He had such an animated and beautiful face.

Then on the way home, we talked about everything we could think of. Arthur loved poetry just as I did. I thought only girls liked poetry. I dreamed he would write me a love poem one day. At my door, he kissed me goodbye. Such a quick kiss, but it held the possibility of a lifetime in its brief touch against my lips.

I was so smitten. How could I even think about all the reasons why women should have the vote? Though I knew they should. I had all the reasons so firmly in my grasp that I didn't think I even needed to prepare. Surely everyone would just agree with me because it was eminently clear that women were as intelligent as men and these days, just as educated. It was evident that we should have the right.

But then, our side lost the debate.

It wasn't entirely my fault though. I blamed the judges as well. One of them was the principal, Mr. Willis. I'm quite sure he had used his exalted position to convince the other two teachers, Miss Stevenson and Miss Smith, that women should stay at home and look after babies.

It was infuriating.

3

The Daily Colonist   December 25, 1927

Wishing All Hearty Christmas Happiness

~~~ ~~~ ~~~ ~~~ ~~~ ~~~ ~~~ ~~~ ~~~ ~~~ ~~~ ~~~ ~~~ ~~~ ~~~ ~~~

I could hardly wait for Christmas dinner. It would be even more magical with my brother Robert, his wife Florence and their two children there as well. I looked forward to more squished peas and squabbles over the seating arrangements.

I hoped that cousin James and his family would go back to Vancouver to be with his closer family at Christmas, but apparently, they could not afford the time and money that would have entailed. So, they were to be at our table once again. I admit I was a little intrigued to see young Margaret again. Something about the child interested me. She seemed hauntingly familiar and yet I knew I'd never met her before.

I'd bought another flapper dress to replace the one Rollo had damaged. Instead of fringes, it had bright sequins. I put it on, hoping it would impress young Margaret and annoy both our mothers. I made up my face and had my usual before-dinner scotch. Then off I sped in my roadster to my family home.

Robert opened the door with his youngest babe-in-arms. I gave my brother a dutiful peck on the cheek and exclaimed over the growth and beauty of his baby, as politeness required. Then, I declined to hold the infant, not because I didn't like children, but because I knew it would make me cry. Babies always made me cry. Robert's oldest child ran by and almost knocked me over, closely followed by his mother. Florence greeted me as she ran past. I watched her grab the boy by the scruff just before he escaped out the open door.

I went into the kitchen, where Mum was at the oven, looking harried as she basted the golden roast turkey whose rich scents assailed my senses. I went over, gave her a peck on the cheek.

She looked me up and down and said, "This is a family dinner, not a dance. Why do you have to dress as a flapper all the time?"

I ignored her question and asked her what I could do to help. She quickly had me setting the table.

At Christmas, the maid had the day off, so I'd been asked to come early. I went into the dining room where the table had been extended to its maximum and the children's card table was again set up in the vestibule with the glass doors open. Through the open door, I could see Lucinda sitting on the sofa in the distant parlour, her two daughters dressed as princesses on either side of her. Her husband, Larry, was holding little Rollo. Looking back in the dining room, I noticed a high chair that my sister must have brought for her youngest was standing against the wall by the children's table.

Grandma came through the open doorway into the dining room, walked over and gave me a hug and kiss.

"It's good to see you, dear," she said. "Can I help?"

"No, Grandma. You just sit down while I set the table."

"I'd rather help," she said.

I gave her a handful of cutlery. "Tell me again how this distant cousin is related to us, Grandma," I asked.

"He's my nephew John's boy," she said as she lay down knives and forks. "His grandfather is my brother, Sam, who left for the Gold Rush many years ago when I was just a girl and ended up in business in Vancouver. Do you remember when we went to Vancouver together and had our first ride in a motorcar?"

I did. How *could* I forget?

"It was John who gave us that ride."

Mum came in from the kitchen to interrupt us. "Make sure the cutlery is all aligned, not just tossed down higgledy-piggledy." She started to straighten the forks that Grandma had placed. "It's such a bother that the maid has to have Christmas off."

Grandma chuckled. "How would you have liked it, dear, not being at home with your family at Christmas?" she said.

Just then, the doorbell rang.

"Why don't you go get it, Mama?" Mum asked. "Come in the kitchen, Edith, and I'll give you the place cards and tell you where everyone sits."

It was not at all the seating arrangement I imagined. The children's table was full, with Smelly, Weasel and their cousin Bob, whom I called 'Bug'. The fourth place was occupied by Lucinda. She'd been placed where she could look after Rollo and all the other children. I was sure she'd love that. It must have been her punishment for Rollo's behaviour at Thanksgiving. Young Margaret was to be at the adults' table. I was sure she'd appreciate the promotion. Mum went back into the kitchen to bring out the serving dishes while I put the finishing touches on the table.

I could hear the bustle and business as Grandma took the guests' coats, ushered them into the living room and introduced them to Robert and his family. I watched the proceedings through the open doors. My eyes immediately went to Margaret. She stood there, smiling shyly, that half-familiar radiant smile. I suddenly knew where I'd seen it before.

It was Arthur's smile!

I stopped what I was doing and grabbed the edge of the table.

Could she be Arthur's child? Was it *possible*?

"Where's Edith?" I heard my father say.

"She's in the dining room," Grandma replied. "I'll go fetch her."

Grandma came through the door. "You look like you've seen a ghost," she said.

"I have, I think."

She looked at me oddly. "Well, pull yourself together and come greet our guests."

I stepped into the living room and shook the hands, first of cousin James, then cousin Margaret, and then little cousin Margaret. Was it my imagination or did I really feel a physical shock of electricity when I touched her hand? She looked up at me and smiled again. Arthur's smile. No doubt about it.

"Well," Mum said, emerging from the kitchen. "Shall we go into the dining room? Supper's ready." She turned to me. "Did you finish setting the table?"

"It's all done," I replied.

We sat down, grace was said, the food was passed around and the plates were filled with the usual Christmas fare: turkey, stuffing, potatoes, Brussels sprouts, gravy poured over all. Then the chatter died down as we began to eat our meal. I could feel two pairs of eyes on me all through the meal. The younger Margaret bestowed glances of admiration, but the elder Margaret's looks could only be called malign. She so evidently disapproved of me and was anxious that her daughter seemed impressed by me.

I pushed the peas around my plate and took small bites, but I had trouble swallowing food. My stomach was doing somersaults trying to imagine how this could be Arthur's child.

After supper, my father invited the men to the living room for a cigar and brandy, while Mum made tea for the ladies — an ancient custom that my mother insisted we perpetuate. Florence took the children to the playroom, at last! They had been restless all through the meal. Florence invited young Margaret, but Margaret was adamant she wanted to stay and have tea. Then ensued a fierce argument between the two Margarets, with the younger insisting she wasn't a baby and the elder insisting she was too young to drink tea. My mother tried to mediate by saying she'd put lots of milk and sugar in the tea, if that helped. Or she could give young Margaret a glass of milk. At last, Margaret the Elder relented and let her daughter stay. Young Margaret sat down with a satisfied smile on her face and looked across the table at me. I smiled back, though I risked a look of wrath from the mother.

As we drank our tea and talked, I became more and more convinced that she must be Arthur's child. I so wanted to kidnap the girl and take her away from her life of misery with that harridan, Margaret the Elder. But that wasn't fair. I'm sure she was a perfectly good mother who only wanted the best for her child.

4

The Daily Colonist   August 5, 1914
British Empire Has Declared War Against Germany

〜〜 〜〜 〜〜 〜〜 〜〜 〜〜 〜〜 〜〜 〜〜 〜〜 〜〜 〜〜 〜〜 〜〜 〜〜 〜〜

Arthur was walking me home after we'd watched another installment of *The Perils of Pauline*. Poor Pauline had been tied up on a railroad track with a locomotive barreling down upon her. Then the hero untied her — at the last second, of course. It was heart-stopping stuff, if a bit silly.

"How did you like the picture?" I asked.

"I didn't pay it much attention," he said diffidently. "I have something else on my mind."

He was thinking about us, perhaps? "What were you thinking about?"

"The war."

I didn't expect that. Britain had just declared war on Germany. What does the war have to do with us? "What about the war?"

"I'm thinking about signing up."

"You can't do that!" I cried. "You're going to university in Vancouver in the fall. You're going to be the first person in your family to get a degree."

"That was the plan," Arthur said, sounding a little sad. "but the King has called on us to fight the Hun in defence of the Empire."

I was stunned. "How can you think of enlisting? How can you leave your home and go to the other side of the world to fight for a king and country you don't even know?"

"Edith," he said. "He's our king and it's the country my father came from, and his father before that. I have a duty to come to its aid."

"But how can you leave me?" As soon as I said it, I heard what a pathetic cry it was.

"Don't be so selfish, Edith. I'm the one who's going to risk my life. Your sacrifice is nothing beside that."

This statement was true, but it hurt me deeply nonetheless. It made me think about what sacrifices I could make. The only thing I could think of was becoming a nurse like Florence Nightingale. I would give up my dream of being a teacher and go save the wounded men overseas. But first I had to finish high school, and the war would probably be over by then.

We were sitting in the front parlour of the Brookes' house on Roseberry. The curtains were drawn and the light was dim in spite of the bright summer sun outside. We were sitting close together on the settee. Even through our clothes, I was acutely aware of the sensation of our legs touching from hip to knee. Arthur's mother was in the kitchen making us some tea and I could sense her disapproval from a distance.

Arthur had signed up and was going away to basic training in two weeks. There was nothing I had said or could say that would make him change his mind.

He looked at me with his serious green eyes framed by long lashes. "I don't want to leave without saying goodbye properly," he said.

"What do you mean?"

"I don't want to die a virgin."

My taut nerves jangled with shock at his statement. "Who says you'll die?"

"War is war." He paused. "I might die."

"Then you'll have to lie with some prostitute over there," I said, hoping to shock him as well.

"No." He looked at me seriously. "I love you and I want to lie with you before I go."

"That's not a *proper* way to say goodbye."

"Oh yes, it is. I want to take that memory with me to the battlefield."

We heard his mother coming down the hall with a tray of rattling teacups and moved apart from each other. She put the tray on the coffee table.

"Look at you two, sitting in the dark." She clucked her tongue at us, went to the curtains and pulled them open.

I squinted in the blinding sunlight. Arthur smiled broadly as he leaned over to pour himself a cup of tea. I waited my turn and picked up the teapot. It was heavy, my arm was shaking and the teapot waved around dangerously. I put it down.

"What's the matter, you silly girl?" Arthur picked up the pot and poured the tea for me. Then he looked at his mother and said, "Could you get us some biscuits for our tea, Mom?"

She sighed and left the room. When we could hear her in the distant kitchen, Arthur turned to me.

"What d'you say, Edith?" he asked. "Will you send me off to war a happy man?"

What could I say? I loved Arthur utterly. How could I deny him anything as important as that? I'd only put up a brief show of refusal for propriety's sake. But I was afraid as any girl would be, especially in those days when we knew so little about sex. The talk between mother and daughter, if there even was one, occurred the day before the wedding. Why would it be necessary anytime sooner? We'd been taught from our earliest childhood that to lie with a man before getting married was a grievous sin.

Arthur and I got off the streetcar at the very last stop and walked until there was nothing but wilderness on either side of the street. The road was little more than a dirt track when we walked into the forest. It was not the dense rainforest that buries you in its damp darkness. It was a Garry oak grove, almost a meadow, with the bent and misshapen limbs of the trees providing us little shade and protection.

We lay down on a patch of soft but scratchy yellow grass between two rocky outcroppings. Above us were the tangles of the oak trees' twisted limbs. And above that, the sky was that deep shade of cerulean blue. The summer sun warmed our skin.

Neither of us spoke. We knew what we had come for — this holy rite of passage.

It began well enough with the long, sweet kissing we had already practised many times before. But then he lifted my skirt, brushing my ankle as his hand travelled the long journey up my leg to my waist where he pulled down my knickers. For a moment, I felt violated, but I couldn't say anything. I had agreed to this.

Next, he took out his willy and I gasped. I had only ever seen my brother's before and only when, as a little boy, he had escaped my mother's clutches after a bath. My brother's was tiny and soft and jiggly and bore no resemblance whatsoever to this long, hard, cudgel-like thing that Arthur was holding in his hand and bringing towards my private parts.

We made love.

Why such a bestial act is named after such an exalted emotion, I cannot fathom. It was awkward as any first-time, unfamiliar physical act is wont to be. And it was painful. That part, I had not expected. I somehow thought — through the forbidden love stories I'd read under the sheets at night with the torchlight seeking out the words on the pages — that the act of love was as smooth and painless as diving into a placid lake. It was not. The act of 'love' felt like having a sharp stick poked in a sensitive wound. And there was blood. I hadn't expected that either.

Afterwards, I lay there as still as if I were dead, looking up at the tangled branches, messy like a child's angry scribbles on a blue sheet.

Arthur lay panting beside me. I could see he had enjoyed it. He turned and smiled at me as if I had done something magnificent when all I'd done was lie there. I tried to smile back at him, but in truth, I felt cheated.

All the writers I'd ever read had made it sound so wonderful. Why?

It came to me like an epiphany. They were all men. They had enjoyed it. I would have enjoyed it too if I was the one poking the stick in someone else. But I was not Arthur — I was Edith and life was damned bloody unfair. I was only beginning to have the faintest notion of that.

The boat was already in the Inner Harbour, waiting to take the new recruits to Vancouver when I went to see Arthur off. From Vancouver, he would take a train across the great Dominion of Canada to Valcartier for basic training. Then he would board a ship from Quebec City down the mighty Saint Lawrence River, out its mouth and across the Atlantic Ocean to Old Blighty. I had traced the journey on the great map in my history classroom, my finger gliding over the pink expanse of Canada across the borders of the provinces and over the printed names of places, then across the blue expanse to the pink island of Great Britain from where our forefathers had come.

The boys in their uniforms marched unevenly down Government Street. They tried to keep step and some of them did with the help of a lively marching band. Our hearts were stirred by the beat of the patriotic music as we followed alongside of them, waving from the sidewalk. The brave young men turned onto Belleville and finally ended their march at the CPR terminal, a great half-timbered house where our crowd joined an even larger throng, waiting to wish the boys farewell.

I could see Arthur, his head above the others in the crowd. In fact, my eyes had never left him during the march. But before I could reach him, his mother and father did. His mother hugged him and cried into his sleeve while his father shook his hand. Arthur looked embarrassed by their attention. He saw me standing to one side and beckoned me closer. His mother glared at me, begrudging my presence.

I went to his side, afraid to make a show of our affection in front of his parents. I wanted to hug him too, but I held back because of his mother. I couldn't cry like her either. I just couldn't do it in public. I don't know why. Did that mean my love was any less than hers?

I so resented his parents at that moment. This was perhaps the last time I would ever see Arthur. But I had given him a memory to take with him to the battlefield. It would have to be enough.

Arthur had other ideas. He put his arm around me and drew me close. "We want to say goodbye in private," he said to his parents.

I could see his father wearing the same embarrassed expression as Arthur. "Well," he said, looking around the steamship terminal, "you won't find any privacy here."

Arthur blinked the way he did when he didn't know quite what to say. "Not exactly in private, but privately."

"Oh, go ahead and kiss her," his father said. "We'll turn away." He took his wife's shoulders and turned her around. "Come along, Iris."

Arthur kissed the top of my head. I turned my face up and he put his hand under my chin and bent down. He kissed my lips sweetly as if sipping nectar from a flower. My heart beat like the snare drums of the marching band.

"Goodbye," he said, looking deeply into my eyes. Then, he let go of my chin. Over my head, he said to his parents, "You can look now."

They turned back.

"Please take care of Edith for me while I'm gone," he said.

My heart swelled.

His father smiled. His mother scowled. And then he was gone, walking up the long plankway to the ship that would take him away. Halfway up, he turned and gave me a goofy grin. I blew him a kiss. Then, I stood and watched until the gangplank was gone and the ship left its berth. I kept watching the ship until it turned out of the harbour into the Strait of Juan de Fuca and I could no longer see it.

5

The Daily Colonist   January 3, 1928

City Workmen Busy with Snow

After the holidays were over, I telephoned the mother Margaret to invite her for tea at my apartment. I had to find out if her daughter was adopted and the best time to ask her outright was when her husband and child, and my family, were not around. Of course, I used the pretext of wanting to get to know her better. I could tell from the sound of her voice that she was skeptical of my motive, but her curiosity got the better of her and she said she would come the next morning after her daughter had gone to school. That worked for me as I was working afternoons and evenings at the time. I gave her my address and told her how to get to my apartment building on foot. She lived in Fernwood, so it was less than a twenty-minute walk away.

I wore the most conservative dress I had in my closet. I didn't want to put her off more than I could help. Then I went about the parlour, putting away books I was reading, straightening pillows and talking to the cat.

"What do you think, Biddy? Do you think that Margaret is really Arthur's daughter? She does look just like him."

Biddy stopped licking her paw and blinked impassively.

The doorbell rang.

I welcomed Margaret the Elder into the tiny dark hallway and hung her coat in the closet. She rubbed her hands together. "It's cold out there," she said. "It's nice to have snow around Christmas time, but it can leave any time now."

I led her into the living room and she looked around. Biddy was curled in a ball on the chesterfield.

"Have a seat," I said. "Make yourself at home while I go make us some tea."

"I don't like cats," she said. "I'd rather we sat in the kitchen." She followed me.

The kitchen table was a mess, covered in more books and papers. I gathered them up and put them on the counter. She seated herself on a kitchen chair, sitting ramrod straight with her back not even touching the chair. I could see that her demeanour was defensive and almost ready for a fight. I didn't know if it was just because she disliked me in general or if she had some kind of inkling of what I was going to ask her.

I made the tea and we talked some more about the snow we'd been having. Now that the Christmas holidays were over and cars were back on the road, the city workers were busy clearing it up. I sat down and poured the tea. We sat in unpleasant silence for a while, having exhausted the topic of the weather.

"You have a lovely daughter, Margaret," I finally said.

"Yes," she said, softening.

"By any chance," I began, trying to think of a way to ask my question without being blunt. "I know this may seem a strange question, but is she adopted?"

She looked totally blindsided by the question.

"Why would you ask such a thing?" she cried. "She's not, but it would be none of your business if she was."

"I think it might be my business. Is her birthday May thirteenth, 1915?"

The look on Margaret's face was full-scale panic. She didn't answer my question, so I assumed that it was.

"I gave birth to a baby girl on that date in Vancouver," I said, "and I gave her up for adoption."

She looked terrified. "That doesn't mean she's your child. Lots of babies could have been born around that date."

"She looks so much like her father," I said.

Margaret was twisting her napkin around and around. I could tell she wished she'd never come. At last, she said, "We've never told her she was adopted. She thinks I'm her real mother. Just think how devastating it would be for her to hear it from you." Margaret was pleading with me, and I could understand her panic.

"Why have you never told her? Don't you think she has a right to know?"

"There never was a reason to."

"There is now."

"Please don't tell her."

I wanted to hate her at that moment, but the look on her face was so abject that I could feel how she was feeling in my gut. I knew what it was like to lose a child.

"I agree that it's not my place to tell her and so I won't. But I believe you ought to tell her yourself."

She seemed relieved to hear that I wouldn't tell her daughter the truth. She put down the twisted napkin and regained her earlier composure. "What my husband and I decide to do about it is our affair and none of yours. You gave her up when she was a baby. We have given her a loving home. You have no right to dictate what we ought to do with our daughter." She took a long swallow of her tea, then gathered herself together. "I will thank you to have no further contact with Margaret. I will not have her upset by your allegations. Now, where is my coat? I'm going home."

I gathered her outer garments from the hall closet where I had hung them. This had not gone well. Perhaps I should have kept my suspicions to myself. Now it was unlikely that I would ever see my daughter Margaret again.

"Please," I said. It was now my turn to beg. "I promise that I won't say anything about it to Margaret if only you'll let me see her from time to time. At family gatherings where there are many people around. If my mother invites you and I'm there, for example. Where you can keep an eye on me. I won't ever tell her."

Her eyes were not much softened. "I'll think about it," she said.

As soon as Margaret left, I knew I had made a mistake. I should have approached my cousin James, not her. He was the more sensible of the two and he didn't hate me, or at least, I didn't think he did. I should approach him now, immediately, before Margaret called him and told him of our meeting.

I picked up and asked the operator to be connected with Mr. James Innis in the Finance Department of the provincial government.

After a few minutes, he answered the telephone. "Hello?"

"Hello, James. It's your cousin, Edith, here. I was wondering if I could take you to lunch today."

"Oh," he replied.

I could tell he was surprised by the unexpected offer and unsure how to respond.

"I suppose so," he said at last.

"We could meet at the dining room at the Empress," I said. "It's close to your workplace. It's my treat."

"All right," he said unenthusiastically. "What's this about anyway?"

"I thought we should get to know each other a little better," I said again. It was lame but all I could think of at short notice. We discussed the specifics of time and place. After I hung up, I put on some makeup and started walking downtown.

A short time later, I was seated at a table in the dining room of the elegant Empress Hotel. As I looked at the gleaming silverware on a white linen tablecloth, I wondered if this was all a big mistake. Where would I get the money to pay for this? And what if James said no to my pleas?

He arrived just as the waiter was about to pour me a cup of tea. I stood and shook his hand.

"Would you like some tea?" I asked.

He nodded.

"Could you bring another cup, please?" I asked the waiter.

James sat down and shuffled uneasily. When he was settled, he looked at me with undisguised dislike and said, "I know what this is about."

Margaret must have called him as soon as she got home. I was at a disadvantage now.

The waiter placed another china cup on the table and gave us our menus. Then he poured James's tea.

When he had gone, James leaned forward and asked me discreetly, "Are you so sure you are Margaret's biological mother?"

"I am," I said. "She was born at the Vancouver General Hospital on May 13, 1915." I took a sip of tea and looked at him. "Does that sound about right?"

James looked nonplussed. He took a sip of tea, then put the cup down. "Still, it doesn't mean she was the only illegitimate baby girl born in Vancouver that day."

"As I told your wife, she's the spitting image of her father."

"And who," he said spitefully, leaning towards me again, "is the father?"

"His name was Arthur Brooke."

"And why didn't you marry him?"

I paused. It was still difficult for me to talk about it even after all these years. "He went off to fight in the Great War." That was all that needed to be said.

The waiter came back to take our order. We hadn't even glanced at the menus.

"What's the special today?" James asked.

"Meatloaf, sir."

"I'll have that," James replied.

"Me, too," I said.

When the waiter had gone, James did not pursue questions about Arthur. He spoke a little more sympathetically when he asked, "And just what do you want us to do about it?"

"Tell Margaret that she's adopted. Tell her I'm her mother."

"That's not going to happen," he said. I knew from speaking to his wife that this was true and, if I persisted, they would never let me see Margaret again.

"Look," I said. "I don't want to upset the life she has with you and your wife. I know that would not be the best thing for Margaret either, and I want what's best for her. As for me, I just want to continue to be able to see her and watch her grow. That's all. I told your wife I wouldn't say anything to her. We could meet at family gatherings just as we did for Christmas and Thanksgiving. I'll be fine with that." I realized full well with some bitterness that I didn't get a vote in their decision.

James looked at me as though he didn't quite believe me. "Do you promise you won't see her alone, that you won't tell her the truth?"

Promise? That was so final. How could I do that? I nodded. A head nod was surely not as absolute as saying the word.

The waiter brought our food and James immediately began to eat.

I picked up my fork and picked at the vegetables on my plate. I wanted to cry. They looked a little overcooked and I had no appetite for food now. I had just made a promise that, with every fibre of my being, I did not want to keep. It was nothing short of giving up my daughter again, but now I had met her and I didn't want to lose her anew.

6

The Daily Colonist   November 10, 1914

Canada's Troops Training Hard

〜〜 〜〜 〜〜 〜〜 〜〜 〜〜 〜〜 〜〜 〜〜 〜〜 〜〜 〜〜 〜〜 〜〜 〜〜

I went back to school. Grade eleven. And life resumed its normal dull pattern, pre-Arthurian period. I missed him terribly. He wrote me copious long letters telling me about his training at a camp in England somewhere. He couldn't tell me where it was, but it must have been near a town large enough to have a cinema because he wrote me about every moving picture he saw. He had become quite enamoured of Charlie Chaplin. I took note of the names of the films he mentioned and then invited Mabel to come see them with me. She couldn't always afford it, but sometimes, when I begged enough, she would let me pay her way.

It was after seeing one of these movies, when we'd stopped to have a soda on the way home, that I told her about my dilemma.

"Mabel," I said. "I'm so worried but I don't know who to turn to."

"What's wrong? Is it something to do with Arthur? Has he been sent to the front?"

"No, he hasn't. It's only to do with me." I paused, took a sip of my soda and tried to find the right words. "I haven't had my menses for three months now. Not since school started."

"What do you mean?"

"My menses, my monthlies, whatever you call it."

"Oh," she said, the light of comprehension dawning in her eyes. "The curse."

"Well, it's not such a curse when you haven't had it. Then you worry about what it could mean."

Mabel had older siblings so she knew more about these things than I did.

"In my experience," she said, "it usually means you're going to have a baby. But only if you've had sexual relations with a man before that." She looked me straight in the eyes.

I looked down and blushed.

"No, Edith! You didn't!"

I couldn't speak. It was as I'd feared.

"Do you feel sick in the morning?" she asked.

"Yes," I said. Just that morning, I'd woken up feeling dizzy and had to run to the toilet. I'd thrown up bile. "But I feel better after I eat something."

"That's morning sickness," she said, a fount of wisdom.

"So, what do I do now?" I asked.

"Well, normally you'd get married to the man who put you in the family way. That's how Alice became my sister-in-law. But I'm guessing that won't be possible in your case."

I shook my head, a feeling of dread seeping into my blood and bones. "What shall I do?"

"Well, you'll have to tell your mother," she said, matter-of-factly, "and go see a doctor to make sure."

"No," I said, "I can't do that."

"You have no choice."

"Maybe I could run away from home like Jack did."

"Don't be silly. Your parents will understand. They're not ogres like mine."

"Your parents aren't ogres, are they?" I asked. That must have been why she never invited me over.

"Just my father. He's the reason Jack left. Mama is okay, though. So is your mother. She'll understand."

"She'll be devastated." I pictured her face when I told her, collapsing as if she'd taken a body blow.

"But she'll come around. You know she will. Anyway, you have no choice."

Neither of us said a word as we walked home from the soda shop. I don't know what Mabel was thinking about but the death of my dream was weighing on my mind. We were supposed to go to normal school together. And when I thought of that, I remembered it was my mother's dream too and my heart ached. I didn't know how I could break this news to her. I wanted so much to run away and hide.

When we got to my house, Mabel gave me a hug and whispered in my ear, "You have to tell her. And the sooner, the better." Then she left.

I watched her go. As if she sensed my eyes on her, she turned back and waved sadly. It was like watching all of my hopes and dreams leaving me.

The next day was Saturday. Mum was making her bed. I walked into her bedroom and watched her.

"Mum," I said.

She flicked her wrist and the white sheet billowed open like a sail. I caught its fresh scent of sunlight as it slowly descended on the bed, lying flat. She made it look so easy. It took me forever to straighten out the sheet when I was making my bed. Mum tucked the edges of the sheet under the mattress.

I stood there, wondering how on earth I was going to tell her.

She picked up a pillow and looked across the bed at me. "Say what you've come to say, Edith. I haven't got all day."

I swallowed hard and said, "I'm pregnant."

She dropped the pillow and stared, her mouth agape. "You're what?"

I knew by the look on her face she'd heard me. Why did she want to make me say it again?

"Did you just tell me you're with child?"

"I did."

She sat down on the bed and said nothing. I stood waiting in agony for the longest time for her to respond.

At last, she turned. I'd never seen such a dark and angry look on her face before.

"Edith," she said. And then, "Who's the father?" And then, when I didn't respond, "Is he going to do the right thing by you?"

"You know," I said, "who the father is!" How could she ask such a question? I'd only ever had the one boyfriend. "So, you know he's on the other side of the world fighting the Hun."

"Oh, Edith. Oh, Edith. I'll have to tell your father."

"Do you have to?"

"Are you absolutely sure, Edith?"

I nodded, though I wasn't.

"Perhaps you're mistaken," she said, and my hopes soared. "I'll take you to the doctor's tomorrow to be tested. In the meantime, don't tell anyone else about this."

I didn't say anything about having already told Mabel. I trusted completely that she wouldn't tell anyone. I prayed it was all a mistake.

We came home from the doctor's office on the streetcar in complete silence. My mother held a piece of paper that the doctor had given her clenched tightly in her hand. I could see her knuckles were white with the exertion of holding it. On it, the doctor had written the name of a 'home' in Vancouver where single women could go to give birth. It was called the Presbyterian Social Services Home. We were Presbyterian. At least, my grandmother and mother attended First Presbyterian Church regularly. I did not, to their chagrin. I could feel my mother's unspoken censure. She was probably wishing she'd forced me to go to church more often.

Well, I was in for it now. I'm sure this 'home' would be non-stop religious instruction with Hell and brimstone thrown in for good measure. What did I need to be told about Hell? This world and this life had become a living hell for me.

We walked up the front stairs to the house and went in. My grandmother was waiting attentively for us. She didn't ask how it had gone. She could see our faces. My mother went straight up to her bedroom without uttering a word.

"Edith," Grandma said. "Come into the kitchen and I'll make you some tea."

I followed her. She pulled out a chair and I sat down.

She sat close beside me and put her arm around me. She had a lovely mature face with soft skin and just a few wrinkles around her eyes. If it weren't for her white hair, bun and long black skirt, you wouldn't suspect her age.

"Sorry, Grandma." I swallowed hard, trying not to burst into tears. Her kindness to me was, in some ways, harder to take than my mother's coldness.

"You don't have to apologize to me," she said. "Sometimes we do things other people consider wrong, but we do them anyway for the right reason. I think that's what happened to you, isn't it?"

I nodded, unable to speak because the tears had started to fall unbidden.

"I understand," she said. "You did it for love."

I had to take a breath because I had been trying so hard to stifle my tears. When I opened my mouth, an ugly snort came out. I had to laugh — a weak, sad laugh that brought on more tears. I put my head down on my arms.

32

"It's all right, Edith." Grandma patted my back. "You have a good cry. Get it all out. You have a difficult row to hoe now."

She got up and put on the kettle. "I'll make some tea."

"What am I going to do, Grandma? What am I going to do?"

"I don't know," she said, looking as perplexed as I felt. "I suppose you're going to have a baby."

"And how am I going to raise a baby on my own?"

"Oh, dear," she said, "but you won't be on your own, will you? You'll have me and your mother to help you. We both know a thing or two about raising babies."

"I don't know, Grandma," I said.

"Well, we have plenty of time to decide about it," she said. "Don't worry now."

7

The Daily Colonist   February 2, 1928

Parliament of Britain Meets Today:
Women To Be Given Equal Franchise

~~~ ~~~ ~~~ ~~~ ~~~ ~~~ ~~~ ~~~ ~~~ ~~~ ~~~ ~~~ ~~~ ~~~ ~~~

I woke up with a hangover. Monday mornings were often like that since I had Sundays and Mondays off. I stayed in bed for as long as my kidneys and my headache would allow. Biddy was curled in a ball on the bed beside me. When she realized I was awake, she purred.

"I'm sorry," I said, "but I have to get up to pee."

I uncovered myself and gingerly removed myself from the bed so as not to disturb her, but as soon as she knew I was getting up, she jumped down off the bed with a thud. I went into the bathroom to relieve myself. Then I poured a glass of water and took an Aspirin.

I carried the glass of water into the kitchen. Biddy did her best to trip me up. Then I put on the coffee percolator and sat down to listen to its soothing, rhythmic suck-and-thrum while I sipped my water. The worst thing about Mondays was there was no paper. Nothing to read while I drank my coffee. Nothing to grab me and root me in the world. No gossip to spread like fertilizer.

Biddy sat on the floor at my feet and stared at me crossly.

"Of course. You want your breakfast. Just a minute, Biddy."

I got up and went to the icebox. Mornings, there were no leftovers. Biddy had eaten them the night before. So, I usually scrambled two eggs and gave one to Biddy. I was not the least bit hungry this morning, so

I broke and scrambled one egg only. Then I scraped it into her bowl on the floor. She started eating it before I finished scraping it. Some of it landed on the top of her head. I tried to brush it off into the bowl. She turned her head to scowl at me and it fell off onto the floor.

Then I poured myself a cup of coffee and sat down. I was depressed. I recognized the signs. Times like this, I didn't want to do anything and anything I did sapped me of energy. All I really wanted to do in times like this was to drink a bottle of scotch till I either passed out or finished it off. But I had a rule. I would not allow myself to drink before noon. Mornings like this, I would sit and watch the clock, waiting for noon. I looked at the clock. It was early yet — a long time even before nine. Why had I gotten up so early? Perhaps I should go back to bed.

Then I thought of Margaret. Not the mother, but the child. Why ever did they name her after her mother? Why couldn't one of them have a nickname at least? But I used to call her May, so I'd call her Margaret May from now on. What would she be doing now? Would she be having breakfast? I wondered what she ate. Of course, today was Monday and she'd be going to school. I imagined her in a hurry so as not to be late, grabbing a piece of toast as she rushed out the door. She'd walk up Grant Street to Fernwood and then south along Fernwood to Central Girls' School. I had a sudden urge to see her. If I got dressed and hurried, I might catch a glimpse of her passing along Fernwood. I wouldn't speak to her — I promised her parents not to — but I might nod in recognition if she saw me.

I stopped imagining and flew to my room to get dressed. I moved too quickly for my throbbing head and I groaned. Fresh air would do me good.

When I was dressed, I put on my coat and walked the five blocks from downtown toward Fernwood. I walked at a brisk pace because I wasn't sure what time school began and, if it was earlier than nine o'clock, she might have already passed by. I stood at the end of her street across from my old high school, the place where I'd first talked to Arthur on the very first day the school had opened. I thrust my hands deep into my pockets, hoping to see Margaret pass by, hoping to catch a glimpse of her face, so like Arthur's. It wasn't the coldest of days but the wind was blustery and standing still made me cold, so I paced up and down the block in front of the high school.

It took ten minutes, but finally Margaret May came walking up the hill on Grant Street with her arms full of books. She looked up, saw me and smiled.

"Good morning, Aunt Edith," she said.

I smiled back and nodded. My mouth filled with bile. I had promised her parents not to speak to her. I turned north as if I had only met her by chance. Then she turned the other way and kept walking toward school. I looked back over my shoulder and she looked back. I waved and she waved back. I turned back towards home at the next block, which was Vining. The rest of the way home, I felt the warm sun on my shoulders like a swelling benediction.

The incident was brief but it filled the rest of my day with bittersweet joy. So, the next Monday, I repeated the same route at the same time. She didn't reappear at the same spot, even though I stood there for ten minutes waiting. Finally, realizing I'd arrived too late, I walked home.

Then the next Monday and the next. After another month, I saw her again. This time, she was with two other girls about the same age and she didn't see me. When I was even with them and still hadn't caught her eye, I broke my promise and said, "Good morning, Margaret."

She looked up, startled. When she recognized me, she smiled and nodded.

One of the girls with her asked, "Who's that?"

"She's a distant cousin of my father's."

I couldn't hear anything more of their conversation as I had passed them. I looked back and saw the girls laughing and talking.

Good. She had friends.

I shouldn't have spoken to her.

Oh, I wished that she knew I was more to her than a distant cousin!

This was too painful for me. Besides, if I kept on meeting her, she might mention something about it to her parents and then they would stop coming to family dinners. But, oh, it was such a long time till Easter!

8

The Daily Colonist   January 5, 1915

New Normal School Opened to Students

~~~~~~

I continued going to school until Christmas. At school, nothing much changed and everything did. Mabel and I pretended everything was the same as it had always been, though it wasn't at all. My heart had gone out of it.

Mum had everything planned. She was going to send me to that horrid 'home' in Vancouver.

"Will I bring the baby home with me afterwards?" I asked.

"I don't think that would be wise, dear," she said. "You wouldn't be able to go to normal school if you did."

Normal school! How could she even think about that? "Then what will happen to the baby?"

"We shall see," she said. "We shall see."

I missed a lot of school because of the morning sickness and my grades began to fall.

The atmosphere at home was toxic. Mum railed at me for my falling grades and then she used them to explain to Robert and Lucinda what was going to happen after Christmas.

"Your sister Edith is going to Vancouver to take a special course in January to improve her grades so that she can go to normal school next year," she said. "Her grades have fallen so much they won't take her at normal school."

Robert and Lucinda exchanged puzzled expressions. Even I wondered what was so 'special' it could save me.

"Where's she going to stay?" Lucinda looked at me suspiciously.

"She'll stay with my cousin John and his family," Mum said. She lied so easily it frightened me.

Robert, who was fourteen, had already lost interest in the conversation. "Can I go now?"

"Of course," Mum said, looking relieved. "You can both go. I have to talk to Edith."

Robert ran off and Lucinda slinked away, slowly watching us. Mum waited till she was out of earshot.

"We've booked you a fare on the Princess Victoria to Vancouver, leaving the day after Christmas. We think it best you leave soon, before you start to show."

I nodded. I'd never been to Vancouver before. It would have been such an exciting adventure under other circumstances.

"Shall I go by myself?" I asked.

"Grandma is going to take you. She wants to visit her brother. You remember your Uncle Sam and Aunt Clara, don't you?"

"No," I said. "Not really."

"Perhaps not. The last time they came to visit, you were only little. But you must remember his son, my cousin John? He used to come with his children, James and Sarah. They're quite a few years older than you."

"Of course," I said. I'd never paid them much mind since they'd not been interested in playing with us younger children. They used to come sometimes in the summer, but not every year and it had been a long time since they'd last visited.

It was a grey rainy day when Grandma and I got on the *Princess Victoria* for our trip to Vancouver. A little part of me was all a-tingle because I'd always wanted to travel and see the world. And another little part of me — no, admit it — a much larger part of me, was terrified, remembering Arthur walking up the gangplank, going to war.

I was leaving my home behind. I was leaving my childhood behind. I would come back, but I would not be the child that had left. I would not go back to school. I would go to work. I knew that Mum expected me to go back to school but I didn't think I could do that. There would be too much gossip and I wouldn't belong there anymore. Besides, in spite of what my mother said, I wanted to keep the baby. It was my link to

Arthur. I expected that I'd be able to find employment when I returned. Because of the war, there was a shortage of workers and Grandma had promised to help me with the baby.

When we found comfortable seats in the ship, Grandma told me she'd never taken this trip before either and she was excited.

"When your parents went to Vancouver, I always stayed home and looked after you children," she said. "I'd never set my sights on travel."

"Why not?" I asked.

"Because it was never a possibility when I was growing up. We were too poor."

"But Uncle Sam went to Vancouver."

"Yes," she said. "Both my brothers left home and went away, but they were boys. I was expected to stay home."

"Both your brothers?" I asked. I'd never heard about another one. "Who's the other one?"

Grandma's eyes clouded. "I had a brother James… Jamie," she said with a faraway look in her eyes. "He died in the Civil War."

It took me a few moments to realize she was talking about the American Civil War. It seemed like forever ago.

"Oh," I said. It was the first I'd ever heard of this. And for the first time since Arthur had left, his dying on a far-off battlefield seemed a real possibility.

Grandma seemed to think the same thought at the same time, for she said "Oh" as well.

The ship was underway now and had left Victoria's Inner Harbour behind. The water was rough and the rolling motion of the ship reawakened my morning sickness. I could feel my stomach coming up into my throat.

"I'm feeling sick, Grandma," I said.

"Let's go outside," she said. "I want to take in all the sights of this adventure."

We walked out onto the deck. The cold air snatched away my sick feeling, while looking out at the ocean made it easier to endure as the ship moved up and down on the waves. There was no horizon and the bottom of the Olympic Mountains was obscured by low-hanging clouds. The peaks towered above the clouds like some kind of heaven floating in the sky.

Grandma and I wandered around the deck as the ship plowed through the waters of the Strait of Juan da Fuca. We were silent as we passed by the Gulf Islands, lush green jewels in the grey sea. I felt my eyes misting as much as the sky as it spit rain at us.

"It's so beautiful," Grandma said, shivering.

I realized how cold it was. "Let's go back inside," I said.

"Perhaps," she said, "we can find the dining room and have a bite to eat."

The dining room was splendid with potted palm trees and antimacassars. The tables were set with white tablecloths and fine bone china. We felt so special being waited on by servants. After examining the menus and seeing the prices, we each ordered a bowl of vegetable soup, but the soup came with bread that helped fill me up. I was glad that my morning sickness was at last chased away with a full belly.

After three hours, we arrived at the dock in Vancouver. Both Grandma and I were surprised to see how big and busy Vancouver was. We were terrified as we stood on the gangplank and looked out at the bustle of the port. Victoria moved at a snail's pace compared with this beehive.

"I hope my nephew has arrived to pick us up," Grandma said. I could hear the excitement in her voice as she turned to look at me. "He's bringing his motorcar!"

Neither of us had ever ridden in a motorcar before.

We got to the bottom of the gangplank and followed the mass of passengers up to the street. I carried my bag in my left hand and had Grandma's arm firmly linked in my right arm. I didn't want her to be knocked over in this crush of humanity. Neither did I want to be separated from her.

We reached the sidewalk and Grandma recognized John standing there, searching among the disembarked passengers. She waved at him. He looked relieved as he made his way over to us. He gave Grandma a kiss on the cheek and took her bag.

"Hello, Auntie Lucy," he said. He didn't speak to me.

"Hello, John. You know my granddaughter, Edith."

He nodded. "Yes," he said. "We're to take her to the Vancouver Home for Girls."

"Yes," Grandma said.

"Righto. Let's get to it then." He turned and walked away without taking my bag or looking at me. We followed him to his motorcar. It was a Model T touring car. I'd seen them before and now I was going to get my first ride in one.

Cousin John first placed Grandma's suitcase, then mine, behind the back seat. He held the back door open.

"You get in here, Edith," he said to me.

So I wasn't invisible!

"And Auntie, you come and sit in the front seat with me."

Grandma looked as excited as a child as he helped her climb into the seat.

"I think it would be a good idea," John said, "to drop you at Papa's before I drive Edith to the home."

"Well," Grandma said. "I was hoping to come along and see Edith is properly installed at the home."

"But Auntie, you've had a long day already with the boat trip."

"I was looking forward to a jaunt in the motorcar," she said.

"I'll take you for a ride on another day, I promise," John said. "Besides Papa is waiting anxiously to see you."

"But I wanted to say goodbye to Edith."

I leaned forward and spoke above the clatter of the motorcar. "That's all right, Grandma. We can say goodbye when we get to Uncle Sam's."

She half-turned to look at me. "Are you sure?"

"Yes," I said.

So we drove to Uncle Sam's house. It was in a nice area with tree-lined streets. When the motorcar came to a stop in front of the house, John jumped out and opened the door for Grandma. Meanwhile, I tried to figure out how to open my door.

An old man came out of the house and walked down the driveway. He met Grandma on the sidewalk and they hugged each other. Over her shoulder, he glared at me.

I reached out and opened the door with the handle on the outside since no one seemed to be coming to help me.

"It's good to see you, Lucy dear, no matter what the circumstances." Uncle Sam glared at me again.

I jumped down on the sidewalk beside Grandma. John arrived then with Grandma's bag. Grandma extricated herself from her brother's embrace and turned her attention to me.

"You'll be all right?" she asked plaintively.

I nodded.

"I was hoping to see you off at the home. I wanted to see where you're going to stay."

"I'm sure it'll be fine, Grandma," I said. "You go enjoy your visit with your brother."

"Yes," John said. "I'll just bring your suitcase in for you." He turned to me. "You make yourself comfortable in the motorcar. I'll be right out."

Grandma put her arms around me. "Write to me," she said.

"I will."

She looked me in the eyes. She was near tears.

"Go on, Grandma. I'm fine."

I watched her go up the walk with her brother until they had all gone inside. Then I climbed back in the car and waited for Cousin John to come back out.

He said not a word to me as he drove the motorcar. The soup and bread I'd eaten at lunch was a distant memory now and my stomach was empty. The jerking motion of the motorcar on the bouncy road made me feel sick. I tried desperately to control it, but I finally had to ask Cousin John to stop. I didn't have time to open the door, so I stood up, leaned over and threw up. I was mortified to see that the vomit landed on the running board of the motorcar and was only grateful that Cousin John couldn't see it. Yet, anyway.

My sickness had only drawn a line under my condition and accentuated my shame. John did not say a word to me even after I sat down. Not a word of sympathy. Not even "How are you doing?"

I reached into my bag and took out a handkerchief to wipe my mouth but it did nothing to help the sour taste there.

In spite of being sick and in spite of the company, I enjoyed my first ride in a motorcar, seeing the city fly past. But Cousin John's silence was almost intolerable. I even preferred my mother's shouting at me. I suppose his own children were angels and had never done anything wrong. Nothing as bad as this, at any rate. But that thought gave me an idea about how to break the silence.

"How are James and Sarah?" I asked.

"Fine," he said.

And I thought that was all he was going to say, but after a moment or two of thought, he continued.

"Sarah has just finished normal school," he said.

Oh, that hurt.

"And James is working as an accountant for a private company. He's been married to his high school sweetheart, Margaret, for three years."

"Do they have any children?" I asked, just to keep the conversation going.

His face darkened. "No," he said. "Sadly not."

"Well, at least he won't have to go to war," I said, "since he's married."

Cousin John gave me another unpleasant look and I decided even silence was preferable to our conversational fumbling. I concentrated on enjoying the trip and not throwing up again.

9

The Daily Colonist   April 25, 1928

Not Eligible as Senators: Constitution disqualifies women from Senate says Supreme Court

Easter arrived at long last and I prepared my outfit with great care.

"What shall I wear, Biddy?"

She scowled at me.

I imagined the delight on Margaret May's face when she saw me in one of my flapper dresses. "But then her mother will scowl at me. Just like you, Biddy."

I got up and went to my closet.

"Something more conservative, then. Perhaps if I can make a good impression on her mother, she might let me see more of Margaret May."

I flipped through my gowns looking for the perfect dress. "Something I might wear to church if I ever went."

Biddy stared at me.

"You want to know why I don't go to church, Biddy? I know it would make Grandma happy. But that's a discussion for another time."

Finally, I found a dress that covered my knees. I'd bought it two years before, but it was still rather stylish with a low, pleated skirt and a matching cloche cap. Margaret May might be disappointed in my attire, but today I was trying to win her mother over. I wanted to be able to see Margaret May on other occasions besides family dinners.

I abstained from my usual pre-dinner scotch so that my breath would be pure when I hugged and kissed my cousins, but I couldn't keep myself from speeding in my roadster to my family home. I took the front steps two at a time.

Papa answered the door. "You're early," he said. "No one else is here yet."

Mum came out of the kitchen into the foyer, scanning my outfit. "Good," she said, nodding her approval. "You can help me set the table."

So, I repeated the Christmas ritual, only this time there were fewer plates to put around the table — three fewer. That was strange. Perhaps Robert and his wife were going to her family's for dinner. After I'd put the plates around the table, I went into the kitchen for the cutlery.

"Who's not coming?" I asked Mum.

"Cousin James and his family have gone to Vancouver for Easter," she said.

I stopped dead in my tracks. They did it to spite me. All this time I'd been waiting to see Margaret May. I had been so good. I had foregone the pleasure of seeing her walking to school. I hadn't taken the nip of scotch I needed to make my family dinners palatable. I was wearing this long dismal dress. And this was how they rewarded me? By going to Vancouver!

"What's wrong?" Mum said, looking at me closely.

"Nothing," I said.

"Well, you know where the cutlery is." She turned back to the oven.

I went to the cutlery drawer and counted out the knives, forks and spoons. But I could barely concentrate. I was angry and I was disappointed. I needed to talk to someone more sympathetic than my mother.

"Where's Grandma?" I asked.

"She's in the parlour on the chesterfield. She's feeling a little under the weather."

"I should go and say hello," I said. "I'll finish setting the table after."

Mum shook her head at me as I walked back to the dining room and put the cutlery in a pile on the table.

Grandma was curled up in the armchair, wrapped in a blanket. She looked as forlorn as I felt.

"What's the matter, Grandma?"

She looked up. "Oh, hello, dear," she responded.

I bent down to give her a kiss.

"It's just a cold," she said.

"Have you taken anything for it?" I asked.

"Just a little nip of brandy," she said, looking a tad guilty.

I smiled. "But you look so miserable."

"Didn't your mother tell you?"

I doubted Grandma would be so upset about the absence of James and his family, so it must be something else. "Tell me what?"

"Your great-uncle Sam died last week."

"Oh, I am sorry, Grandma." I sat down and took her hand in mine. I barely knew him, but he was her brother. I remembered him only as the old man in Vancouver who'd hugged Grandma and scowled at me over her shoulder. I couldn't say that I felt the least bit sorry that he was dead. Then I realized it must have been the reason James and his family had gone to Vancouver. Uncle Sam was his grandfather and Margaret May's great-grandfather. It made me feel a little better to know that their trip was not a slight aimed at me.

"Yes," Grandma said. "Well, Sam was almost ten years older than me. He would have been almost ninety, so he's had a good long life."

"Did you want to go to his funeral, Grandma?" I asked. "I could take you." I remembered our trip to Vancouver together some years before. I would like to do it again under happier circumstances. What irony! To go to Vancouver for a funeral was happier for me than going for a birth.

"Would you?" she asked. "I'd like that very much."

I decided then and there I would tell her about Margaret. I couldn't stand to keep it a secret another second. At that moment, the doorbell rang and Lucinda's children burst into the parlour and surrounded me. I said hello, extricated myself and went back to setting the table.

"Careful of Great-Grandma," I said over my shoulder. "She's not feeling well."

Oh, well. I would have plenty of time to talk to Grandma on the way to Vancouver. It would be a more appropriate time anyway.

The next Tuesday morning, I put together the stories for the Society and Women's Affairs pages as usual and, as usual, there was the list of women's clubs and societies and what they were doing, stories on weddings and parties, and fashion news, including a fascinating story on what to wear at the beach. Apparently, a woman needed to take more than one bathing costume. I tried to remember the last time I'd gone swimming at the Gorge. Perhaps this summer I should make an effort. I thought of a picnic with Margaret May, but that was out of the question. I did have a bathing costume though. I'd even gone swimming at the new Crystal swimming pool.

When I got home, I made a special supper of salmon and potatoes. I knew this would make Biddy happy. And it did. She wound herself between my legs as I stood at the stove frying the filet.

"Yes, I know, Biddy. I'm making your favourite meal and you can hardly stand to wait for it." I bent down to pet her and rubbed the spot behind her ears. "But good things come to those who wait."

I stood up and realized what I'd said. "Or so they say, though it hasn't been my experience."

I gave Biddy half the salmon and then sat down to eat mine. Then I made a cup of tea and picked up the morning paper, which I hadn't had time to read all day. I sat down on the chesterfield and curled my legs under me. Biddy looked pleased and jumped up beside me, curling herself as well.

The little story was on page three buried between an ad for Shredded Wheat and a sale on corsets, entitled "Not Eligible as Senators," subtitled "Constitution disqualifies women from Senate says Supreme Court." I read it through. "The Supreme Court in a decision handed down today... decided that under the present provisions of the BNA Act women were not qualified to sit in the Senate." *Not qualified!* That's what the old fogies at the Supreme Court decided. The British North America Act, according to them, had to be interpreted as the original legislators intended it in 1867. And why was that? Who could know what they'd intended? And did the world not change? Did attitudes not change? I suppose not, since this important story was considered by the male editors of the newspaper not to be worthy of front-page status. It was not even considered something women would be interested in. All morning, I had worked on the part of the paper labelled 'Women's Affairs' and this story about women wasn't even included.

According to the editors at the paper, all that we women were interested in was bathing suits and what cap to wear to the beach. All we cared about was who was marrying whom, what food to feed our children and who was speaking at the Women's Institute this week. Such creatures as women might have the right to vote — horrors! — but they certainly couldn't be senators because they wouldn't be capable of 'sober second thought'.

I immediately set about proving them right by getting out my bottle of scotch. I usually only drank on the weekend, but this evening I was in a proper funk and didn't want to stay sober. I had been so disappointed not to see Margaret May at Easter. I thought of her and realized what a world she was growing up in. I had expected it to be a better place for women after they had the right to vote. But we women, none of us — not me, not my grandmother, not my mother, not even my daughter — were considered to be 'persons'.

Nothing had really changed. The men hadn't changed. And for some reason, the very women who had fought so long and hard for the right to vote stopped fighting once they'd attained their goal. But they had only taken the first step, a baby step. They had no idea how very far they still had to go to win their battle. For, if their battle was true equality, it would not be won until everyone's hearts and minds had changed. In fact, such a battle might never be won.

I was no different from anyone else. I was the same lame person, the same meek lamb as ever. I walked quietly into the newspaper room every day, sat down and disappeared into the wallpaper.

10

The Daily Colonist   January 12, 1915

Third Contingent of New Troops
Leaving Victoria en Route to Europe

Finally, we arrived at the Vancouver Home for Girls, an old building on Cambie Street.

I opened the door of the motorcar by myself, having figured out how to do it. I jumped over the mess I'd made on the running board. I briefly thought about cleaning it up, but all I had was the handkerchief that my grandmother had embroidered my initials on and I didn't want to ruin it. So, I stood there on the sidewalk and looked to see if Cousin John was getting my bag for me or if he expected me to do it. He had gotten out, on the driver's side fortunately, and was reaching behind the seat. I was relieved.

He brought my bag around the motorcar and carried it up the stairs. I followed him through the great doors.

"Thank you," I said.

An austere-looking middle-aged woman came out to the vestibule to meet us. Her hair was pulled back severely in a bun that tightened her face. Her lips were pinched and the lines around her mouth and on her forehead were deeply etched in a frown. She shook Cousin John's hand. Then she turned and shook my hand. "Welcome to the Vancouver Redemptive Home for Girls," she said. She rolled her r's in a strong

Scottish brogue, putting great emphasis on the word 'redemptive.' I hadn't heard it called that before. Was it an inkling of what was to come?

"May I speak with you for a moment?" Cousin John asked her.

"Yes, of course," she said. "Follow me to my office." She looked at me. "You can sit over there."

She pointed to some chairs. I obeyed. Cousin John put my suitcase beside me and went with the woman.

I waited for about ten minutes, wondering what on earth they were talking about in there. Finally, the door opened and Cousin John came out.

He looked even more uncomfortable than he had all the way here. "Well," he said. "I'll tell your grandmother you've arrived safely. 'Bye now."

After he'd gone, it was my turn to go into the office. I followed the woman into a tiny room with a desk, two chairs and a filing cabinet.

"Sit down," she said.

I sat.

"My name is Mrs. Gordon and I'm the matron here. What's your name, child?"

"Edith Robertson," I said.

She took a piece of paper and pen and wrote it down.

"All right," she said. "You mustn't use your last name here. You'll be known as Edith R. We like to protect our girls' identities." She made a weak attempt to smile. "Now," she continued, "normally, the unwed mothers are encouraged to take their babies home with them. We help to find them employment in service. As a single mother out in the world, your sin would be visible to all. That and the responsibility of keeping a child should make you less inclined to waver again."

I nodded. Though it was judgmental, I had no quarrel with the argument.

"But in your case, an adoption for the child has already been arranged."

I stared at her.

"You are a most fortunate girl. I hope that you will take advantage of, and not waste, your good fortune." She stood up. "I'll show you to your room."

She picked up my bag but put it on the desk and left it behind. I followed her swishing black crepe skirt as she walked up the stairs.

"What about my bag?" I asked.

"You won't need it," she said.

I didn't even have time to process this new idea. They were going to take my baby away and she made it sound like a privilege I'd been granted. No one had asked me. I tapped my pocket. At least I still had my letter from Arthur. I'd make sure they never took that.

My feelings were still swirling when we entered a room with four beds squeezed into it. At the end of the room, by the window, were three 'girls' in various stages of pregnancy wearing shapeless sack gowns in the same dismal shade of taupe. They fell silent as we entered.

"Girls," Mrs. Gordon announced in her Scottish accent, "this is Edith."

They nodded at me.

Mrs. Gordon pointed to the first bed on the right. "That's your bed." Then she pointed at a little bedside table with two drawers. "You'll find everything you need in there. Supper is in half an hour. Get changed and don't be late."

Then Mrs. Gordon turned on her heel and left the room. As her footsteps grew fainter, the three young women approached me cautiously. A tall, skinny one with a tiny belly reached me first and shook my hand. She looked even younger than I was.

"I'm Blythe," she said. "This is Gertrude."

A short, shy ginger-haired waif with an enormous belly shook my hand and said, "It's Trudy."

"And this is Carole," Blythe said.

The third girl, who looked older than the others, her hair in tight curls that framed her face, nodded at me. The curls did not move.

"I suppose I have to wear one of those," I said, indicating their garb.

"What?" Blythe asked. "You don't like our mud dresses!?"

"Very fashionable," I said.

"You'd better hurry up," Carole spoke for the first time, "and put it on. You don't want to be late for supper."

"Oh, Carole," Blythe scolded. Though she seemed the youngest, she was definitely the leader. She turned to me. "Carole's scared if one of us is late, we'll all get punished."

"What's the punishment?" I asked.

"Extra chores," Blythe said.

"Yeah," Carole added, "and ain't we got enough of those already. So, shake a leg!"

I pulled open the top drawer of the table and saw knickers and various undergarments. I slipped Arthur's letter underneath them. In the second drawer, I found the large, shapeless sack in taupe and pulled it out.

"Where shall I change?" I asked.

"Right here," Blythe said.

"Unless you're an awful prude," Carole said, "like Gertrude here. Then you hide out in the toilet down the hall."

Gertrude blushed. "It's Trudy."

I took off my dress, revealing my little baby-bulge.

"When are you due?" Blythe asked.

"May," I said. "Early May." I pulled the sack over my head and looked down. Grandma would've said, *It fits where it touches.* It would be some time before I filled it out, if ever.

"I'm due the end of April," Blythe said, "so we're both stuck here for a while."

"What about you?" I asked Trudy. Carole had already retreated to the other side of the room.

"Soon," she said, blushing. "All too soon."

She looked so terrified that I didn't want to ask her anything more.

"Are we the only ones here?" I asked.

Blythe laughed. "No," she said. "There are other cells with other inmates. Some of them are on supper duty, peeling vegetables and setting the tables. We're on clean-up duties, clearing tables and washing dishes. I guess you'll be doing that with us this evening."

"Oh," I said. "Will I ever get my belongings back, do you think?"

"Not bloody likely!" Carole said, as she came back from her corner of the room. "After supper, give your old togs to Mrs. Gor-r-don or she'll have a conniption." She rolled her r's in imitation of the headmistress.

"Let's go, girls," Blythe trilled.

I followed them to the dining room. It was a large hall with five tables and six settings at each of them. I looked around at the sea of girls, some already eating and others in line to get their dinner. It was being dished out by some dour-looking woman who seemed half-afraid of us. I can't say that I blamed her as I looked around at the other 'girls.' In spite of the fact we were all dressed alike in our dumpy shifts, I could tell that the other twenty-five girls were distinctly different. First of all, they weren't pregnant. Secondly, they looked harder. None of them smiled at or spoke to me. They gave me the once-over and went back to whatever they were doing. The ones sitting at the tables hunched over their bowls unhappily.

"What's wrong with them?" I whispered to Trudy, who was in front of me in the line.

"They're fallen women," she whispered back.

"I thought that's what we were," I said naively.

Blythe, who was in front of Trudy, turned around and laughed. "We haven't fallen quite as far." She picked up a plate and added, "Yet."

The lady behind the counter glared at her as she dished out the stew.

Carole, who was behind me in the line, said, "Not all of 'em are whores. Some of 'em are pickpockets and drunks."

I stared around at the motley crew, fascinated. One of them noticed me staring and stuck out her tongue.

"Do you want some stew?" the dour lady said.

I turned back to the business at hand, picked up a plate and held it out while she spooned some glutinous mess onto it. Then she put a bun on top. "Next," she said.

I followed the other girls to our table that was only set for four. When I was settled, Blythe said, "They're not women at all, fallen or not. None of us are women in here. We're girls. It's in the name." Then she did a fair imitation of Mrs. Gordon with the rolled r's and all. "Vancouver *R-r-edemptive* Home for Girls."

We all laughed.

Just then the real Mrs. Gordon appeared. "No more frivolity, girls."

The way she pronounced that last word sent us into gales of giggles again.

"We will now say grace." She glared at us sternly before launching into a prayer. "God, we give you thanks for this generous bounty provided by the kind women of the Presbyterian Church. May we strive with all our might to be worthy of it and of their labour, which has been to Your Honour and to Your Glory. Amen."

As she walked past our table, she said, "Lights out will be half an hour earlier in your room tonight."

That made us stop giggling and turn our attention to swallowing the unappetizing stew.

After supper and all the chores had been done, we sat in the bedroom on our beds while the other girls tried to teach me how to roll my r's like Mrs. Gordon did, so I could mock her too.

"She ain't the only housemother we have," Blythe said. "Tomorrow you'll meet Miss Have-a-shit."

The girls burst out into laughter at this name.

"But don't call her that to her face," Carole said.

"Of course, I wouldn't!" I blushed. "What's her real name?"

"Miss Havisham," ginger Trudy said.

A picture of the poor old, abandoned bride in *Great Expectations* popped into my head and I might have said something but didn't think the other girls would get the reference.

"What's she like?" I asked.

"Uptight mouse," Blythe said. She got up to strut around the room as though she had a poker up her derriere.

There was a knock on the door. Blythe dove for her bed.

"Gir-r-rls." It was Mrs. Gordon. "Lights out in half an hour."

"Yes, Mrs. Gordon," Blythe cooed.

The other girls giggled into their pillows.

As I lay there in the dark, I thought about my mother. I couldn't believe she'd sent me to this place. She didn't even approve of my friendship with Mabel since her family was less well-to-do than ours. Well, the girls here, even the pregnant ones, were quite clearly from a far lower social background than I was. Mum would have been mortified to hear their coarse language and poor manners. And yet, she'd sent me here!

Either she didn't know what the place was like, or perhaps she did know and this was my punishment. That made some sense. She wanted me to see how far I might fall if I continued my wicked ways. Well, I'd show her. I rather liked the other girls in my room, especially Blythe. I was sure we'd soon be friends. As for wicked ways, well, perhaps I'd learn some more while I was here.

11

The Daily Colonist   April 27, 1928

Explanation Is Requested

~~~ ~~~ ~~~ ~~~ ~~~ ~~~ ~~~ ~~~ ~~~ ~~~ ~~~ ~~~ ~~~ ~~~

Grandma and I boarded the *Princess Marguerite* in the Inner Harbour. As I walked up the gangplank, Arthur flashed into my head. I saw him going up a similar gangplank with a big grin on his face and turning to wave goodbye. I caught that wave in my heart and swallowed.

It was a beautiful day, unlike the last time Grandma and I had made this trip thirteen years before in the month of January. We stayed on deck again to watch the ship manoeuvre its way out of Victoria's busy narrow little harbour. We stayed some more to watch the Olympic Mountains. In the rainy days of winter, their snowcaps were often hidden behind the clouds, but in the spring, when the sun was shining as it was now, they were in their glory, still snow-covered and radiant.

It was a calm day and the waters of the strait were not choppy. I didn't have to worry about morning sickness, so we stayed on deck as the ship rounded the end of Vancouver Island and wound its way through the myriad islands of Haro Strait. We could see the majestic peak of towering volcano Mount Baker a hundred miles away in the distance but seeming so much closer because of its size.

Finally, Grandma announced that she was tired and we should go in and sit down. I felt guilty for making her stand so long.

"Let's go to the dining room," I suggested. "Like we did on our last trip."

"I'm not hungry, dear," Grandma said. She always ate like a bird, but she especially had no appetite since her brother's death.

"It's my treat this time, Grandma, and I insist."

"All right," she said. "Some tea would be nice."

We found our way to the beautifully appointed dining room. It was as luxurious as I remembered on that other ship (was it the *Princess Victoria*?) so many years before.

We were seated at a small table and waited on by a handsome young man.

"Does this not bring back memories?" Grandma asked.

I nodded. "Not all happy ones," I said.

"Our last trip was the last time I saw my brother Sam," she said, straightening the knife in its place setting. "He was the last one left of my immediate family."

I persuaded Grandma to order a biscuit with her tea, while I ordered a poached egg on toast with mine. We sat in silence waiting for our food, while I thought about how to tell her my news about Margaret May. The waiter brought us our food and then left.

"Grandma," I said, "I have found the daughter that I lost."

She put down her biscuit and stared. "What do you mean?" She placed her hand on her heart. "How did you find her? Is she in Vancouver? Is that why you wanted to go?"

"One question at a time," I said. "I found her by chance. She's in Vancouver now but she lives in Victoria."

"Who is she?"

"She's Margaret."

Grandma looked at me as if I were speaking another language. "Margaret?"

"Yes, Margaret. Cousin James' daughter Margaret. Margaret Innis."

"But she's not your daughter. She's cousin James's daughter."

"She's adopted."

Grandma frowned. Squinting, she looked me square in the eye. "How do you know this?"

"James told me and his wife admitted it too. They also admitted her birthday is May thirteenth, 1915."

Grandma looked startled. "But in the same family? That's too much of a coincidence!"

"Not so much. Do you remember when John drove me to the Vancouver Home for Girls?"

…na nodded.

Well, he went in to speak to the matron there. I waited outside for ten minutes wondering what they were talking about. I think now he was arranging an adoption for his son, James. He told me at the time they'd been married three years and wanted to have children."

Grandma contemplated her tea biscuit with intense focus, turning it over as if searching for its secrets.

Our waiter suddenly appeared at the table. "Is everything to your satisfaction?" he asked, looking concerned.

"You've put raisins in it," Grandma said. "Very nice."

The waiter nodded and left.

With him gone, I asked, "What do you think, Grandma?"

"It makes sense," she said. "John might very well have wanted his son to have a child from the family. But what are you going to do with this news?"

"I've known for months and I've done nothing," I said. "It's killing me. I had to at least tell someone. So, I told you."

"Better me, I suppose, than Margaret. It would break the poor girl's heart to learn her parents are not her parents."

"Don't you think they should have told her?"

Grandma took a bite of her tea biscuit and chewed. I waited.

"I don't know," she said finally. "I can understand why they didn't." She took another bite and chewed.

I was exasperated. I plunged my knife into the poached egg and it spilled its yellow blood all over the plate. This was not the response I'd hoped for. I wanted Grandma to support me fully. As the elder of the family, I wanted her to speak to her nephew and convince him that all should be revealed to Margaret May. They could do it however they wanted, slowly at first, telling her she was adopted and then, when she was used to that idea, telling her who her mother was. But Grandma was siding with the family.

"I'm disappointed in you, Grandma. I didn't think you would be in favour of all this secrecy."

"Well," she said, putting down her biscuit again, "I'm finding this hard to digest."

I wondered for a moment if she meant the biscuit.

"I can't imagine how such news might affect a young girl like Margaret."

"But Grandma, think of how it's affecting me. I can't sleep. I can't eat. I can't work. I think of her all the time. She's my girl, stolen from me, and I can't even speak to her or touch her or…"

Grandma put her hand on mine. "I know, dear. You've had a rough time of it. But you're an adult and you must have come to terms by now with the loss of your baby."

She was still thinking about it as if it were a miscarriage or a stillbirth, but Margaret May was alive.

Grandma looked at me. "Don't do or say anything at Sam's funeral," she said, looking concerned. "Please."

She said the last word with such a desperate pleading tone that I could only respond "I won't."

The rest of the meal we ate in silence, each lost, I suppose, in our separate thoughts.

12

The Daily Colonist   April 13, 1915
Women's Realm: Caring for the Babies

Shortly after I arrived, we woke up to Trudy's screams in the early morning hours.

"What's going on?" I cried.

The lights came on in the room. Carole was standing at the door by the switch. "T'ain't nothing. Trudy's just gone into labour."

Miss Havisham came running in the room. "Land sakes, girl! Why are you making such a racket?"

"It hurts," Trudy screamed. "Oh, it hurts." She doubled over in an impossible position and cried, "Oh, God, it hurts!"

"That's no reason to take the Lord's name in vain!" Miss Havisham said primly. "Come now. Girls, you take her to the birthing room while I call the midwife."

We helped Trudy get up and Blythe walked with her to the room where she was to give birth as she seemed incapable of doing it herself. I followed and we helped her into bed. Miss Havisham came back and shooed us from the room. I'll never forget the terrified look on Trudy's face as we left.

That evening, Blythe moved into the bed beside me so we could talk together more intimately.

"I'm glad Trudy's okay," I said. We learned at supper that she'd a baby boy.

"Oh yeah," Blythe replied. "What don't kill you makes you stronger. That's what my mother always says, anyways."

"Yeah, but childbirth can kill you." Carole had told us about her own mother, who had died giving birth when Carole was little.

"Yeah," Blythe said. "It can happen. We'd be a lot better off if, instead of Bible study, they taught us about childbirth. But let's change the subject. Tell me about your baby's father. Have you told him you're with child?"

"No," I said. "I didn't find out till after he'd gone overseas. And then... Well, I just thought he's got enough to worry about."

"Yeah," Blythe agreed. "My baby's father's a soldier too. I never told him neither. I mean, what's he going to do about it over there? But when he comes back, he's going to marry me."

"How are you going to look after the baby till then?"

"I begged my mother to look after it — to pretend it was hers. I can't raise a child by myself. I'll go into service until Chris comes back. We'll get married and then I'll take my baby back."

"I never thought of asking my mother such a thing. She was so angry with me and disappointed in me. We never got beyond that." I thought of my grandma. Grandma had offered to help me. But I couldn't imagine Mum pretending the baby was hers.

"Do you think your baby's father'll marry you when he comes back from the war?" she asked.

"Yes," I said. "I know he will."

"How do you know that?"

"He told me in the last letter I got from him."

"Read it to me," she said.

I took it out of my bedside table, opened it up and blushed. "Are you sure?" I asked.

"Come on, read it."

My Dearest Edith,

There is so little we are allowed to say about where we are and what we are doing here. And there is so little that I want to say about it really. I would rather imagine myself somewhere else doing something else and so my mind often wanders back to that summer afternoon we spent together. You cannot imagine the number of times my mind takes me back there and how much I long to see you again.

My fondest dream is to go home after this war is over, and, after taking you in my arms and holding you once again, I will go to the real estate office and buy that piece of land from whoever owns it. Then I will build a house on that spot with my own hands — because now I know these hands can do anything, even the unspeakable, but let's not talk of that.

We will marry and live together in our own little house, and we will have children — as many or as few as you want. That is my dream. It is my fondest hope that it is your dream too, or something very like it.

I decided to end the letter there because the rest of it was too personal for anyone else to hear, even Blythe. It embarrassed me to think that some censor had read it before me.

"That's beautiful," Blythe said. "So, why are you giving your baby up for adoption?" I'd told Blythe about this.

"I never had any say," I said. "It was arranged. No one even asked me."

"But would he still marry you if he knew you'd given away his child?"

"I don't know," I said. I tried to imagine Arthur's face if I told him such a thing. Shock. Sorrow. Forgiveness? "I don't know."

"Best not to tell him then, not if you want him to marry you when he comes home."

Blythe's question gave me pause. Would Arthur marry me if he knew I'd given his child away to someone else? How *could* I do that? And who had arranged this adoption and why? It must have been Mum and the reason must be because she still wanted me to be a teacher and fulfill her dream. I thought these thoughts over and over for half the night, tossing and turning, unable to sleep.

We went to visit Trudy the next day. She was still in the birthing room, where she looked after and nursed her baby boy. We all stood around her bed and cooed over her little bundle. I watched him squirming and kicking off his swaddling clothes and then crying.

That was when my own baby moved within me for the first time and I realized with a sudden, frightening physical knowledge that I was not going to be allowed to take this baby home like Trudy was, like all the other girls were going to do.

I decided I must go and argue my case before Mrs. Gordon. I thought perhaps she would be sympathetic since adoption was not the usual policy of the Vancouver Redemptive Home for Girls.

I knocked on her door. Mrs. Gordon invited me into her office. She looked up from her paperwork. "What is it?" she asked. "I have a lot of work to do."

"I was just wondering, Mrs. Gordon, if I might not keep my baby," I said nervously. "I know that is the usual policy here."

She shook her head. "Usually," she said, "and in the beginning, I was not altogether happy about the adoption arrangement. But I've come to terms with it. You seem quite an intelligent and sensible girl, in spite of your mistake. I understand you want to be a teacher. That'll never happen if you are a single mother."

I'd never told anyone here that I wanted to be a teacher. So, it *was* my mother who was behind this adoption idea. "But I don't want to be a teacher!" I cried. "I want to be a mother."

Mrs. Gordon made a sour face. "You should really be more grateful for your opportunities." She stood up. "Now, I'll hear no more about it."

I left the room, feeling down. Really down. How could my mother have done this to me without my consent?

Blythe and I became best friends as the months passed. I knew I would never see her again after she'd had her baby. And as difficult as that reality was, we didn't try to get any closer than we were allowed. Much as we hated the things that the old biddies at the home said to us, we knew from our own experiences that they were right about one thing. If you got too close to someone, your whole world could be changed irrevocably.

So I never learned Blythe's last name. I knew her only as Blythe S. and I liked to imagine her name was 'Blythe Spirit' like in that poem by Shelley that we'd read in our English class. "Bird thou never wert."

She left sometime during the night of April 29th to have her baby. I didn't go and visit her with the others while she nursed her baby. I couldn't stand to see the mothers and babies together anymore. It brought the pain of my imminent separation to the forefront. She came to say goodbye to me the day she left, without the baby, thankfully. We had once promised each other to exchange names and addresses but we didn't, even then.

Like that, she was gone. An empty bed beside me. But of course, not for long. Almost immediately, it was filled by another young girl — one more quiet, more wide-eyed, more terrified than even Trudy had been. The girls I'd met on my arrival were all gone now, one by one, and they'd been replaced by other one-named girls. I was the only one left of the four who were there when I arrived.

This new girl beside me was named Nancy P. but I scarcely even got to know her before I too was gone, taken by the labour pains in the early morning hours. Instead of having my baby in the Home for Girls, my parents had arranged that I would be taken to the Vancouver General Hospital to give birth. I thought I would never go back to the Vancouver Home for Girls, but I was wrong.

13

The Daily Colonist   April 29, 1928

Society Notes from Vancouver

Scarcely known to each other but bound by blood and robed in black, we stood at the foot of an open grave at Mountain View Cemetery in Vancouver. There were graves as far as the eye could see. Under the imposing glare of mountains, we huddled together to keep warm as a bitter wind came up.

We had come to bury Uncle Sam, or Father, Grandfather, Great-Grandfather, however he was known to us. Only my grandma knew him as Sam, just Sam, her big brother. Only she remembered him as a child. Only she wept.

I put my arm around her. I stared across the open grave at Margaret May, looking small and grim-faced between her 'mother' and 'father'. Her family.

An arrow struck my heart with grief. Not for Uncle Sam whom I scarcely knew, but for the loss of Margaret May, whom I scarcely knew, ensconced in the heart of her family and secretly ensconced in my heart. I felt my eyes grow moist and a single tear fell down my cheek.

The preacher mumbled his cant: "In the sure and certain hope of the resurrection…"

What a strange phrase! There is nothing sure and certain about resurrection. Only death is sure and certain. Death and the impossibility of going back and doing the whole thing over again but the right way this time. But certainly, we hope.

I imagined myself at fifteen, taking my baby wrapped in swaddling clothes out of the Home for Girls and walking into the city of Vancouver. I wondered what would have happened. I wondered that I had not envisioned that scenario at the time. I, childlike, had followed the will of others as if their will was what was best for me. Perhaps it was. But my will was thwarted so that I never discovered for myself what was best for me and best for May.

The preacher intoned "Amen" and our circle began to break up, falling apart into little groups chattering to each other. Cousin John and his wife came over and he took Grandma's other arm.

"Come on," he said. "We'll take you home to our place for tea and cookies."

His car was a lovely blue Packard roadster convertible. I wondered where Grandma and I would sit until he opened the rumble seat.

"Aunt Lucy," he said to Grandma. "You can sit in the front with me." Then he turned to his wife. "Catherine, you don't mind sitting in the back with Edith, do you?"

She frowned as if she definitely minded, then smiled sweetly when Grandma looked at her. "Of course not," she said.

And so we climbed into the rumble seat, which, being directly above the back wheels, lived up to its name on the bumpy streets of Vancouver.

I had never met John's wife before, but I was not introduced to her, so we sat in silence — or more accurately, without speaking — until we arrived at the house. If we *had* spoken, we would have had to shout to be heard over the din and the wind in our exposed seats. Instead, we concentrated on hanging on to our hats. Cousin Catherine had the added difficulty of keeping her neatly arranged locks from becoming disarranged. This was one of the advantages of having a bob. As soon as we arrived at the house, she disappeared to her dressing room to rearrange her hair and I didn't see her again, although she must have been at the reception.

A large crowd made up almost entirely of strangers filled Cousin John's spacious parlour. All the furniture had been pushed against the walls and the chairs were occupied by the elderly. We younger ones milled about in the middle, holding our teacups in one hand and nibbling dainties that perched precariously on the saucers between bites.

I looked about for Margaret May, hoping to talk with her, but I didn't see her in the parlour. There were more guests in the foyer, so I stepped out to see if she was there. I soon felt the presence of Cousin John beside me.

"If you're looking for Margaret, it's best for all that you stay away from her."

I stopped and glared at him. I spoke defiantly. "I promised her parents I would not tell her the truth and I will not, but I may speak to her if I wish."

"Please," he said, "do not make a scene. Come into my office for a moment so we can speak."

I followed him to a little room in the back of the house. He went to stand behind his desk as if he needed a piece of furniture between us.

"You may sit if you wish." He indicated a chair, but he didn't sit, so I didn't either.

"It is most unfortunate that James and Margaret ran into you. I never told them that Margaret was family and I never expected that you would make the connection, but there you are."

He stared at me and I said nothing. So, I'd been right and he *had* arranged the adoption that day he'd spent ten minutes talking to Mrs. Gordon at the Vancouver Home for Girls.

"James," he continued, "has told me that you've made a promise but I wonder if you can be trusted."

"How dare you...?" I began.

"Tut, tut." He put up his hand to cut me off. "No show of false piety. I've been told of your true character by my son and his wife and I won't be persuaded by your theatrics."

"What do you mean by 'my true character'?"

"They tell me you dress immodestly and inappropriately for a young woman. Thus, you reveal yourself as a loose and immoral woman."

"I dress in the fashion of the day."

"I did not say otherwise. But it is clear you are not a suitable relation for Margaret, who is a young and impressionable girl."

"How dare you?" I said again, determined to continue and talk right over him if he interrupted this time. "You took advantage of me when I was just a child, barely older than Margaret is now. Without consulting me, you took her away from me and gave her to your son. I consider that to be immoral behaviour."

He looked astonished. "It was with the full consent of your mother," he said. "And as you yourself admit, you were a mere child and didn't know what was best."

I turned around and started towards the door.

"Before you go, let me offer you an inducement to keep your promise."

I stopped and turned around. "What do you mean?"

"Perhaps you could be induced to stay away from Margaret by a little monetary compensation. Would a thousand dollars be acceptable?"

My mouth fell open, not because the sum was more than I could have made in a year, but because he was offering me a bribe. He must think very little of me indeed. I continued toward the door, turned around, glared at him, then opened it, walked out and slammed it behind me.

Now, instead of Margaret May, I was looking for her mother. I wanted to tell her that she was mistaken about my character. In spite of my dress, I was not a loose woman. It was suddenly important for me to prove this since my opportunities to interact with Margaret May depended on her mother's opinion of me.

There she was, talking to another woman I didn't know. I calmed myself and walked over to her.

"May I speak with you, Margaret?"

She looked askance at me. "Excuse me, Sarah," she said to the woman. "This is our distant cousin Edith from Victoria. Apparently, she craves a word in private."

So, this was James's sister, my cousin Sarah. I hadn't seen her since she as a child. She nodded at me, then dutifully took the hint and left.

Margaret turned to me and whispered. "Well, what is it, Edith?"

"I'm afraid you've formed a very negative impression of me based on my flapper dresses."

"Yes," she said. "That and the fact that you bore a child out of wedlock."

"Her father was a soldier and he was killed in the war. He would have come back and married me. He was the only man I have ever loved."

She looked unconvinced.

"The only man," I reiterated, "I've ever been with in that way."

"We have only your word for that," she said. "Your appearance would suggest otherwise."

"I only dress like that at my mother's dinner parties to aggravate and annoy her. I've never forgiven her for giving away my baby."

"That is childish," Margaret said primly.

"Perhaps," I said.

"You ought to mend your relationship with your own mother before you consider being a mother yourself."

It was annoyingly sensible advice and I hated her for saying it. "Well, you may be right," I said. "I will try. In the meantime, I hope you'll accept my mother's invitations and let me continue at least to see my daughter."

"She's my daughter!"

"All right," I said. "I'll concede that. But all I ask is you let me see her."

"Perhaps. I'll discuss it with my husband."

"Where is she now?" I asked.

"She's playing with her young cousins in the nursery. I'd appreciate it if you didn't disturb her. Now, I must mingle. Excuse me."

Margaret took her leave of me. I went to find my grandmother and take her to our hotel.

We took a taxi to the Hotel Vancouver, a railroad hotel owned by the Canadian National Railway, while the Empress in Victoria was a Canadian Pacific property. Just two blocks away, the CPR had started to build another rival hotel. I wondered if it would be more like the Empress reigning over a spacious landscaped property or if it too would be squeezed on a downtown lot between other buildings like the Hotel Vancouver. Its ornate, Italianate style thrust upwards and reminded me of pictures I'd seen of skyscrapers in New York, on a much smaller scale, of course. But for me, from provincial little Victoria, the scale was quite large enough.

I went to the window of our hotel room and looked down onto the street ten floors below. I had never been in such a tall building and I contemplated briefly what would happen if there was a disaster like a fire. How would I get my grandmother down all those flights of stairs if the elevators didn't work? Then I shook my head and turned away from the window.

Grandma was sitting in an armchair. I went to sit down across from her. We didn't speak for a while, lost in our own thoughts.

My grandmother's muted response to my news about Margaret May and Cousin John's declaration that my mother had conspired with him in her adoption weighed heavily on my mind. What if, in spite of the fact she had been so supportive of me all these years, my grandmother had known about the adoption all along? Perhaps she had even been a co-conspirator.

Such a thought didn't bear thinking. All I had to do to banish it was to ask her point-blank and learn the truth. But what if I didn't like the truth? After all, Grandma was the only person who made sure I was included as part of the family all these years. If it turned out she'd been involved in the adoption conspiracy, I would find myself tossed into the void without a thread to cling to. I loved my grandmother. I couldn't bear to lose her. I wanted to trust her, but I had to know the truth.

"It was a lovely service," Grandma said finally. "And so nice of John to invite us to his house afterwards."

I was not disposed to offer any praise of John whatsoever, so I just nodded. "It was good," I said, "that you got to say farewell to your brother."

"It's more than he did for me when he left home all those years ago. He left without saying goodbye. I was just a child and didn't understand."

Grandma was visibly hurt by this long-ago slight. I left her with her sorrow for a few moments before I brought up the fresher sadness that was on my mind.

"Cousin John told me today that he arranged Margaret May's adoption with my mother's full consent." I hesitated to ask, but I needed to know. "Tell me, Grandma, did you know about the adoption?"

She looked at me, surprised. "Do you mean 'did I know that James and his wife had adopted her'? No, I didn't. Your mother told me that you had agreed it was best that the baby be adopted. I was surprised at the time because I thought you wanted to keep it."

"I did. I really did. I never agreed to the adoption. I just let it happen. I didn't think I had a choice."

Grandma's eyes were sad. "Ah, my dear," she said. "You were just a child. I believed at the time it was probably for the best that you didn't have the burden of motherhood thrust upon you. I believed that you still wanted to go to normal school and become a teacher."

"How could I bear seeing all those children every day?" I was crying by this time and was incapable of further conversation. But I was greatly relieved that my grandmother had not been part of the conspiracy to take away my child.

"There, there, now," Grandma said. "You have a good cry."

14

The Daily Colonist   May 18, 1915

Warns Against False Illusions

I lay in the hospital bed, sweat pouring down my face, my throat sore from screaming and my feet cold. I looked around the sterile, unfriendly room — all the instruments of torture laid out on a tray beside the bed, two nurses and a doctor busy with their work but none looking at me. I had done my labour. Across the room, one of the nurses was wrapping something pink and small. My baby.

The baby wasn't crying. I wondered if it were dead. I had prayed for that often enough, but now I knew it was a wicked prayer. I wanted to ask if I could see the baby but was intimidated by the professional coldness of the doctor and nurses.

The other nurse pulled the blanket over my feet. "You're shivering," she said in a tone of censure.

"Is my baby all right?" I asked.

"She's fine," the nurse said curtly.

So, it's a girl. "Can I see her?" I asked.

"When they're done," she said.

What was all that pain for? What was all that screaming? Did someone slap me when I screamed? It was all a blur — a nightmarish blur — and what was it for? That little creature being whisked away to belong to someone else?

And me lying empty on the bed with nothing but pain and bad memories. I burst into tears. I sobbed. I wanted to drown myself in my tears. I wanted to dissolve.

"Now, now," the nurse said. "If you want to see the baby, you shouldn't act like one yourself."

The nurse on the other side of the room seemed to be finished whatever she was doing. She picked up the baby and started to carry her out of the room.

"Where are you taking her?" I cried. "Can I see her?"

The nurse stopped in her tracks, turned and brought her over. She showed me this little bundle. Only the misshapen head was showing. It looked bruised and beaten.

"Oh, she looks terrible. Is she all right?"

"Yes, she'll be fine. Sometimes the forceps bruise the skin, but it's nothing dangerous."

"Where are you taking her?"

"To the nursery. We'll bring her back to you when it's feeding time."

Then she whisked the baby away.

"You've had a long day," the nurse by my bed said. "You should get some sleep."

I stayed for a week at the hospital. A nurse brought me my baby every four hours like clockwork, then took her away again.

At the end of the week, I was sent back to the home and stayed there for another month while I nursed my baby. Mrs. Gordon thought it was important for a baby to be nursed for the first month of its life. She didn't hold much truck with the modern faith in formulas that were being mixed to replace mother's milk. So, she brought me my baby every few hours for breastfeeding. She would not let me keep the baby in between feedings at all. If one had been available, I'm sure she would have preferred to hire a wet nurse.

"I don't want you to grow too attached to the little one," she said. "Don't name it or anything foolish like that."

I promised I wouldn't. It was too wonderful to be allowed even a few moments with my child every day.

Mrs. Gordon would come into my room with the infant screaming at the top of her lungs. I would take her and talk softly to her until she quieted. The sound of my voice seemed to soothe her. We would look into each other's eyes and I would croon softly. She would slowly stop her screaming and sob gently, then curl into a ball in my arms. I would bring her to my breast and she would latch on. At the beginning, this was not an easy thing for her. We had several false starts until the nurse at the hospital taught me how to squeeze my nipple small enough to fill the baby's mouth. Then she would begin to suck vigorously. She sucked until it seemed she would suck the soul from me. It was painful and, at the same time, the most beautiful experience of my life.

In the brief time I spent with her, I stared into her face, not with the doting fondness of most mothers, but with the greed and avarice of a thief. I wanted to memorize every part of her tiny precious face — her little button nose, the determined well-set jaw, the smooth skin that every day progressed from bruised blue to yellowish-green to a pale pink, the head that grew rounder, the pouting smacking mouth that groped for my breast, the perfect arc of brow above the indigo eyes, the frown of them, the way she stared as if she too were memorizing my face, the way she seemed to smile, though Mrs. Gordon said it was just gas.

I tried to imagine how her face would change as she grew — what her button nose would become, what colour her eyes would be, how her hair would grow and what colour it would become. Now, it was straight and light brown. I tried to see through her to her soul. I tried to eat her whole, like a meal, for I knew I would soon be starving for her.

I smelled her — the milky smell of her breath, the talcum powder smell of her skin, the urine smell of her bottom.

I counted her pink toes, I fondled her baby fingers (all of them were babies) — tiny, the skin peeling as she grew. She was perfect in every way.

How was it different from every other mother's bonding with her baby? Every moment was imbued with a knowledge of loss — that this might be the last time. So, every moment was filled to bursting with love and with memory already happening, already crowding my heart till there was room for nothing else.

I didn't even find room to realize that I could run. I could put on my clothes and walk out of there with my baby in my arms and never look back. To my undying shame, I never even thought of it, not once. I thought only of stealing her image and placing it on my heart as if I were the thief and not the rightful owner. To my undying shame.

I would let her suck for as long as she wanted while I sang to her. Mrs. Gordon would come back for her and find us like this long before either of us was ready.

She would walk into the room. "That's enough for now," she would say.

We would not stop.

"Enough," she'd repeat, more forcefully.

Neither of us would pay any attention to her, locked in our own little world. Then Mrs. Gordon would lean over and press her finger against the breast that the baby was sucking. The suction would break, the baby would howl and Mrs. Gordon would take her up and carry her away until next time.

I tried not to name her, but I had to call her something. It came into my head that she was born in May, so that's what I called her. When they took her away from me, I would remember the day she was born and I would always celebrate her birthday.

All good things must come to an end and, one morning, Mrs. Gordon walked into my room without the baby.

"Her mother and father," she said, "have come and taken her to her new home."

"Just like that!" I cried. "With no warning."

"It's better that way," she said.

Better for whom? Certainly not for me. "But I didn't even get to say goodbye."

Then Mrs. Gordon left before I could ask any more questions.

The next morning, I awoke still empty. Some great piece of myself had broken off and would never be replaced. I would live with this emptiness for the rest of my life. I would have to get used to it. Was this grief? But no one had died.

Mrs. Gor-r-rdon said it was just selfishness and that I should be grateful for my new freedom.

Miss Have-a-shit said I had to pay.

I had to wait a few more days at the Vancouver Home for Girls until my father came to fetch me. Without my baby, I was moved out of the birthing room but, even as cruel as they were, my two captors would not put me back among the expectant mothers, so I was moved to a room with the whores and criminals. I kept to myself and tried to ignore them.

What I remember most vividly of those few days was that they bound my breasts. I remember the excruciating pain of my swollen, tender, milk-producing breasts being squeezed tight as a cloth was wrapped around and around them. Miss Have-a-shit assured me this would stop the milk production. But it didn't seem to work. Every time I heard a distant baby cry, I could feel the tingle of my milk glands and then the wetness that soaked through the binding cloth to my nightgown.

I imagined each time that the crying baby was my baby and that she was attached by some invisible thread to my milk glands. When I heard her cry, I couldn't help myself. We were still connected and I longed for her. I longed to see her, to hold her, to feed her. The longing was painful. It was situated in my breasts and the milk that flowed from them were the tears of that unquenchable longing we had for each other. I longed to leave that place, but I had to wait for my father.

I was lying in my bed the night before my father came to take me home, crying into my pillow as usual, and a young woman crawled into the bed beside me. Her skin felt clammy.

"What do you want?" I asked, terrified for my safety.

"Oh," she said. "Oh! What are you doing in my bed?"

"No," I said. "This is my bed. You're in the wrong bed."

I climbed over her and went to turn on the light. The girl on my bed winced from the sudden glare. She was a sickly grey colour and I could see she was trembling all over as if she were terrified too.

"Turn off the light," she said.

"Not until you leave my bed," I said.

The other two women in the room woke up and started swearing at me.

"What's going on?" one of them said.

"She climbed into my bed," I answered, pointing at the sickly creature.

One of the women laughed. "What! You don't fancy a little cuddle?"

"This is my bed," she said, taking her hands from her eyes. "You can tell by the picture." She turned and faced the bare wall. "See the picture." Her hands caressed the empty plaster. "Isn't it beautiful?"

Then she suddenly stopped and started to wail like a banshee. My roommates put their hands over their ears and continued to swear.

Miss Havisham came running into the room.

She went and sat on my bed beside the woman. "What is all this fuss about, Phyllis?"

"Is she mad?" I asked.

Miss Havisham looked at me. "No, she's not mad. She's a drunkard. I'm afraid she may be suffering from delirium tremens."

"What's that?" I asked.

"It's withdrawal from alcohol. Watch her for me and I'll go get her some medication."

"I didn't think that women drank," I said.

"There's no end," Miss Havisham said, "to the perversions women can get up to." She turned to me. "I hear you're leaving tomorrow."

I nodded.

"Well, you have been most fortunate in being given a chance to start over again. Do yourself a favour and resist the wicked debaucheries of these women."

She looked around the room at the other women. They turned away and put their blankets over their heads.

After Miss Havisham left, Phyllis started scratching her arms so hard that they were bleeding. "Get them off of me!" she shouted.

I stood there and watched her, afraid and unsure what to do.

Miss Havisham re-entered the room with a glass of milk and a spoon.

"Oh, dear," she said. "She's having hallucinations. You take her arms and hold them down. I'll give her the medication."

I looked skeptical.

"If she doesn't get some soon, she may go into a seizure. Come on. Hold her."

Much as I did not want to be involved in this rescue operation, I could see no way out of it. Besides, my sense of humanity made me grab the woman's arms and pin them down at her side.

"They're crawling all over me!" she cried. "Do you want them on you too?"

Miss Havisham stirred the milk and it turned a beige colour. It smelled awful. She managed to pour some of it into Phyllis's mouth, though she struggled mightily. It was all I could do to keep her arms at her side. As she swallowed the little mouthful she had, she started to screech.

"It burns! It burns! You're killing me!"

I looked at Miss Havisham, perhaps a little accusingly. "What is that awful stuff?" I asked.

"Paraldehyde." She looked back at me. "If she doesn't take it, she might die," she said, pouring more into Phyllis's mouth.

It took all of my strength to keep her in one place as she twisted and turned. Most of the medication landed on Phyllis's face and smock and some of it was on my arms.

Finally, the glass was empty and Miss Havisham said to Phyllis, "Now, let's get you back into bed."

Phyllis stopped struggling. Miss Havisham led her to her own bed and tucked her in. I wiped the stinking medicine off my arm.

"Try to sleep," Miss Havisham said to Phyllis. She turned to me. "And you," she said, "go back to bed and let this be a lesson to you."

I went back to bed and promptly forgot the lesson.

15

The Daily Colonist   May 13, 1928

Mother's Day Recalls Sacrifices of Mothers

〰〰 〰〰 〰〰 〰〰 〰〰 〰〰 〰〰 〰〰 〰〰 〰〰 〰〰 〰〰 〰〰 〰〰 〰〰 〰〰

It was my habit every year on May 13th to celebrate my daughter's birthday. I usually invited my grandmother to my apartment for supper. She was the only one in my family who acknowledged my daughter's birth at all. For my parents, it was a taboo topic and my siblings had never even been told of it.

But Grandma understood what the date meant to me and she always came to my place to celebrate and commiserate with me. This year I was less keen because, having told Grandma about the discovery of my daughter, I was disappointed in her reaction.

"Should I invite Grandma to celebrate May's birthday," I asked Biddy, "or should we just have a party, the two of us?"

Biddy looked at me crossly.

"You're right," I said. "We should punish her."

Biddy shook her head and started to lick a paw.

"Do you think she may have thought some more about it and reconsidered? Perhaps we can persuade her to our point of view. You do agree with me, don't you, Biddy?"

Biddy ignored me, got up and left the room. Alone, I decided I couldn't let May's birthday pass without including Grandma, so I called to invite her.

Mum answered the phone and I asked to speak to Grandma.

"She's ill," Mum said, sounding frantic. "I don't think your trip to Vancouver was such a good idea. She caught a cold and now it's worsened to pneumonia."

I promised to come over right away to visit.

Mum let me in and took me up to Grandma's room. As we went up the stairs, she quietly asked me not to stay long and tire Grandma out. I said nothing. As usual, I was put out by my mother's statement and thought it was simply meant to spite me. But when I saw Grandma's state, I repented of my suspicions.

I went into the darkened room where Grandma was lying on the bed. Her breathing was loud and raspy. She didn't open her eyes when I said "Hello." I'm not sure she was even aware of my presence. Nevertheless, I sat down beside the bed and spoke to her.

"Grandma," I said, taking her hand and squeezing it gently to let her know I was there. "It's May's birthday today."

I looked at her to see if she had heard me, but she showed no signs of it. Still, I continued.

"You must get better soon," I said. "And when you do, I promise I'll take you out to celebrate May's birthday. It'll be very special, I promise."

I could feel the tears starting to sting my eyes, so I left quickly. I didn't want to cry in front of her.

I opened the door, blinked at the bright lights and went down the stairs. Mum came out of the kitchen.

"Would you like some tea?" she asked. "I'd like to talk to you."

I followed her into the kitchen. Somehow, I knew this wasn't going to be a good conversation. I sat down at the table and watched her bustle about, putting on the kettle and fetching her best china cups.

"How long has she been like this?" I asked.

"A few days," Mum said. "You shouldn't have taken her to Vancouver."

I could tell Mum was frantic with worry and looking for someone to blame for Grandma's illness. As usual, it was to be me.

Mum put the teapot on the table and sat down across from me. "I should not have let her go," she said.

So, it was *not* all my fault then. That was a little better.

"She told me about Margaret," Mum said, looking at me.

That was disingenuous. "You knew about Margaret," I said. "You've always known about Margaret. That's why you didn't invite me to Thanksgiving dinner last year." I picked up the teapot and poured the tea.

"Well," Mum said. "I don't want to argue about it right now. All that matters is that Mama gets better." She stood up and went back to the counter to arrange cookies on a plate.

I didn't feel like arguing either. "Has the doctor been to see her?"

"Yes, he thinks she might recover in spite of her age."

"Yes," I said. "She's very strong." Perhaps that was why this was such a shock to me. She'd always been my rock.

Mum put the plate of cookies on the table in front of me. They were home-baked. Waves of childhood nostalgia came over me and I sobbed.

Mum looked at me sympathetically. "Don't worry," she said as she poured milk into her teacup. "I'm sure she'll be fine."

No, it wasn't that. I was crying because it had been so long since my mother had been like a mother to me. Ever since she'd learned I was pregnant, she had held me at arm's length. I wanted to chastise her for arranging Margaret's adoption.

But then, no. She was just beginning to be nice to me at last and if we argued at all, she would push me away again. In the face of my grandmother's illness, I needed my mother's support and she seemed to need me too.

I picked up my tea and put my hands around the hot china cup.

"Well," Mum said. "I have to go get ready. Lucinda has invited me and your father for supper tonight."

I was surprised.

"For Mother's Day," she explained. "In my day, we never had such frivolous holidays."

I felt deeply embarrassed. I had been so wrapped up in my own thoughts and hopes for Margaret May that I hadn't even thought about my own mother. She might not have been much of a mother, but she was the only one I had. "Happy Mother's Day," I said, feeling foolish.

Mum took off her apron and started to leave the room.

"If you're going out," I asked, "who's going to look after Grandma?"

"I've asked the maid to stay with her this evening."

"I could stay with her," I offered. "It's the least I can do for you for Mother's Day."

"Thank you," she said. "I'll ask the maid to fix you a bite to eat before she leaves." Mum got up and went to the door. "I do appreciate it."

I watched her go and then I finished my tea. It was appropriate that I looked after my grandmother on Mother's Day. She'd been more like a mother to me these last ten years or so than my own mother had been. I thought of Margaret and Margaret May. They would be celebrating

Mother's Day together. After all, Margaret was the only mother she'd ever known, and I'd been even less of a mother to her than my mother had been to me.

16

The Daily Colonist   June 23, 1915
Peace Rumours Denied

Papa had arranged a job piloting a freighter that brought him to the port of Vancouver. Then he rented a horse and buggy to pick me up at the Vancouver Home for Girls and bring me to the port. We were to go back on a pilot boat. I was glad my father, a man of few words, was bringing me home because I did not feel much like talking. I was still in grief over the loss of my baby and all I really wanted to do was weep.

Before we boarded the ship, my father took me to a small diner for lunch. The food was not the best, but it was still better than what I'd been eating for the last five months and it filled the void in my belly.

"Did you have a good stay at the home?" Papa asked. He still retained his English accent.

"Yes," I said. "It was fine."

"And the birth went well?" He did not look at me when he spoke but ate his food.

"Yes," I said.

"No complications?"

I shook my head. "It was a girl," I said.

Papa nodded. Then he didn't speak for a while. I could almost hear the gears turning in his head as he buttered his bread and thought about what to say to me.

I ate a few mouthfuls of corned beef hash and looked out the window. It was well and truly spring. New fresh green leaves were unfurling on all the trees.

"I suppose," he stated, "Arthur Brooke was the father."

I nodded.

"Have you told him?" he asked.

"No," I said. "And I won't."

"He should know," Papa stated flatly.

I shook my head.

"His parents should know. They could pay some of the expenses."

So, it was about money. I didn't suppose my parents had to pay anything for my stay at the home, which was a charity. But they would have made a donation and they would have had to pay the hospital bills.

"I'll pay it all back," I said, "once I have a job. You won't have to pay a cent. Only I don't want Arthur to know. Nor his parents. It's my mistake and I'll pay for it."

Papa looked uncomfortable. "It takes two," he said, "to tango. It's not right that you take on the burden all by yourself."

I remembered then the conversation I'd had with Arthur about the sacrifices he was making. I'd wondered then what sacrifices I could make. I'd never dreamed that my sacrifice would be this great.

"Arthur," I said, "is taking on the burden of fighting for our country. I won't ask him or his parents for anything more."

Papa looked at me then with an expression I could only interpret as pride. "You've changed, Edith," he said. "You seem much more mature."

"I'm not a child anymore."

"I can see that," he said. "I don't know whether to be glad or sad."

Then we settled into silence. I'd spoken more than I wanted to and said nothing that I wanted to say. I was angry at my mother for setting up my child's adoption and I wanted to know if my father had been involved too. But then, I didn't want to know. A part of me wanted to keep my anger purely and simply on my mother. To focus it. How could she?

On the pilot boat, Papa showed me to a cot in a darkened room and I slept. Anger and grief are exhausting and my father was busy working while we were on the ship.

My brother and sister were at school when we arrived home. Mum leaned forward to give me a perfunctory kiss and I turned my cheek to her lips. She gave me a look and took my suitcase from my father.

"I'm going back to work," Papa said, going back out the door.

"Where's Grandma?" I asked.

"She's lying down," Mum said. She made it sound as if somehow this was my fault. "Come with me."

We went into the kitchen.

"Martha," Mum said to the maid, "will you take Edith's suitcase upstairs? I want to talk to her."

When I was seated at the table, Mum said, "You must never tell anyone what you've done. It would bring shame on the family and especially your sister. It would spoil her chances of marrying a good man."

She looked at me sternly. She had not even asked me about the baby, about her grandchild. I nodded, since she seemed to be waiting for some kind of response from me.

"Is that clear?" she asked firmly.

"Yes."

"Your father and I expect you to go back and finish high school next September so you can go to normal school," she said.

He hadn't said anything of the kind. In fact, he hadn't argued with me when I said I would get a job and pay him back for the expenses they'd gone to.

"I don't want to," I said. "I want to get a job and pay you and Papa back all the money for the hospital. I'll pay for room and board."

Mum sat there in stunned silence. She shook her head. "You will not throw your life away after all that I've done for you."

"You arranged the adoption!" I shouted. "You didn't even ask me. I wanted to keep the baby."

"Stop shouting!" she said. "You'll wake your grandmother."

"I wanted to keep the baby," I whispered. The softness of my voice flooded me with the grief I was feeling and I started to cry.

"You have no idea what you're talking about," she said. "We'll talk about this again when you've had time to come to your senses."

I couldn't speak anymore anyway. I got up to go to my room to unpack.

My bedroom was much the same as I'd left it and yet it looked as though it belonged to someone else — someone far younger than me, someone who was still a child. A few of my favourite old dolls stared at me from where they were sitting in a line on top of the bookcase. Oh, they would have to go! I couldn't have them glaring at me accusingly all day, every day.

I heard a gentle tap at the bedroom door. "Can I come in, dear?" It was Grandma.

"Of course," I said, going to open the door wide. I opened my arms and gave her a hug. She squeezed me back.

"Mum told me you were lying down."

"She wanted to speak to you alone."

"Yes, she did." I didn't want to talk about that. "Have a seat, Grandma."

She sat on the spare kitchen chair in my room and looked at me sympathetically. "Was it very awful at the home?" she asked.

A wave of memories swept over me. Yes, some of them were awful, but most were of the companionship I'd shared with the other girls. I shook my head.

"We were not mistreated."

It was true. They had not beaten us. We had been well-fed. Our physical needs had been provided for.

"How was the birth?" She spoke so quietly I could scarcely hear her but I could tell, though it was difficult for her to ask, that she really wanted to know.

How do you speak of childbirth? No one, not even another woman, wants to know all of the details, but then to say, "It was fine," seemed such a lie. "There were no complications." That was a little better.

"Girl or boy?" Grandma asked.

"Girl," I said.

"Did you get much time with her?"

Across the room. A scant glance. My eyes filled with tears. "No," I said. "Only enough time to nurse."

Grandma got up from her chair and gave me a hug. We stood like that while I cried. She patted my back gently.

My tears got noisy and messy and I snorted while trying to stifle them.

"Don't," she said. "Just let the tears come. Just let them out."

I sobbed and heaved and wept as she stood there holding me — a little old woman as strong as a Douglas fir swaying in the wind. I wondered why my mother was not more like her. Why there was no bend in her love. She was strong and cold as steel.

17

The Daily Colonist   June 10, 1928

Guest at Tea Party

I called every evening to ask after Grandma and visited her on the weekend. Each day, she was a little better until, one day, she was sitting up in a chair beside the bed and talking to me like her old self.

"Well, Grandma," I said. "I promised I'd take you out to celebrate May's birthday when you got better. Do you think you're well enough to go out next weekend?"

She looked at me kindly. Either her eyes were a little rheumy still or there were tears in them.

"Well, dear," she said, "you don't have to take me out anywhere. I usually just go to your place for a meal."

It was true and, in the beginning when I hardly had anything to eat, she used to bring the food.

"Grandma," I said, "surely you don't want me to break my promise to you. Besides, I know just the place I want to take you."

"Where's that?" she asked.

"It's a surprise."

I wanted to take her to a place that meant a lot to her — Gorge Tramway Park. We'd gone there often when I was growing up and Grandma used to tell us of her childhood a little farther up the inlet that we called 'the Gorge'. Grandma says they used to call it 'the Arm', which makes more sense really, because it's a long inlet and the gorge is only a small part of it. She'd come to Craigflower Farm as a little girl and only moved into Victoria ten years later. She told us what it used to look like before the British Columbia Electric Railway Company had transformed it into an amusement park. As children, we'd played in that park, watched shows, listened to music and swum in the Gorge waters.

Then, three years ago, a fire destroyed Gorge Tramway Park's bandstand, concessions and trees. But the Japanese tea garden was still there. The year after the fire, it had opened up as usual on Victoria Day and I had been sent to talk to the owners, Hayato 'Harry' Takata and his brother, Kensuke. I'd interviewed Harry, who came to Victoria with his friend Yoshitaro (Joe) Kishida in 1907. Joe's father, Isaburo Kishida had designed the tea garden and the teahouse. Harry gave me a tour of the garden with its arched bridges, ornamental stream, stone lanterns and authentic teahouse renowned for its brunch and afternoon tea. A year before the fire, Joe had gone back to Japan, selling his interest in the teahouse to Harry's brother. I wrote an article but the newspaper never ran it. Instead, they ran a story about the gymkhana at Willows Beach. Still, the Takata brothers served a lovely tea and I thought Grandma would enjoy it.

I went to pick her up on the first Saturday of June. It was a warm, sunny day. Grandma came out of the house to meet me, leaning on her cane. Grandma had carried a cane before her illness, but then it had been a jaunty accessory. She had not seemed to depend on it before as she did now. I took her arm to steady her as she walked down the front stairs and slowly made our way to my red roadster.

Grandma smiled as I opened the door to let her in. "It's a beautiful day," she said. "Aren't you going to take down the roof?"

"I thought it would be too windy for you. After all, you've only just recovered from pneumonia."

"You're right," she said. "It does get rather breezy, especially the way you drive." She grinned at me.

"Get in, Grandma," I said, feigning annoyance.

She sat down and arranged her long skirts around her. When everything was tucked inside, I closed the door and went back to my side.

Soon, we were off. We drove down Pandora and over the new Johnson Street Bridge with its ominously large concrete counterweight overhead.

It was painted dark grey. The car shuddered over its ribbed-grill surface and then shot ahead on the pavement in Vic West. After a few twists and turns, we were speeding along Craigflower Road towards Tramway Park. We drove over the tramway tracks and up the drive to the parking lot. Grandma had a great smile on her face when she realized where we were. I helped her out of the roadster. She stood, leaning on her cane, and took a deep breath as she gazed around her at the trees, the garden, the Gorge waters.

"It smells the same," she said.

I took a deep breath myself and inhaled rain forest and salty fresh air.

"Come on, Grandma," I said. "Let's go to the teahouse."

We walked slowly along the uneven paths of the Japanese garden. Wind rippled through the pale green leaves of trees and bushes as we passed, their dancing dappled shadows reflected on the pathway. We walked across a wooden bridge that arched over a trickling stream on our way to the bamboo structure that housed the teahouse. The sound of running water was the background music to the dance of shadow and light on the footpath.

Harry Takata met me at the entrance to the teahouse and held out his hand to shake mine. I let go of Grandma's arm to shake it.

"Miss Robertson," he said. "It's so good to see you again." He turned to Grandma, who was leaning on her cane and looking proud of me. "And who is this?"

"This is my grandmother, Mrs. Macaulay," I said.

"Welcome," he said, taking her arm.

She smiled.

"Let me show you to a table." He walked with her to the nearest table and pulled out the bamboo chair for her to sit down. "I'll get your menus," he said.

"Well," Grandma said, looking around at the swaying Japanese lanterns. Tiny windchimes tinkled in the light breeze. "This is nice. How do you know that gentleman?"

"He's the owner," I said, then I told her about the unpublished story I'd written for the paper.

Just then, Harry came back with our menus and our waiter, who was dressed in a coat as white as the linen tablecloth.

"This is your waiter, my cousin, Kenji Takata. He's here from Japan for the season."

"Please forgive my English," he said. "I'm just learning."

"Thank you," Grandma said as she took her menu.

"If you have any questions, just ask," Kenji said.

Tea at the Empress

Both men bowed before leaving us to peruse the menu. It was a deep Japanese-style bow, not the head nod we were used to. I felt deeply honoured by the gesture.

"What would you like, Grandma?" I asked.

"I think I'll have a tea biscuit and some tea."

"Are you sure you don't want anything more?" I asked. "They make a lovely poached egg on toast."

"That does sound good, dear," she said. "But my appetite has not entirely returned. You go ahead and have that if you like."

I looked around to catch the waiter's eye and saw that he was looking at me. He seemed a little embarrassed to be caught staring. He came quickly to our table and I gave him our order. He took our menus and bowed again. Before leaving, he gave me a look that I can only describe as admiring. It was an expression I hadn't seen in a long time.

I watched him leave, admiring in return his slim figure and upright posture.

I turned to Grandma. She noticed me noticing him, but she said nothing. It was a good thing, too, because I had not brought her here to talk about men. I couldn't wait to talk about Margaret, about the great-granddaughter she had lost who we'd called May all these years when we'd celebrated her birthday together.

"Have you thought any more," I asked, "about my news about May?"

"Perhaps we should have some tea," she said, "before we talk about that."

Our waiter returned with a pot of tea. We were silent as he poured it into our china cups.

"There is cream and sugar here, miss," he said to me, "and madam." He bowed and turned to leave.

"He likes you," Grandma said.

"That's neither here nor there," I said, as I stowed the information away somewhere. "What I wanted to talk about is May."

Grandma poured some milk into her teacup. Then she picked it up and sipped it slowly. She put the cup down.

"Well," she said, "we are here to celebrate her birthday."

Just then, Kenji arrived with our food. My poached egg was perfectly round. It looked like a cheerful pale sun. I immediately pierced it with a knife to watch the liquid gold pour out onto my toast.

Grandma buttered her tea biscuit.

I took a bite of my yolk-soaked toast and smiled. Grandma took a nibble of her biscuit, chewed and, with a faraway look in her eyes, said, "It tastes almost as good as the ones Mam made."

90

It took no time for me to finish my egg and toast. It was so delicious and I was so hungry. I put down my knife and fork, picked up my teacup and looked across at Grandma, still nibbling on her biscuit.

"Can we talk about Margaret May now?" I asked.

Grandma put her biscuit down. "Yes," she said. "I've been thinking about that. James and his wife must not have known you were the mother or they wouldn't have risked bringing her to our house. I guess John didn't tell them that the baby was family." She took another bite and chewed. When she'd finished, she asked, "How did you discover that she was your child?"

"Margaret," I said, "looks so much like her father."

"It seems strange to say this," Grandma said, "but I met Arthur so few times that I can't remember what he looked like."

His face with its many coy mannerisms flashed into my memory. It was uncanny how Margaret May had such similar mannerisms.

"I want to own her as my daughter. I want to tell her, Grandma."

She looked at me sternly. "You will not," she said. "You are a grown woman and you have gotten used to the loss of your daughter. She is but a child. You don't know the harm you might do her by telling her this secret."

"But don't you think her parents should at least tell her she's adopted?"

"Perhaps it would have been better if they'd told her when she was very young. But I think such news would not be well-received now."

"But she would get used to it. Then, in a few years, when she's old enough, they could tell her that I'm her real mother."

"If they told her in a few years that you were her mother, she might no longer trust them because they'd known all that time and didn't tell her."

"Then *I* could tell her!"

I put my fork and knife on top of my plate and pushed it away to indicate I was finished.

Kenji came and took it, giving me a sly glance as he did so. "Would you like anything else, miss?"

"No, thank you," I said. "What about you, Grandma?"

She shook her head.

It was clear to me I would not get the comfort and support of my grandmother as I had hoped. I was on my own.

18

The Daily Colonist   August 3, 1915

Canada's Casualties Mounting Higher

I fell into a depression so profound I find it difficult to write about even now.

I woke up in the morning after a restless night of tossing and turning. My legs felt like cement. I could not find the energy to get up and so I lay there.

At nine o'clock, my mother came into the room, chirping like a bird in the springtime.

"Rise and shine," she said as she pulled the curtains open.

The summer sunlight stabbed my eyes. I closed them, covered them, moaned.

"Get up, sleepy head. The day is half over."

"Go away."

She stared at me for a few moments and then left.

I summoned all the energy I could muster, let my feet drop to the floor, staggered across the room and closed the curtains. Then I hurled myself into my bed, pulled the covers over my head and fell asleep. Or tried to.

At ten o'clock, the chirping bird returned, but this time she was more like an angry bird. She yanked the curtains wide. I moaned. She plunked a tray down on the table by my bed.

"I brought you breakfast and the paper. Now, eat it and get up. I've got chores for you to do."

Ah, yes. Words to make me want to jump out of bed.

I pulled the covers tighter around myself and put my face into my pillow. At some point, she left the room. I drifted in and out of sleep.

Grandma came in later. She sat in a chair beside my bed and said nothing until I recognized her presence and spoke to her out of the depths of the pillow.

"Good morning, Grandma."

"It's well into the afternoon, child."

I'm not a child. Why did even Grandma annoy me now? "If you've come to get me up, I'm not going to," I said.

"All right," she said. "You're grieving. It's normal to feel grief when you've lost a child. I know I did."

I turned over and looked at her.

"Did you never wonder why I had only one child?" she asked me. "I had difficulty bringing a child to term. I lost several babies, all stillborn."

I could hear the catch in her voice that meant she was near tears. Was this story meant to cheer me up? "It's not the same thing," I said sullenly.

"Every grief is different," she said.

Oh, wise woman, go away.

"I think your mother's right though," she said. "You should get up and face the day. Even if you only go through the motions. Eventually, you'll come out the other side of grief."

"Not today," I said, turning back into my pillow, wrapping my cocoon around me.

I heard her go. I was sorry about how I'd treated her, but I couldn't find the energy to be nice to her or anyone else. Not even myself.

After weeks of lassitude, one day, I finally got up.

I put my feet on the floor.

I lifted the thumbworn newspaper off the tray beside the bed and saw the piece of cold toast beneath it.

I took a bite and chewed and swallowed.

I put my feet inside my slippers.

I shuffled across the room and peeked out the curtains.

It was a warm, sunny day. Bright flowers glowed in the border garden. The lawn was the colour of straw. August, then?

I went back to my bed and sat down.

Mum came sweeping into the room as if she'd been listening just outside the door for any sounds of life within.

"Good," she said. "You're up." She looked at the tray by the bed. "It's Sunday. We're going to church in half an hour. Do you think you could join us?"

I shook my head.

"It'll do you good," she said.

"I doubt it," I said.

"Grandma would be pleased."

"Oh, go away," I said.

Mum sniffed and looked insulted. "All right, then. Stay at home by yourself and mope." She left the room.

I went back to bed and slept on and off.

A few hours later, Mum knocked on my door and came in. "Look who's here to see you?"

Mabel came in behind my mum.

"She was at church," Mum said, "and asked about you. I told her you'd be glad of some company."

I knew how much Mum didn't like Mabel. She must be getting desperate.

Mabel came to my bedside and sat where Grandma always sat.

"I'll leave you two alone then, shall I?" Mum said, heading back out the door.

"I've missed you, Edith," Mabel said. "I didn't even know you were back. You never called."

I could tell she was a little miffed. I'd written to her a few times from the home, but I hadn't called since I'd been back.

"I've not been well," I said.

"So, your mother tells me. Should you not go see a doctor?"

"What could a doctor do for me?" I said.

"You sound like my father." Mabel laughed.

Laughter. I'd forgotten what that was. Like ripples shimmering on a lake swept by a sudden breeze. I smiled.

"It's a beautiful day today," Mabel said. "Do you want to come swimming with me at the Gorge? We could take the streetcar."

It sounded nice, plunging into cool waters, but it also sounded far too difficult — finding my swimsuit and towel, packing them, walking to the tram stop, taking the tram filled with noisy children, changing in the changeroom…

"No, thank you," I said. "Not today. Perhaps another day."

"Well, we could go downstairs and have lunch. Your mother has invited me."

Yes, Mum was getting desperate. "All right," I said.

I supposed I could manage putting some clothes on and going downstairs. It would be challenging but easier than going swimming with the screaming masses.

As I got changed, Mabel talked about going back to school in September. She seemed excited about her final year. She mentioned the clubs she would join, the teachers she would have.

"And what about you?" she asked.

I pulled up my skirt. "I don't think I'm going back to school," I said.

"What?"

If the thought of going swimming seemed beyond my reach, the thought of going to school seemed like climbing a mountain.

"You've always wanted to be a teacher!" she said. "Are you going to give it up?"

"The desire has gone," I said, buttoning my blouse.

"But if you go back to school, it might come back again."

I went to the dresser and looked in the mirror. There were black semi-circles under my sunken eyes. I pinned up my hair.

"I'd have to repeat a grade."

"But that's nothing for you. You're clever. Come on," she urged. "We were always going to go to normal school together."

"But by the time I get there, you'll be gone." I knew her family could only afford to send her for one year. After that, she'd be sent to a school in a distant small town in British Columbia. Teaching jobs in the city were only for students who spent two years at normal school.

She had no comeback for that.

"Let's go to lunch," she said.

"All right," I said, "but don't say anything to my mother about me not going or she'll have a fit. I'll tell her in my own time."

Mabel nodded, but she looked crestfallen.

19

The Daily Colonist   July 3, 1928

Royal Assent Given to Equal Suffrage Bill: London

It had been three months since I'd seen Margaret and then only a glimpse of her across an open grave. Never had time passed so slowly. Now, it was summer and I couldn't even spy on her on her walk to school. I needed something to take my mind off the burden of my secret that had become my obsession.

"What do you think, Biddy?" I asked. "Would it be a desecration of Arthur's memory to go and find another man?"

She looked very disapproving.

"But it's been such a long time. Don't you think he'd want me to get on with my life?"

Biddy answered by getting up and leaving the room.

"Well," I cried after her, "if even you desert me, what choice do I have?"

So I got in my car and found my way to the Japanese tea garden at Gorge Tramway Park. It was late Saturday afternoon. I strolled along the pleasant walkway through the serene Japanese garden and found myself at the teahouse. Kenji Takata stood at the entrance as if he had been waiting for me there ever since my last visit. He smiled discreetly and showed me to a table. Then he handed me a menu.

"Would you like the poached egg on toast again?" he asked.

My mouth watered. "Yes, please," I said. "Can you make it two poached eggs? I'm famished."

"Yes, of course," he said.

All through my meal, we exchanged meaningful glances, but no words were spoken until he came with my bill.

"Would you like to go out with me for a drink?" he asked, looking shy.

I was too surprised to speak at first.

"Please excuse me if I'm being too forward. I am not familiar with the customs here."

"It's quite all right," I said. Perhaps he was being forward, but I'd already decided to overlook the indiscretion. "I'd like to go out with you for a drink."

"I have no car, so we would have to take the tram into town."

"That won't work," I said. "Victoria is dry."

"What does that mean?"

"It means you can only buy alcohol at a government liquor store or private club. But don't worry. I have a roadster. We can drive out to Six Mile House where there's a beer parlour."

Kenji bowed. "I would be honoured," he said.

I detected a note of dishonesty in his words. Surely, having a woman drive him on a date might feel dishonourable to him.

"What time are you off?" I asked.

We agreed to meet later in the parking lot.

Later that evening, Kenji was smiling in the seat beside me as we sped further along Craigflower to the Island Highway. Whatever qualms he might have had about being driven seemed to have vanished as soon as he saw my roadster, and he certainly enjoyed the speed at which I travelled.

I slowed down as we passed the old Craigflower Manor. I liked to give it a silent salute because it was where my grandmother and great-grandmother had begun their lives in this country when it was still a colony.

Then we picked up speed as we passed the Four Mile House and continued another two miles to the old Six Mile House at Parson's Bridge.

Kenji and I went in the door marked 'Ladies and Escorts'. It led us into the room where only women and the men who had brought them were allowed. Unlike those in most dark and dingy beer parlours, the room for ladies at Six Mile House was bright with windows letting in the sun. There was a red and inviting carpet on the floor. Unfortunately, the dozen or so other patrons of the establishment looked far less inviting. I was shocked by the scorn in the stares of the dozen or so men and women in the beer parlour. They were gaping at my escort as if he had two heads. Kenji seemed not to notice and led me to a table where we sat down.

I tried to ignore them. After all, I was used to being an outcast. My own family had ostracized me. I wouldn't have even been invited to family gatherings if it hadn't been for my grandmother. But Kenji was so much better than I at ignoring the rudeness of these strangers. I decided to enjoy my time with him and overlook the stares. I smiled at him as we sat down at a table and waited to be served.

We waited a long time, but no one came. There was a waiter behind the bar, but he passed his time wiping up the counter with a rag and avoiding eye contact.

I asked Kenji if he had a job in Japan and he said he worked in his father's manufacturing business. He told me his father had thought it would be a good idea for Kenji to come to Canada to improve his English because he wanted to expand his business and export his products to America. Kenji never asked me about my job. Perhaps he didn't imagine that women could work outside the home. Eventually, we ran out of things to say to each other and there was an awkward silence.

Finally, Kenji asked, "Do you think I'm supposed to go to the bar to order the drinks?"

I shook my head. "No, the waiter is supposed to come to us."

Just then, the waiter flung the towel over his shoulder and poured two beers from a tap. He walked over to the next table where the couple's stares were particularly hostile. He put the drinks down, then picked up the empty glasses. Without saying a word to them or turning in our direction, he started to walk away from the table.

Kenji called to him, "Excuse me."

The waiter glanced in our direction. "Just a moment," he said. Then he walked back to the bar, put down his tray with the empty glasses and finally sauntered over to our table.

"What can I get you?" he asked, looking pointedly at me.

"A beer," I said.

Then he looked down his nose at Kenji. "And you?"

"Do you have anything stronger than beer?" he asked.

"We don't," the bartender said. "We have beer."

"I'll have beer then."

The waiter walked away from our table and then disappeared through a door behind the bar.

"Why did he bother asking what we wanted if they only have beer?" Kenji asked me.

"It's a good question," I answered. "Perhaps he wanted to prolong our misery."

Again, we waited a very long time before he reappeared. While we waited, I looked around at the hostile faces that glared back at me.

The man at the closest table leaned his pockmarked face closer to mine and whispered, "What are you doing with that chink?"

I glanced at Kenji, but he seemed not to have understood.

Then the man said, "Come out with me and I'll show you a real man."

The woman he was with ignored his slight and stared at me haughtily.

I considered responding with, "He's not Chinese," but then decided his comment was not worthy of a reply. I turned my back to him and stared at the door where the waiter had disappeared.

"I would have liked to have some scotch," Kenji said to me. "I've never had any. My usual drink back home is sake. Beer seems so weak to me."

"You can only get hard liquor in liquor stores," I said. "But at least you can get it. In the States, you can't even get beer under Prohibition."

Kenji shook his head. "Such barbaric laws," he said.

Finally, the door behind the bar opened and the surly waiter came out. He filled two glasses with beer from the tap. He placed them on a tray and brought them to our table. Then he announced the amount we owed him and stood there waiting for us to pay.

"Put it on our tab," I said.

The insolent waiter shook his head. "You have no tab," he said.

Kenji didn't argue but took out his wallet and paid the waiter, who finally left our table. When he was gone, Kenji picked up his glass in toast position. I picked up mine and clinked his.

"Cheers," he said, then took a large gulp.

I sipped mine and smiled back. I would have gulped as much as he did under other circumstances, but I didn't want to empty my glass too soon and then have to go through the humiliating process of ordering another one. Besides, I wanted him to think well of me. No one else did. At least, not in this place. Next time, I thought, I would invite him to my apartment and he could finally get to taste scotch. He could take the tram.

It was dangerous, though. A single lady did not entertain a man in her apartment regardless of his race. I could be evicted for such behaviour.

After a few moments of silence, I decided to tell Kenji a little more about myself. I told him I had a job at the newspaper.

He looked astonished. "What do you do there?" he asked.

"Sometimes I write stories for the society page," I said.

"We have no women journalists in Japan."

"No?" I responded. "Well, there are damn few of them here and we're on a short leash as far as stories are concerned. I spend most of my time fetching copy and filling orders for coffee. Occasionally, I'm asked to attend a ball and report on what the women were wearing." I didn't know anything about fashion, but the men at the paper assumed, because I was a woman, I would naturally care about such things. Fortunately, Grandma helped me with that part of my work, explaining technical terms regarding women's wardrobes. When I'd started, I couldn't tell a 'flounce' from a 'ruche'.

Kenji stared at me, unable to comprehend my bitterness. "It is only surprising to me that you are able to write at all."

Now it was my turn to be surprised. "Women in Japan cannot read or write?" I asked.

"Perhaps the finest ladies learn calligraphy," he said. "But to work outside the home writing stories in newspapers. That is totally unheard of!"

"Well," I said, "One day, they will. You wait and see."

He shook his head and I couldn't tell if he thought it would be for good or for evil. "I knew," he said, "that women had the right to vote here, but I had no idea they had the right to work outside the home. Surely, when you marry you have to leave your job."

"That is true," I said. "But I'm not married and so I work."

"It is very brave of you," he said.

"Do you mean to say you have no working women in Japan?" I asked.

"Of course. We have geisha."

"What is that?"

"Women whose job it is to please men," he said.

"Like prostitutes?" I asked.

He shook his head. "Not exactly."

"What's the difference?"

"Sex is not the only way to please men," he said, smiling.

"I'm glad to hear it," I said, taking a final sip of my beer. I was unable to nurse it any further.

"Would you like some more?" he asked.

"I'm afraid not," I said. "It's far too painful an experience."

"I'm sorry you didn't enjoy yourself."

"It's not your fault," I said. "But next time you'll come to my apartment where the company is more agreeable and I can offer you some scotch."

"That would please me very much," he said.

Then we got up and left the beer parlour before any serious hostilities broke out.

20

The Daily Colonist   September 7, 1915

Help Wanted — Female: Girls! Girls! Girls! Splendid Positions

After much persuasion on her part, I had promised Mabel I would give school one more try. My mother was excited and bought me a new outfit for my first day back. It irked me to be doing what she wanted me to, but if I didn't go to school, I would need to go to work. Finding a job required even more effort than putting on my clothes and going to school, something I had done since I was a child.

So, I walked to school and went in the girls' entrance. I went up the stairs and saw the wide hall filled with students milling around noisily. I looked for Arthur's curly head above them all, then my heart fell when I remembered he was gone. He was a letter I received every month, a few words scribbled in blue ink on white paper.

I found my classroom and sat at a desk. The other students looked at me as if I were an alien invader. Two girls started to twitter behind their hands while they stared at me. They weren't very good at keeping their gossip secret. Soon, whatever they'd been sharing was making its course around the room and more eyes were staring at me.

The teacher called the class to order. Then he called the roll. When he got to my name, the room erupted in laughter. The teacher scolded them. He called my name again and I responded, ignoring the persistent, if quieter, titters.

Then the teacher droned on about what we were going to learn that year.

The classroom gawkers kept on gawking. They knew. They all knew my shame. How was I going to keep coming to school every day with everyone staring? I wanted to get out of the room. I couldn't stand it.

My eyes drifted out the window to the distant blue Sooke Hills. In the sky, seagulls dipped and soared. There was a world out there, another beautiful world. There were people who didn't know my past. There were jobs that soldiers had left behind waiting to be filled.

What was I doing here? Arthur was not here anymore, though the halls were haunted by his presence.

I looked around the room at the gawkers. I put my pencil and notebook in my satchel. I got up.

"Where are you going?" the teacher asked.

"I'm leaving," I said.

I felt a sudden liberation, an exhilaration such as I had not felt in many months.

I was dressed now. I could go anywhere, walk anywhere. I could go downtown and look for jobs if I wanted to. I didn't have to sit here being an object of pity or scorn or curiosity.

I walked to the door. "Goodbye," I said, closing the door behind me.

I walked down Grant Street until it ended at Cook, looking at all the houses as I went. Their windows revealed nothing of what went on inside them and I supposed that was a blessing. There was enough heartache in my own home to deal with. I kept on walking toward town, past the new First Presbyterian Church building that looked like a fortress. The hymn "A Mighty Fortress Is Our God" came into my head accompanied by loud flourishes on the organ. *A fortress against what?* I wondered.

Last Sunday, my mother had finally convinced me to go to church with the family. I'd thought it would be nice to see Mabel there. But it had been just like the first day of school with people staring and sharing their gossip. Mum and Grandma pretended not to notice but I saw it. Not much of a fortress against gossip and hypocrisy. Even the minister looked at me askance. I vowed then and there never to go back to church. And now I would not go back to school either.

A few more blocks and I was downtown and looking in shop windows for Help Wanted signs. When I saw one, I peered in the window and saw a shop girl speaking to an old gentleman. Could I do such a job? Could I feign that kind of confidence? I suppose, but did I want to? Not especially.

A newsboy on the street corner was shouting out the headline. "*Hesperian* torpedoed off the coast of Ireland! Twenty-five missing! Germans give no warning to passenger liner!"

The war was still going on over there in Europe. It wasn't safe, even for innocent civilians. What Arthur must be enduring! Every day, we heard more war stories — the glorious ones repeated in the newspaper, the less than glorious ones told by soldiers in their letters home. At least, the ones that made it past the censors.

I bought a paper from the newsboy and went to the London Bakery to sit down and read it. I turned immediately to the page that listed the casualties for the previous day. Arthur's name was not there. I breathed a deep sigh of relief. Then I called the waitress over and ordered a cup of tea to celebrate.

When she was gone, I checked the Help Wanted ads. Under 'Female', there were mostly service jobs — housemaid, housework, cook, mother's helper. Things hadn't changed much since my mother's day. There was one job for a saleswoman in a needlework department, but you needed experience. A good job for my grandmother, then. Nothing else. Perhaps leaving school hadn't been such a good idea after all.

I stared at the newspaper. Why couldn't women do more? Why couldn't I do more? And if I was allowed to do more, what would I want to do? I stared at the newspaper. And suddenly, it came to me. I used to write stories for the *Camosun* newspaper at school. Why couldn't I write stories for the *Daily Colonist*? How much more difficult could it be?

Women were writing for newspapers these days. At least, they were in other places. And I could write. I'd always been considered a good writer at school. I took out my pencil and started to write a little story called "The New Century," filled with all the strides we women were going to make in the 1900s.

The waitress came over and put the cup of tea on the table. "Would you like something to eat, dearie?"

I could tell by her tone she was not happy, so I ordered a piece of toast. Then I went back to writing about all the 'firsts' that women would achieve in this new century. First of all, we would soon have suffrage and then… women could be doctors and lawyers and politicians, women could be businessmen and — why not? — even newspaper reporters.

When my toast arrived, I put aside my story and ate it. I thought about how I would pass the afternoon. I knew that I should walk to the newspaper office and ask for a job, but the thought of it terrified me.

Then I thought about Arthur in the trenches over in France. I imagined the courage it took him every day to face the enemy's guns. What was I afraid of? Walking down the street into an office and asking for a job? Before I could lose courage, I put my story in my satchel, paid my bill and went to the *Daily Colonist* office on Broad Street.

Somehow, half-conscious of the way I'd arrived there, I found myself in the office of the editor-in-chief of the newspaper: Mr. Charles Lugrin, as the sign on his door announced him. He was a gruff man with a large bushy mustache, under which he puffed on a cigar as he perused my story. He did not appear to be reading it so much as looking it over in much the same manner as he'd looked me over when I'd walked in.

"Hmph," or some such sound, he made as he put it down in less time than it would ever take to read it. "It's not exactly news, is it?"

"It's a sample of my writing is what it is." I held my hat in my hand, pulling on the rim in my nervousness.

"Ever work on a paper before?"

"I worked on the *Camosun* at Victoria High School," I said.

"And after high school, did you go to college?"

I could feel that newspaper writer job slipping out of my grasp. "No," I said, "but I'm a good worker."

"Well, we already have Miss Lawson writing the column 'Women's Realm.' She's a former teacher and an educated woman. You must have read her stories?"

"Yes," I said.

"So, we don't need any girls. But we do need a new copyboy, someone to run errands and the like. Do you suppose you could do that?"

"I may look young," I said, "but I'm not a boy."

"Yes, that's just the problem, isn't it? All the boys are running off to war and we're left with the girls. But back to my question, do you think you could do the work of a copyboy?"

"I can do anything you ask me to," I said.

"Good," he said. "We'll call you a 'copygirl' then, shall we?"

I was young, just seventeen, and this was an entry-level position. As soon as I learned the ropes of the newspaper business, I would surely graduate to writing copy. At least, so I hoped.

"You can start tomorrow and we'll see how it works out."

Mr. Lugrin stood up and held out his hand to me. I shook it, hardly believing how easy it had been. Too easy. I walked back through the smoky, messy, noisy newspaper office and I could feel a heady excitement growing in me. This was a place where the clatter of typewriters meant something. Reporters shouted across the room at each other in a strange vocabulary I would soon have to learn. The room vibrated with a sense of urgency and immediacy. And tomorrow, I would be here in the middle of all of this. My trepidation vanished, to be replaced by anticipation.

21

The Daily Colonist   July 10, 1928

Men of My Heart

Somehow, I managed to smuggle Kenji into my apartment. He laughed when we got inside. From the pocket of his suit jacket, he pulled out a mickey of scotch.

I showed him into the parlour and went to the kitchen for glasses. When I came back, he was looking through my bookcase. That's exactly what I would have done in a stranger's house — there was no better way to get to know someone. He would have found all the classics there, though I don't know if he would have recognized them as such. I can't pretend that I'd read them all, but I was trying. On the table beside the sofa was my current read, *A Room of One's Own* by Virginia Woolf. I'd hurried to the bookstore and bought the first copy on the shelf. It was easy reading and enlightening, not like the hard slog of some of her novels.

Kenji turned and smiled. I handed him a glass. He poured his scotch into it and handed it back to me. I gave him the second empty glass and he poured it.

We saluted each other and clinked our glasses together.

Kenji took a large gulp of the liquid. He smacked his lips. Then he smiled. "It burns like sake," he said, "but it has a sweet mellow taste after."

"Yes," I said. "I like it."

We sat down together on the sofa, side by side. I felt a little uneasy, but Kenji poured me another swig of scotch and I knew that all unease would soon be gone. That's what I wanted at that moment.

Yes, yes. I knew I was headed for trouble. I was a train wreck waiting to happen. I knew that. Have you ever felt yourself in a situation like that? You know you're doing all the wrong things, but you do them anyway. It's not that you're powerless to stop them. Or is it? Is it just some kind of perverted curiosity to find out how low you can fall?

Growing up Presbyterian, I had this redemption story playing out in my head. I had to sink to the bottom to rise up to the top again. I had to test God's love and power to forgive. I had to believe in a higher power to do this; otherwise, I was doomed. I had to believe God was more like Grandma than she was like Mum.

And so, I kept pace with Kenji. When we finished off his mickey, I brought out my bottle. I had found a fellow drinker. But he underestimated me. He didn't know my tolerance for alcohol. He didn't know how much I consumed on lonely nights when I was feeling sorry for myself.

So, when he thought I should be drunk senseless, he made his move and came for me. I let him kiss me for a while. Kissing is always pleasant. I dallied with him, but when I felt he was going a little too far, I pushed him away. I had no intention of returning to the Vancouver Home for Girls at my age!

He looked surprised.

"Do you have a French safe?" I asked.

"What is that?"

I explained the prophylactic device to him. They must have them in Japan as well because he quickly understood and admitted he didn't have one.

"Well, I don't want to get pregnant," I said, adding again in my mind.

"Can I stay and sleep on your couch?" he asked. "I feel too drunk to make it home."

He looked so downhearted I almost relented, but I didn't have a lock on my bedroom door, so I couldn't risk sleeping with a horny man in my apartment.

"I'm afraid you'll have to leave," I said, feeling cold.

Poor Kenji got up and staggered out. It was late enough that no one would be up and we didn't have to take any measures to conceal his departure. I just urged him to be as quiet as possible. In his drunken state, I was afraid he might stumble down the stairs and wake my neighbours.

After he was gone, I felt sad. I hoped it wasn't the last time I saw him. I rather liked him. Perhaps he would come back again with a French safe next time. Though I didn't really wish it. My only other experience with sexual intercourse had not been positive.

Kenji did come back. He called me a few weeks later and we made another date.

He arrived at my door with another mickey and a French safe. I must say I was terrified by the sight of one of these items, but seeing the other gave me a little courage.

The evening unfolded pretty much as you would expect it to. Kenji and I talked for about half an hour while we drank. Then we necked for another half an hour and we drank.

After that, the evening becomes a little blurry in my memory. I know that I was in such a state of inebriation that my defences were totally shut down. I felt like someone blindfolded swinging at a piñata and wildly missing time and again. Until I finally hit the target, which spilled its 'candies' over me.

At some point, Kenji must have put on the French safe. At least I hope he did. Frankly, I was not in a state to be one hundred percent certain of anything. I'm not even certain if I enjoyed my second sexual encounter. I say that with a great deal of regret and some shame.

What I felt afterwards, besides shame, was that I was linked to Kenji and he was linked to me. If I got pregnant by some stroke of luck, he would marry me and all would be well. But whatever happened, he would stay in Victoria after the summer was over and remain a part of my life forever.

I thought about what it would be like to bring him home for dinner. I didn't have to imagine my mother's scorn, having felt it often enough. I knew my grandmother would be supportive. Nothing about having Kenji as my partner would change my relationship with my family. But, having been in the bar with Kenji, I knew that we would face more public contempt now. Perhaps it would be a relief — to have my sins open and visible. If Kenji loved me, then I could bear it.

He seemed to feel the same way. He telephoned me a couple of times a week and he visited every weekend evening. He couldn't stay the night because he worked on the weekend. I drank less on those evenings so that I could feel more, and my feelings for Kenji grew until I could say that I loved him.

Kenji was the first man I had been with since Arthur. Before Kenji, I had not allowed anyone to get close. I'd always compared every man with Arthur. Especially their service in the war. If they hadn't enlisted, I wouldn't even go out with them. If they had enlisted, well, they hadn't died, so nothing they had done in the war seemed enough.

It's crazy, I know. I was crazy when it came to Arthur.

Why had I let Kenji near my heart? Perhaps because he was foreign and thus couldn't have been expected to fight in the war. And he couldn't be expected to look anything like Arthur. And I liked him, so what could go wrong?

22

The Daily Colonist   October 5, 1915

Housekeeping Rooms

Mother was angry. I couldn't call her 'Mum' anymore because 'Mum' is a cozy and loving word, while Mother was angry.

She railed at me for leaving school. She was unimpressed with my job on the newspaper. She grew so loud and vociferous that Grandma had to take her aside to calm her down. After that, she glowered at me.

Underneath her anger, I sensed a deep and abiding pain because I had destroyed her dream. She had set so much store in my success. She had wanted to live vicariously through me. I didn't care. She'd taken away my child without even asking me.

I was angry too. And I was angry first.

The atmosphere at home was strained because of me. Mum had told Robert and Lucinda that I'd gone to Vancouver to improve my grades at another school, yet I had come back and missed a whole year. My siblings had trouble understanding why I had so hastily left high school when I used to love it so much. They knew I'd always wanted to be a teacher. My explanation that I'd changed my mind just didn't ring true to them.

Then there was my mother's change in attitude towards me. She'd always held me up to them as a model student to be emulated but, now, she was distinctly cold to me.

So, on this one particular Sunday morning when I was still in my nightgown reading the newspaper in the parlour, I overheard twelve-year-old Lucinda challenging my mother in the kitchen.

"Why do I have to go to church when Edith doesn't have to?"

"Edith is a grown woman," Mum responded. "She can choose to go to Hell if she wants to."

I heard my grandmother respond to this, perhaps some sort of protest at my mother's language, but her voice was so low I couldn't make out what she said.

Mum continued, "But you're still a child and you'll do as I say. Now go and get dressed, because you're going to church."

Lucinda stomped off to her room then and my mother came into the parlour. I looked up from the paper, sensing trouble.

"You ought to look at the classified ads," she said, her voice calm, though I sensed the suppressed fury beneath it. "Because you need to find your own place to live."

I was speechless.

"I can't have you living here anymore. You're a bad example for your sister."

I was stunned. I had only just got a low-paying job and I was barely seventeen. I wasn't ready to be out on my own yet. "Would it make any difference if I went to church with you this morning?" It would be a small price to pay in order to be spared this punishment of exile.

"No," she said. "You're an embarrassment to me. I don't know who knows or who suspects, but I am sure people will look at us and people will talk. I'm afraid Lucinda might hear things I'd rather she didn't."

"Whether I leave or whether I stay, she may hear things."

Mum shook her head. "I'd rather you left," she said.

And that was that. I started looking at the classifieds right away.

Grandma came into the room and set a cup of tea on the table in front of me. Then she sat down beside me.

"I'm sorry, dear," she said. "Would you like me to stay home with you this morning?"

I wasn't crying or anything. In fact, I felt as cold as a stone inside.

"No, Grandma. You go to church and pray for me, if you wish."

"I always do, dear. I always do." She patted my hand. "Now, you drink your tea."

She got up and went to her room.

It's difficult for me to relive my feelings from that time. In the deepest pit of myself, I felt the rejection. Grandma was the only one to show me sympathy at the time. She came and sat with me as I packed up my few scanty belongings. She said little. I knew she would never speak against her own child, but I sensed her support of me all the same. She would never have sent me away. She felt as I did that some unspoken rule had been breached by my exile.

I wasn't making a lot of money and I couldn't afford much. I got a place above a shop downtown. It was just a studio sitting room with a hot plate on the counter and a shared bathroom down the hall. I bought a small table and chair and put a mattress on the floor in the corner. I started saving up for a bed the day I saw a mouse run across the mattress and hide under the skirting boards.

It was an embarrassing accommodation, but fortunately no one came to visit me there. Except Grandma. One Sunday afternoon, she arrived at my door winded after walking up the stairs. She stood in the doorway and looked around with a faraway look in her eyes. "This reminds me of the first place I lived in when I came to Victoria," she said with a deep sigh. "I was twelve."

"Come in," I said, "Have a seat." I offered her the only chair.

"I went to work shortly after that when I was fourteen," she said, settling into the chair. "And your mother started working when she was sixteen. She wanted so much more for you."

"So did I," I replied.

"I'm sorry she's so harsh with you."

"It's my own fault, Grandma."

"Now, don't be so hard on yourself, Edith. You've had a string of bad luck, but you're cream. And I know that you'll rise to the top one day."

I've never forgotten those words. No one had ever said such a thing to me before. Any time I've had any success in my life, I've looked back and remembered what she said that day.

She looked around the room. "There's no icebox and no stove."

"I've got a hot plate. I can boil some water for tea if you'd like some."

"Next time I come," she said, "I'll bring you a proper cooked meal."

I got up to put the kettle on for tea.

23

The Daily Colonist   September 11, 1928

Leaves for East

I went to the teahouse on the second Saturday in September. I had to see Kenji. He hadn't called all week, though usually he called at least once to tell me what time he was coming on Saturday evening. Some nagging little insecurity made me go.

Harry Takata greeted me at the entranceway.

"So good to see you again, Miss Robertson," he said. "You're becoming a regular."

I demurred. I looked around the teahouse furtively, as if I were searching for a table.

"There's a table with a nice view of the garden right here," Harry said, leading me to one beside the bamboo wall.

I felt confident Kenji would be my waiter. Harry handed me a menu and I declined to take it.

"No need," I said. "I know what I want."

Harry took the carte and said, "I'll send your waiter right away."

I was on pins and needles waiting for Kenji to appear. But a few minutes later, some other Japanese fellow with an almost indecipherable accent appeared at my table.

"What you like?" he asked.

"I'll have tea and a poached egg on toast," I said.

He bowed.

"Before you go," I said. "Is Kenji working today?"

He looked at me without comprehension.

"The other waiter, Kenji Takata?"

He shook his head. "No. Not here."

I sat in silent turmoil, my stomach turning fiercely. It was only his day off, I told myself. No need for alarm. But he didn't usually take Saturdays off, my gut responded.

Harry was standing idly by the entrance, so I caught his eye and called him over.

"Is everything all right?" he asked.

"Oh, yes," I replied. "Everything's fine. I was just wondering where your cousin is. He's usually my waiter."

"Oh, he was only here for the summer," he said. "He's leaving on Monday."

"Oh," I said.

"We'll miss him. He was very popular, especially with the ladies." He turned on his heel and left.

Frankly, I felt that last comment was turning the knife in the wound. I also felt a great chasm open in my heart. How could I continue to sit here, eating poached egg on toast and pretending to be just fine? Especially with Harry Takata still observing me from the entranceway when he wasn't greeting and seating guests.

The waiter brought me my tea. How could I have been such a fool? Didn't I know better than to trust a man? I took a sip of my tea. It was too hot.

Any man. Even one of a different colour. They were all the same, no matter what race. They didn't care about women.

The waiter brought me my perfectly round poached egg sitting like a sun on the toast.

Women weren't really human. Only this spring, the Supreme Court of Canada had ruled that women were not persons.

I took a bite of my egg and chewed. I didn't know how I could swallow it. I was sure that my roiling stomach would toss it right back up, something to be discarded and rejected. Just like a woman.

I tried to will a peace within me so that I could finish my meal. I took a sip of tea to help me swallow. I took a few more bites and sips. I ate slowly until I had eaten more than half. Then I covered my plate with my napkin, put some money on the table, got up and made a dignified exit from the teahouse.

When I got home, I went to the bathroom and threw up my egg. Then I went to my liquor cabinet and drank till I passed out. I only woke up the next day when the telephone rang. It was Kenji.

"Can I take you to dinner tonight?" he asked.

I was angry. I wanted to shout at him. *So this is how you are going to say goodbye? In front of a lot of people so that I can't scream and carry on!*

"No," I said as calmly as I could muster. My head was throbbing. My whole body felt as though it had been invaded by trembling rabbits. "I already know you're leaving tomorrow."

"But I want to say goodbye properly."

I had heard that before! "There is no proper way to say goodbye!" I shouted. My own voice made my head ache harder and jangled my spidery nerves. I took a deep breath. "I thought you were going to stay here. I thought you would marry me."

"Are you crazy?" he asked. "We could never marry."

"I wouldn't mind other people's prejudice."

"Even if that were true," he said. "I have a wife and child back home in Japan. I have…"

I don't know what he said after that because I slammed the receiver down. I hoped the sound it made hurt his ears as much as it hurt my head.

How could I have missed that fact? I was usually so careful about married men. If a man was my age or older, I was very wary. Kenji looked younger. Besides, he had come to Canada for the summer to learn English. I hadn't considered he could have left a wife back home. I had taken pains to find out that he was here by himself and stayed in a room at his cousins' home. And I had been deceived.

I thought of Kenji's wife at home in Japan. She had been deceived too, even worse than I was. Could any man be trusted ever? Why would I ever let my heart be broken again?

I thought of Arthur alone and far away in a foreign country. Had he deceived me too? Of course not! Arthur would never have done something so evil and baseless. Arthur would never have deceived me. He loved me utterly. But Arthur was not coming back.

I went over to the liquor cabinet to begin another day of drinking.

24

The Daily Colonist   May 13, 1916

Women's Realm: Work for All

~~~~~~

May would have been a year old that evening in the month after which I named her. Grandma came to visit me, bringing a casserole dish filled with stew. She sat on the bed watching while I ate it.

"You know, don't you, Grandma?" I asked her between mouthfuls.

"Know what?"

"That it's May's birthday?"

"May?" she said.

"That's what I call her. I have to call her something, so I call her May. I'm glad you remembered."

"Well, I wrote it down in my diary. She *is* my first great-grandchild, after all. I want to remember her too, even though I've never met her. And I knew you'd be sad today."

My hand stopped on the way to my mouth. I didn't think I could eat another bite without choking on my tears. I put down my fork.

"Let me make you some tea, Grandma."

"Good," she said. "I've brought cookies too, for dessert."

"You'll have one of those?" I asked.

"Yes," she said. "They're good with tea." She looked around my shabby room. "Don't you think that you've lived here long enough?"

"This is all I can afford, Grandma."

"But you have a good job at the newspaper, don't you?"

"I may have overstated that to Mum in order to impress her. Which it didn't. But I'm really just a copygirl. The bottom rung."

"Well," Grandma mused. "I know you're a good writer. You won all sorts of prizes at school. Perhaps it's time you went to the boss and asked for a promotion."

"Well, I do work hard, Grandma." Truth be told, I was a little slave to the reporters and other copyboys — running around doing whatever tasks they felt too high and mighty to do.

"There, you see? Hard work should be rewarded."

"All right, Grandma. I'll go see about getting a writing job tomorrow," I said. "Now let's have tea."

The next day, with my grandmother's words ringing in my ears, I plucked up my courage and waited to talk to Miss Lawson. She wrote the daily column called 'Women's Realm'. Every day, there was a poem and then a story about some important British noblewoman or other and what she had done for the war effort. She also wrote stories about what the women of Victoria were doing, such as sending boxes of sweets to soldiers at the front and sometimes advice such as how women should feed their children or how they should buy locally.

She had a small office in a corner of the building and she came in every day, usually in the morning for a few hours. Then she took her handwritten copy directly to Mr. Lugrin's office. I kept my eye on her office door, hoping to see her when she arrived.

Finally, I espied Miss Lawson opening her door. She reminded me a little of my grandmother. As I walked toward her, she looked me in the eye.

"Yes, miss," she said sternly. "What do you want?"

Even if Mr. Lugrin hadn't told me, I could tell by her commanding voice that she used to be a schoolteacher.

"Good morning, ma'am," I said meekly. "I've come to ask you a favour."

She spoke a little more gently. "And what do you do at the paper, miss?"

"I'm a copygirl," I said. "I've been here a year and a half, ma'am."

"It's 'miss'," she said, correcting me.

"I'd like to talk to you, miss, if you have a few minutes."

She opened the door and asked me to have a seat.

"Thank you, miss." I sat in a chair.

Miss Lawson sat down behind the desk, facing me. "What is the favour you'd like?"

"I appreciate your column, 'Women's Realm'," I began, hoping a compliment might soften her. "I read it every day."

"That's nice, dear."

Clearly, praise did not soften her. "I've always wanted to write for the newspaper and I wondered if you'd be willing to see some of my stories. Perhaps you could include some of them in your page."

"What kinds of stories?" she asked.

"I have an idea what would interest younger women, Miss Lawson. I think they would be interested in the fight for women's suffrage, for example. And perhaps the kinds of work that are available to them now with the war on as another example."

"And you don't think that my stories interest young women?" she asked, clearly miffed.

"Of course they do," I said. "But I would like to try my hand at writing too. I could help you with your column."

"Other than being a copygirl," she asked, "what kind of experience do you have?"

"I used to write for the *Camosun* at Vic High," I said.

"Did you go to college?" she asked.

"No," I said.

"That's enough," she said, dismissively. "I have a column to write and I'm sure you have work to do as well."

I got up to leave, feeling miserable.

"If you want," she said without looking up, "you can bring one of your stories tomorrow for me to read."

I felt terrific. That night, I hardly slept as I wrote and rewrote a story about the wondrous strides I still hoped that women would make in this new century. Miss Lawson had been brusque with me, but that must be the manner she'd learned as a single woman competing with male writers. I thought surely she must have some sympathy for a fellow woman trying to make her way in a man's world. After all, in the end, she had relented enough to read my story.

Finally, after many agonizing revisions, I was satisfied the story was my very best-crafted writing. Even if she didn't agree with the content, she would have to see that I could write well.

With high hopes, I brought it into Miss Lawson's office and left it on her desk.

She sought me out the next day and told me that I wrote well, but my story was far too political to her way of thinking.

"It's not," she said, "the kind of story I envision for 'Women's Realm'."

I'd certainly been wrong about Miss Lawson. I shouldn't have been surprised that she'd rejected my story. I'd read all of hers, and it was clear that she was a firm, committed supporter of women's place in the social order. Perhaps she thought of herself as the exception that proved the rule. At the very least, in her opinion, a woman needed a college education to be a reporter, and I hadn't gone to college. If she only knew I was a high school dropout, she probably wouldn't have even read my story.

None of the men who wrote for the newspaper had gone to college. Not one. It wasn't considered necessary. But if you were a woman, you had to be better than a man. You had to pay much higher dues to get into the club.

25

The Daily Colonist   September 18, 1928

Velvets and Satins Vie for Fall Wear

I woke up to the sound of a knocking in my head. Every bang pounded inside my skull. I shook my head. The pounding continued. I opened my eyes. The brightness of the room screeched in. I shut my eyes. The knocking sound continued. It was outside of me. The door.

Bang. Bang. Bang.

How to stop it? I slipped out of bed. My blankets fell on the floor. I glanced down. I was in my nightie. At least I'd made it to bed last night.

Bang. Bang. Bang.

"I'm coming." It hurt to speak. It hurt to walk. Everything hurt. I staggered to the door. "Who is it?"

I heard a faint answer. It sounded like a woman. What day was it? *Sunday.* Oh, no!

First Presbyterian Church was just across the street. *Oh God, do not let this be one of those rare occasions when Mum and Grandma drop by after church. I should put on my robe.*

"Just a minute," I said, going back to my room to look for my robe.

Bang. Bang. Bang.

"Shit! I have to make it stop."

I hurried back to the door and opened it.

Grandma was there. Alone. *Thank God.* And she had a brown paper bag with her.

"Come in," I said.

"Oh, my," she said, looking at me.

She went straight to the kitchen and put the bag on the counter. She took a casserole out of the bag and turned on the oven.

"I'll just heat this up, shall I?" She looked at me again. "Would you like some tea, dear?"

"Coffee," I said. "I'll have coffee. I just got up."

"I can see that," she said. "Are you not well?"

"No," I said. "I'm feeling terrible. Let me go get dressed while you make that."

I turned and went back to my bedroom. I had the terrible feeling that she could see right through me to the truth. I didn't want her to know the truth. I didn't want her to know what a despicable person I was.

I got dressed and went to the mirror to make myself look presentable. There were those bloodshot eyes and that yellowish skin. God, I looked awful. I put some skin cream on and rubbed my face. My head ached. I went into the bathroom to take some Aspirin. Was that coffee I smelled? I came out at last.

Grandma had the plates filled with salmon, rice and vegetables. My stomach turned at the sight. I had no appetite except for booze.

She poured me a glass of water. "Drink this while you're waiting for the coffee to be ready."

The percolator whooshed its soft and soothing sound. I sat down and drank the water.

"You've been drinking," she said.

How could she know?

"My father was a drinker," she answered my thought. "I know the signs. How long has this been going on?"

"A while," I said.

She nodded. She looked tired and frail and I felt terrible burdening her with my problems.

"Have you missed any work?" she asked.

"A few days last week," I said.

"Aren't you worried you might lose your job?"

My sacred job! How I hated it. And yet, what would I do if I lost it? I nodded, but it hurt to shake my head even gently.

"What is it that drives you to drink?" she asked.

"When things go wrong," I said, "as they so often do."

"Do you mean about May?" she asked.

"Yes, that's part of it."

Grandma nodded. "I don't want to pry." She looked around my spacious kitchen. "You've done well for yourself, you know. This is a lovely apartment and you have a good job. I just don't want you to lose it all."

"I know, Grandma. And I should be trying to make myself worthy of my daughter. I'm just doing such a terrible job of keeping myself together."

"You go ahead and eat," she said. "I'll pour you a cup of coffee."

I looked at the plate of food. Still no appetite. But I picked up the fork, took a small bite and nibbled at it. "Why is Mum not at church this morning?" I asked, changing the subject.

"She's not feeling well herself. She has a cold."

"How did you get to church?"

"Your father gave me a ride."

"I'll drive you home," I said. "You know you don't need to bring me meals anymore. Though it is delicious."

Grandma poured me a cup of coffee. "Are you in a fit state to drive?" she asked.

"Of course," I scoffed.

Grandma sighed.

"Oh, look, Grandma," I said. "I don't want to let you down." I pushed some food around the plate. "I don't want to let May down either."

"It's yourself you shouldn't let down," she said.

"I always do, though, don't I? I've been a screw-up since the day I was born."

Grandma shook her head. "No," she said. "You made one little mistake once. And you've been paying for it ever since. It seems to me the debt should be all paid up now. It's time to get on with your life."

I snorted. "And just how do I do that?"

"Pull yourself together. Apply yourself at work."

"I hate my job."

Grandma looked shocked. "I thought it was a dream job to be a writer on the newspaper."

"I'm not a writer, Grandma. At best, I'm a re-writer. At worst, I'm a dogsbody."

"Well, be the best dogsbody you can be then."

I loved Grandma. I didn't want to disappoint her. She was trying to help. For her, I would stop drinking today. For her and for May. And I would damn well try to be the best dogsbody I could be.

It was always a struggle getting up to go to work on mornings after my days off when I drank too much. Even with a day off from drinking, It wasn´t much easier. It wasn't as if I found the work inspiring either. Yes, I did get to write the occasional piece for the Social and Personal page. Stories like "Miss Sheila Gillespie is visiting friends in Vancouver for the weekend" or, even better, "Outstanding wedding of the season."

The column that Miss Lawson wrote, 'Women's Realm', the one I had scoffed at with its poetry and stories about women who were doing things to better our position, was gone now, replaced by the Social and Personal Page. And I was still a 'copyboy' essentially, doing whatever job was needed. Sure, I'd learned the newspaper business, but I was going nowhere.

Still, I pulled myself together on Tuesday morning and dragged myself into the office where I made a great urn of coffee for the reporters. I loved the smell of the newspaper office. The noisy clattering of typewriters and voices shouting here and there. Sometimes they'd be shouting for me: "Edith, get me a coffee!", "Edith, take this copy to editing!" The hustle and bustle would revive me along with the copious cups of coffee I drank myself.

It was easier for a woman to hide her drinking problem than for a man. First of all, it was unthinkable that a woman would be a drinker, especially not an aging suffragist. Suffragists were known for their stand on temperance. Men who drank too much would often beat their women, and so suffragists considered drink a leading cause of family breakdowns. After getting the vote, they'd turned their energies to prohibition. As if that had turned out so well. In British Columbia, it had failed utterly, and now, smuggling had become an industry and drinking was considered chic among the young.

No matter how I dressed, I didn't consider myself very chic anymore. I must have looked quite a fright coming into work Tuesday mornings with my bloodshot eyes. You'd think someone would have caught on. But all I had to say was "I'm not feeling well today." And if they pressed me on it, which almost no one did, I said, "It's women's problems." That would shut them up completely. It was shameful of me to use their ignorance and fear against them. It was shameful of me to blight the cause of women with my fake excuses. But I must confess, I was shameless at the time.

Still, I had to pull myself together — not just for Tuesday morning, but also for the day of Remembrance and Thanksgiving that was fast approaching, November 11. It was ten years since the war had ended. Hard to believe! Ten years since all those young men had died needlessly. For the last two years since it had opened, I'd gone to the Cenotaph in front of the Parliament buildings in the morning. There, we would stand in silence for a moment and remember the dead. I liked the silence. I liked remembering Arthur's face. Usually, after the silence, I would leave because I didn't like all the noisy fanfare — the trumpet flourishes, the squealing bagpipes, the instruments of war. I didn't like the speeches and the prayers for the dead or the hymns either. They reminded me too much of church and of the glorification of war.

Then in the evening, I would go to my family home for Thanksgiving dinner. Thank you, God, for war. Thank you, God, for death. Yes, thank you, God, I'll have another bun. Let's be happy. Let's be jolly. Let's eat, drink and be merry. Well, let's eat and be merry anyway. God forbid you should take a drink.

But I really did try to reduce my drinking in the days leading up to the Armistice anniversary and Thanksgiving. I couldn't wait to see Margaret again. It had been almost a year. I wanted to see how she'd grown. I could hardly wait and I wanted to be my best self for her. If that meant less of the scotch, then so be it.

26

The Daily Colonist   April 10, 1917

Canadians Take Ridge of Vimy

One of the perks of writing for the *Colonist* was getting a free copy of the paper as I came in every day. Usually, I waited for my morning break to read it, but this morning the headline was "Canadians Take Ridge of Vimy." This intrigued me so much that I sat down and read the story immediately. I pored over the details, wondering as I so often did when I read war stories, whether Arthur had been in the battle. "Canadians Proud," the story said. "Our men were splendid, and are proud that they were counted worthy to furnish a striking force in so important an operation as the recapture of Vimy Ridge."

I pictured Arthur all puffed up with pride. *How would it be possible to live with such a man?* I thought, imagining the arrogant look on his face. He would be so proud and I would be so humble. I was still wondering what I should say to him. Should I tell him that I — that we — had had a child and that I had given her up for adoption? Or should I keep it a secret and not tell him, because, if I told him, how would he ever forgive me?

His father came to tell me the news. He must have gotten my address from my mother. He looked around my small and shabby room but didn't really see it. He wept as he tried to find the words, but his tears told me everything I needed to know without them. Still, he laboured on telling me the details of the Battle of Vimy Ridge as they pertained to his son's death, as if that was important to me. It was not.

Arthur was dead and, beyond that, I could not see or feel or hear anything. Nothing touched me in the solitary inner space where I withdrew to contemplate this news.

In that moment, my whole world changed. Nothing that had mattered so much to me one moment before meant anything to me now. All of my worldly concerns became as dry leaves and blew away.

And where was I on this bleak horizon of this strange new world? I did not know. I only knew it would take me a long time to find myself again and I would wander in this wilderness a while until I did.

I was numb. I said nothing, or perhaps I mumbled something inconsequential.

He didn't seem to expect me to perform any conversational niceties. In fact, he caught me up as I was about to fall and he held me in his arms and cried. His tears brought mine to the surface. I was not used to men showing emotion. If he could break down, then so could I.

I don't know how he managed to come to me and deliver this news when he was still grieving himself. It showed that he understood the depths of my feelings for his son and that he didn't belittle me or think me of no consequence to Arthur. For that, I was grateful. After a few moments of grieving together, he told me when and where Arthur's memorial service would be and then he took his leave of me. I decided not to go. I couldn't listen to the kind of cant a minister would spout. I couldn't stand to have his mother look down on me. I couldn't bear to keep the secret of his child in the face of all of that.

I should have written to Arthur as soon as I knew to tell him he had a child. He should have known that before he died. How important was my shame now? Death lets you see what's really important, but this learning comes too late to make any difference.

I went back to the newspaper story I'd read about Vimy Ridge, this time with new eyes, searching for a testimonial to Arthur there. I read: "Of the casualties it can only be said at this moment that they are surprisingly light, especially in view of the importance of the ground won." *What a gross and arrogant lie! Light! What a word to use. And* casualties. *Another shocking word. How can someone's death be light and casual? And what for? A piece of ground! How could a piece of ground be more important than a man's life?*

How could Arthur have died and I not felt it? Surely his soul should have come to touch mine in its flight from this earth. I should have known.

I had prayed for Arthur to live and he died. I had prayed for my baby to die and she had lived. *Do not pray anymore*, I told myself. *Do not pray anymore.*

27

The Daily Colonist   November 11, 1928

Armistice Anniversary Will Be
Observed by Service at Cenotaph

~~ ~~ ~~ ~~ ~~ ~~ ~~ ~~ ~~ ~~ ~~ ~~ ~~ ~~ ~~

I walked down to the new Cenotaph in front of the Parliament buildings to watch the veterans march in. November 11, 1928: ten years since the war ended, since all those men had died needlessly. It was hard to believe. Ten years. There was to be a special ceremony this morning.

A crowd of more than a thousand had gathered before Parliament Square. I was surprised to see so many since, being Sunday, the service coincided with church services. In order to get as close as I could to the cenotaph, I jostled my way in among the people huddled in their winter coats, hats on in case of rain. Many had a red poppy pinned to their lapels as a symbol of remembrance of those who had died on the killing fields. They looked as solemn as the occasion demanded. At last, I got close enough to see the cenotaph that had been unveiled just three years earlier by the lieutenant governor. It was a tall granite pillar with a bronze statue of a soldier atop. He had a rifle in his hands and his feet spread apart as if ready to step into battle.

Did Arthur look like that as he went to his death?

This was the place where I'd seen Arthur off to war fourteen years before. Where I'd seen him for the last time. Kenji had been on my mind so much lately that I hadn't given much thought to Arthur. I'd been so proud of myself, starting to move on and go out with other men, but now I felt as if I'd betrayed his memory. Arthur was the only good man I'd ever known. The service hadn't even started yet and the tears were threatening, so I squeezed my eyes tight and looked around.

Beyond the Cenotaph, I saw some roped-off chairs and I wondered who the dignitaries were who had the privilege of sitting during the ceremony. A few people were being wheeled in chairs to the seats. Amputees. Then a group of young women dressed in black. Widows like me. Except that I was not recognized. I couldn't sit with them. I had to stand on the other side of the street. Then I saw Arthur's parents in solemn dress, finding their way to their seats. Mrs. Brooke dabbed her eyes with a handkerchief. I looked away.

It was still too soon for tears. I didn't want her sorrow to remind me of mine. Besides, we'd never liked each other. Why pretend now? I looked back at Mr. Brooke. He wouldn't cry. He sat in dignified and stoic silence. I wondered if they had any grandchildren besides the one they knew nothing about.

I could hear the distant swirl and squeal of bagpipes. They were coming. The men who had fought and not died. The ones who could not live up to Arthur's valour, no matter how hard they tried. Soon, the sound of the bagpipes grew louder and louder as the parade made its way along Belleville.

The soldiers marched in uneven steps as they went up the road towards the Parliament buildings. Just like the new recruits who had gone off with Arthur. I wondered if they had ever learned to march in step or if they had just forgotten after ten years of civilian life. Most of them were in civilian clothes, though a few had dusted off their regimental gear. Most wore medals on their breast — bright-coloured coins and ribbons pinned in a row. I watched them till they'd all arrived. Some continued marching in place until a sergeant major hollered something incomprehensible. Then, they all stopped.

We heard the firing of the cannon at Work Point, a bang in the distance. Then a bugler beside the Cenotaph began to play the Last Post. I glanced at my watch. It was almost eleven. I could hear other buglers playing in the distance. At the end of the bugles' playing, there would be two minutes of universal silence.

But the silence was broken by the squeal of a seagull above us protesting the fading noise of the bugle. The man standing next to me shuffled from foot to foot. I tried to imagine the silence of the tomb. I tried to imagine Arthur's face. I caught glimpses of it in my mind. His smile, then on top of that, Margaret May's smile. That same twinkle. Then, both faded.

Two minutes is a long, long time. Memories gripped and washed over me. In and out, like the tide. Arthur, dying. Margaret May, being born. One made the other more bearable. Both were my burdens. I glanced over at the widows and families of the Dead. I should be there. But I was not. I should be a mother. But I was not. And all because of the lack of a piece of paper saying that Arthur and I were man and wife.

Finally, the silence was broken by the sound of the bugle again, this time playing Reveille. It was time to wake up from our thoughts of death and dying and return to the land of the living. It was also time for me to leave. The preachers in their long black gowns were coming to the podium to begin their sermons and prayers for the dead. Soon, we would be expected to screech out hymns. "O God, Our Help in Ages Past" and "O Valiant Heart." Even though it was a Sunday, I never attended church anymore and I wouldn't do so now.

You might very well ask me why I went at all then. Why didn't I just stay at home and observe a moment of silence? I liked to be in the middle of a crowd of grieving people. I liked to look around and see the faces and know that all of them had known at least one person who had died in the Great War. I looked back at all the people and caught a glimpse in that moment of the numbers of soldiers who had gone to their deaths. I was not alone in my grief. I was not alone.

It had been so long since I'd seen Margaret May and I was eager to see her again. I went early to help my mother and her maid. I was setting the table when the doorbell rang, so I put down the plates I was holding and went to open the door. James and Margaret stood there. The smiles drained from their faces when they saw me. I looked beyond them and saw Margaret two steps behind as if she wanted to distance herself from them. Her arms were crossed in front of her as if she were cold, though it was a mild evening. A glimpse of her face led me to know that it was just part of her act of hostility.

"Come in," I said effusively. "Come in and make yourselves at home." They came in.

"Can I take your coats?" I put out my arms and gathered all their coats to hang them in the closet. "Go on into the parlour."

They left me alone to hang up their coats. When I was finished, Mum was already calling everyone into the dining room. This Thanksgiving, it was my brother and his wife's turn to eat with our family and so we were eleven adults and five children, if you counted Margaret May, but that was not a given. So, we found our names at the table and crammed around it. Margaret May frowned and folded her arms when she found she had been placed at the children's table that had been set up in the vestibule to make more room in the dining room.

My mother looked embarrassed. "There are just so many of us," she said. "And I thought you wouldn't mind."

Margaret May continued standing.

"Margaret, sit down," her mother ordered.

Margaret May glared at her mother. "I'm not a child."

"I didn't say you were, but it would be good for you to learn to look after the little ones. It will be practice for you when you have your own."

Margaret May's chin jutted out, making her look proud and defiant. I had seen that expression before and I knew that she would not back down or, if she was forced to, she would do a terrible job of child-minding.

"Why don't I be a good aunty and sit at the children's table?" I volunteered.

My mother and sister looked astonished. I was rather astonished too. It was not something I wanted to do. I hated looking after the little ones. I half-hoped that Margaret May would offer to sit at the children's table with me, but she didn't. So, I was denied the privilege of watching her and listening to her.

Instead, I was left to cut turkey into manageable bites for the little ones, wipe up spills, urge toddlers to eat, spoon food into their mouths when they didn't and head off sibling fights. Occasionally, I glanced through the open doors and caught glimpses of May's sullen unyielding face and snatches of her ongoing bickering with her mother.

At first, I'd felt happy to see the state of affairs between Margaret May and her mother. Then it reminded me too much of my own attitude to my mother when I was that age. I began to pity Margaret the Elder when I realized that I too, as a mother, would have been subject to such behaviour. It almost made me think perhaps pouty May should have been consigned to the children's table.

Finally, dinner was over and my father invited the men to the parlour where they could smoke cigars and perhaps even drink a snifter of brandy. The children quickly fled the children's table and found their mothers, while I went to sit in my father's seat at the head of the table.

Mum came out of the kitchen with the teapot and sat down. She looked at me with an expression of gratitude I had rarely — no, never — seen in the last fourteen years.

Margaret May was still glaring daggers at her mother.

"Show your appreciation," Margaret's mother said, "for your cousin Edith's kindness in letting you sit at the adults' table. Something which you did not deserve, by the way."

I was embarrassed to be included in their feud.

Margaret May looked down at the tablecloth, gathered herself and looked up at me. "Thank you."

"You're welcome," I said.

"Now, let's have tea," Mum said.

Margaret May turned to me and said, "I really am sorry you had to sit with the children."

I laughed. "My mother would say that I'm still a child too! So, it's fitting."

Margaret May smiled. She poured milk to top up her half-cup of tea, then took three spoonfuls of sugar and stirred them in. She sipped it, made a face and stirred another spoonful of sugar in.

"You don't have any children?" she asked, knocking me for a loop.

Her mother glared at me.

"I'm not married," I said, not really answering the question but getting out of it in an acceptable manner.

Margaret's mother nodded in approval and took a sip of her tea.

"Why not?" she asked.

Again, I had to think up an answer that didn't tell the truth but didn't exactly lie. "I'm happy working," I said. Now, *that* was a lie.

"You work for the newspaper," Margaret May stated. "That must be exciting work."

I nodded, not wanting to make any more dishonest statements.

"You see, Mom," she said, turning her attention to her mother again. "You don't have to get married and have children to be happy."

I was back to being a pawn in their game.

"I want to be like you when I grow up," Margaret May said to me.

"I thought you already were grown up," her mother said spitefully.

Margaret May stuck out her tongue.

Oh, Margaret! I thought. *You are such a child! I wish you were mine. I wish you were sparring with me.*

"That's enough!" her mother shouted.

I think even Margaret knew she'd lost that battle. She quietly drank her tea and answered my occasional harmless question about school.

28

The Daily Colonist   October 8, 1918

City Will Act To Check Epidemic

The newsroom was abuzz with word of the epidemic of Spanish influenza that had swept through Canada and the U.S. in September. The 'flu had found its way to our island at last. Early in October, Victoria had its first casualty. The next day, the city shut down all the churches, theatres, schools and meeting places.

The reporter who covered City Hall had a droll wit and liked to read aloud the humorous bits he had buried in his long dry stories. According to him, City Council meetings were exempt from the Public Health order to close because "the atmosphere of the Council Chamber was so heated that no germ could live in it."

I was in the newsroom ten days later, waiting for his copy, when he read this bit on the same subject: "The board made the request, however, that the public should refrain from attending the council meetings and rely instead on the reports to newspapers, whose representatives were held to be 'germ-proof.'"

That got a few good guffaws from his fellow scribes. I smiled too as I took his story down to be typeset.

By October 22nd, there were already more than eight hundred cases of influenza in the city. The old Fairfield firehall that had closed down a few months before was being renovated and equipped as an emergency hospital because the isolation hospital was at full capacity. There was still a shortage of nurses, though.

The Medical Health Officer, Dr. Arthur Price, made an appeal in the *Colonist*.

> Here is an opportunity for young women of Victoria to render a splendid service to their city. In fact, it is more than that. It is a matter of duty to their country, just as it has been a matter of duty for men to go overseas to fight. Here is a chance to fight a formidable enemy right in our own homes. We need nurses to assist in fighting Spanish influenza. They don't need to be competent. Any young women will do. The only qualities necessary are a good head and a pair of willing hands.

Dr. Price certainly knew the right words to persuade me at that time.

> There naturally must be self-sacrifice in this work. Just as our soldiers left all behind and started out to battle, the women throughout the country are rallying to the new colours.

Arthur's sacrifice was so fresh in my heart and I felt useless sitting at home on my days off. As the doctor said, my sacrifice would be "comparatively small." So, I decided I would dedicate two days a week to nursing the sick. I went down to the makeshift hospital in the old Fairfield fire station and signed up. I let them know that I could only work for two days. They were disappointed but desperate to take whatever they could get.

It was a great stark hall where the fire engines had been kept and it was filled with beds where the sick lay. Around the perimeter of the building, several coal-burning stoves vented to the outdoors kept the cavern warm as the poor patients suffered from fever. The smell of the warm dampness of burning coal permeated the place as I bustled about changing bedclothes, emptying bedpans, cleaning out buckets of vomit and whatever other horrid tasks the real nurses would order me to do. Talk about dogsbody work!

Two days of this convinced me I did not have what it takes to be a nurse and I very much looked forward to going back to my work on the newspaper on the third day.

I worked one day back at the newspaper, but on the next day I couldn't. I was sick — so sick I could scarcely get out of bed. I managed to crawl to the parlour and pick up the telephone. I asked the operator for the *Colonist* and I told them I was sick. Then I placed a call to my mother and was put through to her.

All I said was, "I'm sick."

"Oh no," Mum said and then there was a long pause. "I'll be right over."

Mum didn't come alone. Grandma was with her. She had insisted on coming and brought chicken soup. I smelled it, then ran down the hallway to the bathroom and threw up in the toilet. I came back to my bed and crawled in, my head spinning. Grandma pulled the covers up and tucked me in. I shivered.

"However did you catch the 'flu?" Mum asked, looking with disgust around my one tiny room. It was the first time she had visited me. "Did someone at the newspaper have it?"

"I volunteered as a nurse on my days off."

"Oh, Edith!" Mum cried. "How could you? Don't you think that was foolish of you? And now you're sick."

"Now is not the time, Maggie," Grandma said.

I was grateful for her intervention. I couldn't listen to Mum's tirade today. I had no comeback and my head was spinning.

"We should take her temperature," Mum said.

"We have no thermometer," Grandma said, laying the back of her cool hand on my burning forehead. "She has a fever."

"I'll get a cold compress," Mum said.

That was more like it. It felt nice to be nursed by both of them. I lay in bed and enjoyed listening to the sound of their banter until I fell asleep. Hours later when I woke up, Grandma was still there.

"Your mum had to go home to make supper," she said. "Would you like some soup now?"

I moaned and turned over, incapable of even replying. I felt like hell. I should have known better. I was the one who had chastised Arthur for believing it was his duty to go fight for his country and look what happened to him.

And now it was happening to me. If someone tells you something is your duty, run, don't dally, run in the opposite direction. You have no duty to die for someone. And that day, and the next, I lay in that bed and felt for sure I was going to die. In fact, I felt so bad sometimes that I almost wished for death.

The next morning, Grandma was there. I was not aware whether she had stayed the night. I had no other bed, so she would have had to sleep beside me on mine. I was glad I was not alone. I didn't want to die alone. She put a fresh cold washcloth on my forehead and a spoonful of porridge to my lips. I tried to take a sip, but I couldn't swallow it. She brought me a glass of water. Then Papa arrived, dropped off Mum and took Grandma home.

When they were gone, Mum told me off again. "Think how you'll feel if Grandma gets sick now." She shook her head and clucked at me. "And what are you doing living in this dump? Once you're well again, I'll help you find a better place."

Oh my God! I felt terrible. I couldn't feel worse. I would have hoped for death — then if Grandma got sick, I wouldn't know it and I wouldn't feel guilty — but Mum's negative lectures left me struggling to get well enough to send her home so I wouldn't have to listen to her anymore.

Grandma didn't come back. Mum wouldn't let her. She was angry that Grandma had stayed overnight with me. She was angry with me for being so selfish. Mum was right. Two days later, Grandma was sick and then the day after that, Mum was sick. Dr. Price had talked about 'self-sacrifice'. He hadn't mentioned anything about how I might infect others but I knew that I wasn't 'germ-proof', even if I did work on a newspaper. If I hadn't felt so sick, I would have thought to send my grandmother home. Instead, I took her care and gave her the 'flu in return.

Though I was feeling better, I didn't go back to work. I moved back home and nursed both my mother and grandmother. I wouldn't let Lucinda or Papa anywhere near them, and Robert was away at college in Vancouver. I didn't want anyone else to get sick. The maid did the cooking and housework while I did sickroom duty. Duty! There's that ugly word again. But this time it really was my duty. I had brought the terrifying spectre of death to the ones I loved, so my penance was to banish the demon forever.

I was sitting at Grandma's bedside, listening to the sound of her laboured breathing, when there was a timid knock on the bedroom door.

"Yes," I called. "What is it?"

"Supper's ready," Lucinda answered. "The maid sent me to fetch you."

"I'll be right there."

Lucinda waited for me and we walked down the stairs together.

"I like your dress," she said.

Ankles were showing that year and I always dressed in the latest fashion. Poor Lucinda looked quite forlorn in her out-of-date long black skirt and hair tied up in a tight bun.

"I really want to have my hems shortened," she said, "like everyone else, but Mum won't let me."

Mum held the reins on poor Lucinda tightly and I knew it was because of my transgression. She thought that somehow she could keep Lucinda from repeating my mistake. It was having the opposite effect. Lucinda was apt to rebel, her frustration palpable. But I dared not suggest to Mum she should loosen the reins. I only hoped that Grandma could do that when she got better, God willing. Perhaps I should have spoken to Lucinda myself.

There was only Papa, Lucinda and I at the table for supper. The maid had put together a light meal of leftovers in a stew.

"How are your patients?" Papa asked.

I knew he was anxious about Mum especially and I was glad I could put his mind at rest. "Mum is recovering nicely," I said. "I think she should be up and around by tomorrow."

"And Grandma?" Lucinda asked.

"She's having a tougher go," I said, feeling worried. "If she's no better tomorrow, perhaps we should call the doctor."

They both looked worried.

"Let's talk about something else," Papa suggested.

"What do you think," I asked, "of our first woman member of the legislature, Mrs. Ralph Smith?"

Papa glared at me. "I don't approve of talking politics at the dinner table," he said.

"But Papa," I replied, "just think what young women can aspire to these days. When Mum was young, she had little choice but to be a maid."

Papa said nothing.

"Perhaps Lucinda could even be prime minister one day," I continued. "What do you think about that?"

Lucinda made a face. "I would absolutely hate it," she said. "Imagine being like one of those stuffy old men." She shook her head vehemently.

"What would you like to be then?" I asked.

She shrugged.

Papa pointed his knife at me. "I'll thank you not to put any ideas into her head," he said. "Having to educate Robert is costing me quite enough already."

Robert was now attending the newly opened University of British Columbia in Vancouver, the school that Arthur was supposed to have attended.

"What is he studying?" I asked.

"A lot of useless nonsense like history, French and literature," he said. "Lord knows what he's going to do with all that book learning when he finishes."

Robert was the first person in our family ever to go past high school and I'm sure it was a great expense for my parents that he had to go away to another city for university.

"Perhaps he could go into the civil service," I said. "There's always room for bright young men in the civil service." *There's always room for bright young men everywhere,* I thought bitterly. *There's just no room for bright young women anywhere. Still.*

"What about the newspaper business?" my father said.

"Yes, of course," I said, "but I think civil servants are paid better."

Mum recovered as quickly as I had done but, for Grandma, the 'flu sunk deeper into her chest and it was touch and go whether she would make it for a few days. I watched her sinking slowly, and I prayed as I have never prayed before or since. I vowed that if she lived, I would be a more considerate granddaughter. I chastised myself for wanting to be a hero, to sacrifice myself. I should have known better after what had happened to Arthur.

But then I watched her rise again, slowly but surely. My joy at her recovery was infused with relief. Grandma was going to live and I would not have to live the rest of my life with the heavy burden of guilt on my conscience.

I hadn't killed her.

29

The Daily Colonist   December 15, 1928

Is 'Flu' Returning?

I went Christmas shopping. I wanted to find something for Margaret May. It was hard to know what a churlish thirteen-year-old could want. I found toys for all my nieces and nephews in short order, but they were young and it was easy. Everything I looked at for Margaret May was either too old or too young. I thought about what I would have liked at that age and all I could think of was a book. But what book? There were hundreds of books. Which one would be the perfect one?

It should be by a woman. It should be about a woman. I thought of the Brontës and immediately dismissed them. They were too romantic. Girls of Margaret May's impressionable age should not be subjected to such romantic nonsense. It could only lead to tragedy.

Then I thought of Jane Austen, of *Pride and Prejudice* fame. She had a much more sensible voice. Still, it wasn't very modern. It was all about finding your mate, the only real opportunity for women in those days.

This was the twentieth century. Women could vote. Women could write for newspapers. Not here perhaps, but somewhere anyway. Surely, I could find some twentieth-century novel by a woman about a woman that Margaret May would like. I'd just finished reading Virginia Woolf's latest novel, *To the Lighthouse*, and I wondered if that might not be appropriate. It spoke to this new century, to people left behind after the war. Perhaps Margaret May would like that. I dropped into a bookstore and picked up a copy.

I came home from shopping and was putting away my purchases when the phone rang. I picked it up. "Hello?"

"Edith." It was my mother. She sounded upset. "Your grandma is ill. We've just taken her to the hospital."

"To the hospital! Why, Mum?"

"She needs nursing care around the clock and I'm too busy."

"How are you too busy? Only Lucinda is at home now."

"Christmas," she said. Then, she broke down and cried.

"Never mind, Mum," I said. "Can I go visit her?"

"Yes, of course." She gave me the ward number. I wrote it down on a piece of paper, put my coat back on and rushed out.

At the nurse's station, I stopped to ask for Grandma's room. The nurse explained to me that Grandma had pneumonia.

"She's had that before," I said. "Why did she need to be hospitalized this time?"

"It's," she said, "a particularly virulent case."

"Can I see her?" I asked.

"Of course," she said. "She fades in and out of consciousness, but I'm sure she'll be comforted by your presence."

Grandma looked small and helpless in the hospital bed. She was asleep as the nurse had warned. I sat down beside her bed and took her hand. It was warm.

"I'm here, Grandma," I said. "I'll stay with you until they kick me out."

Her eyelids fluttered. I knew she heard me.

"Thank you for your pep talk, Grandma. I've hardly touched a drop since our talk together."

Well, there'd been a few slip-ups, I admit, but I was doing a lot better and wasn't missing any work. It was better than I would have done without the talk. Then, in my head, I did a terrible thing. I made a deal with God that if He spared my Grandma, I would never drink again. I should know better than to make a deal with God. It was as bad as praying.

So, I sat there with Grandma, telling her about the sorts of things I'd been doing at work. I had a part to play in putting out the newspaper, a product I was proud of. It was a small part, but I knew Grandma would be glad to hear about it. I may have exaggerated my part a little, to be sure, but that was also a function of the news business, wasn't it?

I'd only been there nattering for half an hour when the nurse came in to tell me visiting hours were over. I bent over and gave Grandma a kiss on the forehead. It felt warm.

"Would you like some water, Grandma?" I asked.

"I'll give her some," the nurse said. "Now, you be gone."

"I'll be back to see you tomorrow, Grandma," I said. "I promise."

At one o'clock exactly the next day, I was at Grandma's bedside again. This time when I took her hand, it felt cooler. Good. The fever was gone. When I spoke to her, there was no response. She seemed in a deeper sleep today.

I sat down and started to chatter. I was talking about Margaret May and about Christmas, when my mother, father and sister bustled in the room. Mum gave me a peck on the cheek. I stood up and offered her my seat. She sat down.

"How is she?" Mum asked.

"She's sleeping soundly," I said. "I think the fever's gone."

Mum put the back of her hand on Grandma's forehead and nodded.

"Why can't you look after her at home, Mum?" I asked.

Mum looked distressed but said nothing.

Papa spoke up. "Your mother has enough to do at home. Now is not the time to bicker."

I saw a warning in his eyes that said I shouldn't push her. Never mind how much she pushed me. I stepped away from my grandmother's side and went to the foot of the bed so that Lucinda and my father could get closer.

"Her breathing is shallow," Mum said, sounding alarmed.

I looked at Grandma again. So much at peace. So little here with us. I hoped it was the prelude to her recovery, but then, I had never seen death before. Perhaps it was just like this. No, it couldn't be already. What about my bargain with God? I stood at the foot of the bed and watched.

She had survived so much. The Spanish flu at the end of the Great War. She had survived that. And only last year, another case of pneumonia. She had survived that. I had come to believe there was nothing she couldn't survive.

And I needed her. God, how I needed her. She was my rock, my everything. She was the one who loved me and believed in me unconditionally, even knowing how messed up I was. No one knew me and loved me like she did. I had promised God I would give up drinking if He spared her, and without her, I wouldn't have the strength to do it.

Looking down, I watched her breathe her last. It was so quiet and uneventful that it didn't seem to have even happened, but my mother started to howl and my father took her in his arms. Then the tears came into my eyes and I backed myself against the wall.

No. It couldn't be. Not Grandma. No.

My sister came, put her arms around me and cried into my shoulder.

At that moment, Robert came into the room and I saw on his face a reflection of our distress. He quickly grasped the truth I was not yet ready to accept.

30

The Daily Colonist   January 1, 1919

Returning Soldiers

The men were coming back. Day by day, more ships came into the harbour bringing back 'our boys'. People went down to the Inner Harbour to wave and cheer. I couldn't. All I could think of was that Arthur would not be on any of those ships. I remembered cheerfully waving goodbye to his ship, but there would be no welcome back.

He wasn't the only one not coming back. The man who'd had my job before me did not come back either and so I was not required to give it up. But now, many men were applying for jobs and I knew I was an unnecessary appendage. The few other women who worked for the paper had left. Either their jobs were reclaimed by returning servicemen or their husbands had returned from the war. Many of the younger ones didn't need to work; they were living at home and eager to find young men to marry them. Still, I did not want to give up. I certainly didn't want to go back home and now I had a new, more expensive apartment to pay for.

When Mum had seen my place, she'd said she'd help me find a better place. She didn't know that I had continued living there so long because I was saving my money to buy myself a motorcar. I had wanted to buy one ever since my first ride in Cousin John's Model T touring car, even if it was to the Vancouver Home for Girls. But Mum insisted on keeping her promise and, even though I knew that the war would shortly end and I might lose my job, I indulged her. It was nice to have a little positive attention from her for a change.

So we'd set to it and found a lovely apartment in a brand-new building on Quadra Street. It was right across the street from her church. Perhaps she liked the location because she thought I might slip across and return to the fold. Or, at least, she could keep an eye on me on Sundays after service. At any rate, I liked it because it was near downtown, and well, frankly, because it was better than "a room of my own" — it was a whole apartment of my own.

Mr. Swayne, the new editor-in-chief, called me into his office. I assumed this was not a good thing. I knew I was going to be asked to leave. I puffed myself up and prepared to fight for my job. I hadn't gotten married. There was no legal reason I should be required to leave.

"Come in and sit down," he said. Once I was seated, he continued. "What are your plans?"

"Excuse me?" I asked.

"What are your plans now the war is over?"

"I have no plans," I said.

"Well, with all these young men returning, surely you'll find the right one for you and settle down."

"The right one for me," I said, "as you call him, was killed at Vimy Ridge, so it may be too late for that."

He looked startled. "I'm sorry," he said. "But you're young yet. You'll find another."

"Perhaps," I said. "But it may be a long time. In the meantime, I plan to keep working here."

"Oh," he said. "I just thought you might leave and make room for the men returning. They need a job more than you do."

"I don't think so," I said. "I have an apartment to pay for."

"You don't live at home?" He seemed astonished.

I shook my head.

"But you could move back home?"

I shook my head again. "No," I said.

He looked disappointed.

"Have you any reason to complain of my work?" I asked. I had always done my best.

"No," he said. "You do good work."

"Then, surely you have no objection to my staying on?"

He looked as though he had every objection in the world, but he couldn't bring himself to say anything.

"No," he said. "If you insist on staying, you can stay."

He waved his hand at me to suggest I leave. I got up and went out.

His perfunctory dismissal was a harbinger of things to come. For the next few months, even years in some cases, I was met with the same cold attitude from my co-workers. I had been expected to leave and it was churlish of me to stay on when men were looking for work. My less-than-friendly workplace turned hostile, but still I persisted.

31

The Daily Colonist   January 10, 1929
Women Again Offer Protest

Christmas was cancelled that year. Mum was deeply grieving and couldn't bring herself to put up decorations, shop, cook, clean and have people over for supper. We all grieve in our own way. Although, I'll wager most alcoholics grieve in the same way I did. I know I should have been more faithful to Grandma's memory, but there was that little matter of my bet with God. He hadn't kept his part of the bargain, so damned if I was going to keep mine.

Of course, getting drunk is not really grieving. In fact, it's just grief postponed or denied, an attempt not to feel anything. I spent the entire week between Christmas and New Year's in a drunken stupor. Why not? I took another week off from work. I had no place to be, no one to see. I drowned myself in booze and self-pity. And then, the last day before I had to go back to work, I allowed myself to feel all the pain of my self-loathing. My whole body trembled. I threw up and up and up. I lay in bed and cried until my head ached.

It was time to live up to Grandma's expectations. I made a resolution for the New Year that I would give up drinking and I would work hard and do everything I could to advance myself in my work. The very next day, I needed to go into my boss's office and ask for more. A raise. A promotion. A writing job. Something — anything — that would lift my spirits and give me something to live for. I had been working for the newspaper for fourteen years. I was not a girl anymore, I was a woman. This year, I would turn thirty. And this year, Margaret May would turn fifteen. That was the age I was when she was born, when I bore her. I was exactly twice her age. This was some kind of omen to me, but I wasn't sure what it meant.

And the thought of Margaret May reminded me of something else I had missed at Christmas. I had not seen her, I had not given her gift to her yet. So now, I wouldn't get to see her until Easter. I'd spent too much of my life waiting. Yes, it was time to face my boss.

I put the urn of coffee on and screwed up my courage. Before I had time to doubt myself, I went and knocked on his door. He beckoned me in. Jack Kerne was a young man, hardly more than a boy, but he was trying hard to emulate his boss, Senior Editor Mr. Swayne. I noticed a cigar sitting on the edge of his ashtray. It wasn't lit, but it was cut and ready for lighting.

"Good morning, sir," I said.

"Morning," he said. "What is it? Are we out of coffee again?"

"No, sir. I've come to make a request on my own behalf. I know that I've just taken a week off…"

"Yes," he said, looking at his shoes and then at his desk, but not at me. "I was sorry to hear of the death of your grandmother."

"But," I continued, "I've worked here for fourteen years and I've never once had a promotion or anything."

"Got a point."

He picked up his cigar and took some pains to light it. I watched the ritual and waited impatiently. Finally, he got it lit, took a puff and squinted at me through the haze of stinky smoke.

"I could," he finally continued, "use some help writing articles on the Social and Personal Page. Would that suit you, do you think?"

He didn't seem to remember that I already did that and I hated it. That was the one part of the paper I never read, filled with useless stories about where Mr. and Mrs. Tyrwitt-Drake spent their holidays or who came visiting the Pembertons and what women were wearing these days. Still, if the work I did all the time anyway was finally being recognized, then it would mean a promotion and a raise.

"What would the job entail?" I asked.

He squinted at me again through the blue haze of his cigar smoke. "It entails writing is what it entails — writing whatever I tell you to write. Do you think you can do it?"

"Of course I can. Does it also entail a promotion?"

"We are pushy this morning, aren't we?" He squinted at me some more, but I said nothing. "All right."

He pushed his chair back, scraping it noisily across the floor. He put his cigar in his mouth and offered me his small, soft hand to shake.

I shook it. "Do I get a desk?" I asked.

He took the cigar from his mouth and placed it back in the ashtray. Then he waved his hand dismissively. "Just sit at one of those desks out there in rewrite."

I left quickly. Best not to press my luck. It wasn't much of a job, but I was, at last, one step up on the ladder.

My boss, Jack Kerne, was hardly out of grade school and eager to get ahead. I think he hated working on the society page even more than I did. He tried to be tough and hard-bitten like the senior editors, but he was still a sensitive boy underneath. He couldn't bring himself to put me down and stomp on my ambitions. In fact, I think Jack saw me as his liberation. If he taught me the job well enough, I could take it over and then he could find his rightful place in real news where real men belonged.

Not that I wanted to be trapped on the society page forever, but for the first time in my life, I saw the possibility of being in charge of something, of being the one who made the decisions. If an eighteen-year-old boy could be the editor of the society page, then I could do it too, and even better.

In my mind, I had ambitions for the page. After all, it was the one page that most women read. I could make it the Women's Page. I could write stories that women like to read — fashion and celebrities, yes, but also, stories about the issues women were facing in a world that was stacked against them. Of course, it couldn't happen all at once. Whatever I did would have to develop slowly. I knew better than to threaten too directly the superior position of men in this male-dominated world. But we would see. We would see.

Now, there was a possibility of advancement at least, and maybe, eventually, one day, if I worked long and hard enough, I could become a real reporter writing real news about the affairs of the day.

32

The Daily Colonist   August 5, 1919

Soldiers Returning

May would have been four years old when I had my first after-Arthur date. I was twenty. My beau picked me up at my apartment and we rode a streetcar to the end of the line at Gorge Tramway Park. We walked into the park and through the lovely Japanese Gardens. It always seemed strange to me that what the Japanese called a garden had so few flowers in it. Instead, there were trees, waterfalls, quaint wooden bridges and stones. But it was a lovely day. The sun shone through the Japanese maples with their tiny red leaves casting dappled shadows on the path in front of us.

It was so beautiful that it reminded me of that summer's day with Arthur and I looked up, expecting to see him, but instead I saw John, the handsome, but vapid, young man that worked at the paper. There, he had a desk and a typewriter and I used to stand and watch him pecking away at the keys and wish I had a typewriter too. One day, he had noticed me there and asked me out on a date.

"Shall we have tea in the tearoom?" John asked me now.

I nodded and we went into a bamboo building along the path. He ordered two black teas, with milk, without asking what I wanted. I would have liked to try Japanese green tea because I was feeling adventurous — I was finally going out with another man after all.

159

But when I looked at the menu-board on the wall, I noticed there was nothing Japanese on it.

We sat in silence for a time and I searched my mind for something to talk about.

"So," I eventually asked, "what did you do in the war?"

"I was in the merchant marine," he said. "We ferried ships with supplies from the States." When he saw I didn't look too impressed, he added, "Lots of boats were torpedoed. We were lucky to get out alive."

"Yes, you were."

I thought of Arthur and how unfair it was that this man had survived but Arthur hadn't. And then I chastised myself for such an unkind thought. We drank our tea, mostly in silence. I did not want to engage him in more conversation about the war and he seemed disinclined to bring up any other topic.

After our tea, we walked along the waters of the Arm. The way the eelgrass was flowing showed that the tide was coming in. I searched the water for seals or otters. I saw none, but a great blue heron was standing in the shallows still as a statue, waiting for the flash of a fish among the grass.

We came to the Gorge itself and walked out on the bridge to watch the white water below pouring over and between the rocks. Every time I'd been here before with Grandma, she told me the story of going through those rapids in a canoe as a little girl on her way to her new home on Craigflower Farm. She told me how terrified she'd been at first, but when the canoe shot out of the rapids like a cannonball, it had been the most exciting experience of her life.

My escort took my arm and broke my reverie. We walked back up the hill to the streetcar stop.

"This has been lovely," he said.

I nodded. Perhaps I was being unfair. Perhaps he would grow on me if I took the time to get to know him better.

At the door to my flat, he gave me a kiss. At first, he was gentle, but when I responded, he stuck his tongue between my teeth and thrust it into my mouth, reminding me harshly of the horror of making love. Well, I knew I would not go out with him again.

After that, over the years I had many first dates. Occasionally even second dates when I could talk myself into them, but not more than that. And I cursed Arthur and how he had spoiled me for other men because none of them frankly measured up to him. And why should I share my bed with any man who was less than he was?

33

The Daily Colonist   March 31, 1929
Easter Has Drawn Many from Afar

Three months after Grandma's death, Mum was feeling well enough to invite all the family for Easter Sunday dinner.

"Mama would have wanted it," she explained to me on the telephone.

"Yes," I said, "she would have." After all, Grandma loved family get-togethers and always made sure I was included.

It had been four months since I had seen Margaret May and I'd thought of her every day. She and Grandma were the reasons I'd stopped drinking as my New Year's resolution. Tomorrow would mark three months of teetotalling. I felt good and I was enjoying my new job as a writer even if I didn't have my own desk and typewriter. I wasn't always thrilled about what I had to write — Jack Kerne hadn't accepted any of my ideas for improvement of the page, but no matter. My writing was recognized and I didn't have to run around doing odd jobs anymore. At least, not as often.

Robert and his wife had gone to dine with her family and, of course Grandma was gone, so we were less crowded at the table. Lucinda supervised the children's table, so I had the privilege of sitting at the table with my own daughter, even though she didn't know that's who she was. As far as I knew, her parents still had not even told her she was adopted. It wasn't right. She would be fifteen in less than two months.

That was my age when she was born. If I'd been old enough to have a child then surely she was old enough to know I was her mother.

I watched her discreetly as Papa said grace. His graces were long and formal, like those of the Church of England he grew up in. Margaret May looked less hostile than she had seemed at Thanksgiving. She kept her head bent and her eyes closed through the long prayer. I wondered if she went to church and, if so, which one.

"Amen," Papa said, and we all looked up and started dishing food onto our plates.

"Do you attend church, Margaret?" I asked.

"Yes," her mother answered. "Of course she does. What a question!"

Both Margaret May and I gave her a look which made her turn away, take an offered dish of sweet potatoes and spoon some on her plate.

I turned back to Margaret May and asked, "Which church?"

"We go to Emmanuel Baptist. It's on the corner of Fernwood and Gladstone, only two blocks from where we live."

Baptist. Weren't they the Holy Rollers?

Margaret May spooned a healthy helping of potatoes onto her plate, joining the chorus of dishes and spoons that punctuated our conversation.

"Do you like it there?" I could feel a cold glare from her mother.

"Yes," Margaret May said, glancing at her mother. "Of course."

"And how about school? I presume you go to Vic High now?" I took a few Brussels sprouts and put them on my plate.

"Pass the mustard," Papa said, so I did.

"Yes," she responded. "I love it." She seemed enthusiastic.

"Do they still have the Portia Society?"

"Yes." She looked at me with newfound respect. "All the most popular girls belong to that club," she said. "Did you go to Vic High too?"

"Yes," I said. "We were the first class in the new school building in 1914 — the year the Great War broke out. And I belonged to the Portia Society. We used to have such spirited debates. What groups are you a part of?"

"I belong to the Modern History Club. We have interesting speeches and debates as well."

After that, our conversation slowed as we ate. When dessert was done, the men went off to the parlour for cigars and the rest of us had tea in the dining room. When the tea was drunk, Mum asked me to clear the table while she and the others joined the men in the parlour.

"I'll help," Margaret May said.

Her mother looked askance.

"Thank you," I said. "I'll be glad of the company."

"It's better than listening to dull adult-talk," she said. "Besides, I want to ask you all about your job at the newspaper. I have an assignment at school to write about an interesting occupation."

"Well, come on into the kitchen and I'll tell you all about it."

Margaret-the-mother cast a worried glance at me as she walked out of the dining room. I stacked plates and carried them out to the kitchen and Margaret May followed me.

There we had a conversation in which I used all my creative powers to embellish the chores that I did every day. We ended up clearing the table completely, putting away all the food and doing the dishes. I had my hands in dishwater and Margaret May was wiping a plate when her mother came into the kitchen to see what was taking us so long.

Margaret-the-mother stated the obvious. "You're doing the dishes."

"Yes," I said. "We just got carried away talking."

Margaret-the-mother cast a warning glare at me. "Well, don't take too long," she said.

When she'd closed the door behind her, I asked, "Would you like to come to my workplace and see what I do every day?"

"Thank you for the offer, but I wouldn't be allowed to miss school."

"Margaret," I said, hunting in the dishwater for utensils at the bottom. "I never gave you your Christmas present. You have a birthday coming up. Perhaps I could take you to the Empress for afternoon tea one Saturday to celebrate your birthday in May."

"How do you know when my birthday is?" she asked.

"I must have heard you mention it," I said, pulling a knife out of the water. "Would you like that?"

"Tea at the Empress! Yes, of course, I would."

Then I realized that I was not supposed to see Margaret May on my own. "But your parents would never allow it."

"Why not?" she asked. "What harm would it do?"

I had to think of something quickly. "They think I'm a bad influence on you."

"They told you that? They had no right. Well, I just won't tell them about it," she said. "When should we go?"

It was wrong and I should have said so right away. "What day is your birthday?" I asked.

"The thirteenth," she said.

So they celebrated the actual date. "How about the Saturday before your birthday — May eleventh? I'll meet you at the Empress tearoom at three o'clock."

"It's a deal," she said, putting down her dishcloth and offering her hand.

I dried mine on the dishcloth and then shook hers.

"I can hardly wait," she said.

"Let's go join the others."

34

The Daily Colonist   March 7, 1920
Smart Models for the Spring Season

I sat in the barber's chair, quaking with fear inside and hoping I didn't look half as nervous as I felt. The sweet, greasy smell of pomade, or whatever it was that men put in their hair to make it shine, made me feel queasy.

"Are you sure you want to do this, miss?"

In the mirror, I saw the barber clicking a pair of scissors ominously and squinting at me. He had a perfectly trim little mustache curling on his upper lip and his black hair was slicked tight to his scalp. He didn't look too happy.

Of course I wasn't sure I wanted to do this!

But short was how forward-thinking women were wearing their hair and skirts these days, and I wanted to be one of them. My skirts were already creeping up — it made it so much easier to ride my bicycle — and now my hair would go that way too.

It had been two years since women had gained the full right to vote in Canada, so now, in the very next election, I could vote. I was proud of that achievement and I wanted to identify with the women who had worked so hard for it.

"You surely" the barber asked, "don't want to be mistaken for one of those suffragette women, do you?"

He had said just the right thing to push me off the fence. "Yes, I do. Cut, please."

He scrunched his face as if he'd bit into a lemon. "People will think you're a man. Men won't want to go out with you. You know that, don't you?"

I knew no such thing and it didn't scare me, even if it were true. I thought of the recent date I'd had with my colleague and how banal it had been. What did I need a man for anyway?

"Cut," I said.

He took the scissors, held a clump of my hair and hacked at it.

"In wartime," he said, "they cut off women's hair like this when they've been consorting with the enemy."

"Don't cut it all off," I said. "I just want a bob."

I showed him again the magazine photo of a fashionable young woman in New York.

He looked at it and shook his head. "Still looks like a man to me."

He continued clipping in hostile silence.

I watched as a long brown curl of my hair fell to the floor.

Snip.

I looked in the mirror and saw my sad face.

Snip.

I glanced down. The curls were forming a pile on the floor.

"Keep your head up."

I looked up.

Snip.

My face in the mirror frowned at me.

He stood between me and the mirror and combed my hair in front of my face. *Snip, snip, snip.* He cut my bangs short.

He stepped away from me. "There you go," he said.

I looked at myself in the mirror again. It wasn't so bad. My face was still the same but now it was framed with bangs and short, clipped hair. The barber removed the towel around my neck. I stood up, trying not to look at the pile of my long, dark beautiful curls lying on the barbershop floor, but seeing them anyway. Trying hard not to cry.

He named a price that was higher than the one that was posted, thus more than he charged his male customers. When I objected, he just said, "You had a lot more hair to cut off."

"Enough," I said, "so that you could probably sell it and make even more money."

"I doubt it. Not with all the young women like yourself coming in to get their hair cut off."

166

Well, I thought, *I won't be recommending your shop to any of them and I won't be coming back either.*

The day after my haircut, the copyboys at the paper began giving me a bad time. Copyboys never stayed in that position very long and these were a new crop of younger boys. I must have seemed a novelty to them — slightly older and perhaps wiser in the ways of the world.

"Edith," Ed said. "Your hair is so short that you look like one of the 'boys' now."

Everyone laughed.

"Yeah," Ivan said. "So, why don't you come with us when we go for a drink after work?"

Now, this invitation might not seem like much to get excited about, but in the past I had rarely been acknowledged as a fellow worker. I said yes without thinking.

So, we all piled into Zack's car and drove to his house. There, we sat in his parlour and he brought out a bottle of alcohol. I was astonished. Prohibition was still on in British Columbia and it had just begun in the U.S., so it was very difficult to obtain liquor.

"Where did you get that?" I asked.

"Don't ask and I won't tell. Some things it's better not to know."

"Bootleg, then?"

"Of course."

"Is it safe?" I asked.

"I couldn't say," he replied.

Ivan ribbed me and said, "What does it matter to you? You suffragettes are all teetotallers, aren't you?"

It was true that we were supposed to be. I felt I'd very much let my team down by going out to drink with the boys instead of chastising them for their bad habit. I shrugged. It was too late to get all preachy. I was here and might as well live the experience.

The boys thought it was hilarious to initiate me into drinking by giving me bootleg whisky. A glass with a few fingers of the amber liquid was placed in front of me. I swirled it and watched it coat the inside of the glass. Then I sniffed it and the fumes burned the inside of my nostrils.

"You have to drink it fast," Ed said. "In one gulp." He held up his drink.

I looked at the amount in my glass and thought that shouldn't be too difficult.

"Let's go," he said. "Three, two, one."

I tipped the glass back and felt liquid fire slipping down my throat. Instead of drinking his, Ed had put down his glass and was watching me. I knew I was supposed to be the entertainment and cough or sputter or at least make a face, so I did none of those things. Everyone laughed anyway.

"What's wrong, Ed?" I looked at his glass. "You can't keep up with me?"

He turned red, then swigged his drink. Then he wiped his mouth with the back of his hand. I think he was hiding his reaction.

"I'll have another," I said, slamming my glass on the counter. "But this time, I plan to drink it slow and enjoy the taste."

Again, everyone laughed. Ivan poured me another drink.

I did drink it slowly, but it tasted absolutely dreadful. I watched the others downing it quickly and realized that was the only way to drink the awful stuff. So I chugged the next glass.

Suddenly, I felt like a child again — free from pain and guilt, *happy*. I felt as though I was soaring on a breeze, flying high above these mere mortals down below. I wasn't so high that I would let these boys take advantage of me, though God knows they tried. I ended up escaping their clutches and getting out of there unscathed. I had to walk home, but at least my dignity was intact. And they would keep their distance from me in the future.

Even though the boys never asked me out again, I was well on my way. A year later, prohibition ended and I could buy my own bottles of whisky. The legal liquor from the government liquor stores was marginally better-tasting than the bootleg stuff. Especially the scotch. It became my drink of choice and I always enjoyed it alone in the privacy of my own home.

35

The Daily Colonist   May 12, 1929
To Give Mother Foremost Place

~~~ ~~~ ~~~ ~~~ ~~~ ~~~ ~~~ ~~~ ~~~ ~~~ ~~~ ~~~ ~~~ ~~~ ~~~ ~~~

I was going to meet Margaret May for tea at the Empress.

I stared into my closet, pondering what to wear. I stood there trying to decide. I stood there longer than I would have if I were going on a date. So much more was at stake. I was going to meet Margaret May.

Biddy wound herself between my legs as if asking me why I was standing in one place so long. I looked down at her questioning eyes.

"She loves my flapper dresses." I took the sparkly one out of the closet and shook it. It glimmered in the light.

Biddy meowed.

"But I know it's not appropriate," I said, putting it back in the closet. "I'm her mother. I should set an example."

Biddy looked disgusted.

"You think I should set an example of how to have fun?"

My everlasting shame flooded me.

"I can't encourage her to become what I am."

I reached in the closet and took out a sensible suit and blouse and flung them on the bed.

"That's what I'll wear, Biddy. Something sensible."

Biddy jumped on the bed on top of my clothes as if to keep me from getting dressed. I pulled a slip out of my drawer and put it on.

"I know what you're thinking. She doesn't know I'm her mother. But one day she will, and I have to set an example."

I pushed Biddy off my skirt. She glared at me.

"No, I'm not going to tell her today. I promised I wouldn't and I won't."

I picked up my skirt and pulled it on. Then my blouse. As I did up the buttons on my blouse, I looked at my dresser top for some jewellery to pin on my suit. Everyday stuff — nothing suitable. I walked over and opened my jewellery box. Among the chains and pins, I saw a little blue box.

"What's in there, Biddy?" I asked.

As usual, she said nothing, so I opened it.

"Oh!" My heart skipped a beat. "Oh, Arthur."

Inside was his high school ring. He'd given it to me before he left for the war. It never fit me so I'd put it in this box for safekeeping. And forgotten it.

"How could I have forgotten this, Arthur?"

I took it out and put it on my finger. Still too big! I untangled a chain from my jewellery box and put the ring on it. Then I attached it around my neck.

"Why have I never worn it like this?" I said.

In my heart, I heard the reply, *Because it's too painful.* I turned to the cat.

"Every time I touch it, I see Arthur's face, so I hid it away."

I undid the clasp and put the ring and chain back in the blue box. Biddy was staring at me.

"What do you think, Biddy? Should I give it to Margaret May?"

Biddy licked her paw.

"But what would she want with it?" I put it back in the jewellery chest and closed the lid.

Inside, I felt a fierce fire burning. *She's my child. Give it to her.* It was Arthur's voice.

I had to sit down. I sat on the dressing table chair. Since his death, Arthur had never spoken to me before. I took a deep breath and let out a sigh.

"All right, Arthur," I said. "I owe you that much at least."

I took the blue box out of the chest and sat with it wrapped in my hand until the anguish inside of me had subsided and Biddy had fallen fast asleep. Then I got up and finished getting dressed.

We met in the lobby of the hotel. There was an awkward moment when I gave Margaret May a hug which she wasn't expecting, then we stood and looked at each other.

"Let's go find the tearoom, shall we?" I said.

When we found the tearoom, I followed the maître d' and Margaret followed me, through the elegantly dressed tables with their white tablecloths and bone china settings. The maître d' pulled out a chair for me, then one for Margaret. I sat down on the great big, comfortably stuffed behemoth and tried to pull it closer to the table. It took all of my strength to scrape it along the floor one inch.

Then I ordered the afternoon tea and sat back and looked at her.

"Look at you," I said. "All grown up."

Margaret's face reddened and she looked down at her place setting. The pattern had lovely yellow tea roses. My china pattern was similar except the roses were pink. I resisted the urge to turn it over to find out its name.

"So, tell me, how old are you now?" I asked, as if I didn't know.

"I'll be fifteen in two days," she said.

"We'll have to ask them to bring a special cake for you."

"No, Auntie Edith." She reddened. "I'd rather you didn't."

"No more of this 'auntie' business. You're practically a grown-up now and I'm not your aunt. Call me 'Edith' from now on."

She smiled.

The waiter arrived with a pot of tea and put it down beside me. I turned and told him that it was Margaret's birthday and would he bring her a piece of cake for the occasion?

Margaret blushed again, unrolled her napkin and busied herself arranging it on her lap. Meanwhile, I peered into the teapot to see if it was ready.

When we were both settled again, facing each other and feeling awkward, I smiled.

"Well, then. Tell me about yourself, Margaret. Do you have a boyfriend?"

"No." She answered too quickly, I thought. "Of course not."

"Why not? An attractive young girl like you. You must have some admirers."

She shook her head. "Not a one," she said.

"But there is someone that you admire," I said, persistently.

She blushed and said nothing.

"There, I knew you did," I said. "Unrequited love. It seems like the worst thing in the world when you're young. But it isn't really. In fact, I must say I think 'requited love' to be far worse. It can have drastic consequences as you'll come to know. And besides, you're far too young to have a beau. Now, let's talk about other things. Would you like some tea?"

I suggested that she put the milk in her cup before she poured, which she did, then marvelled at the way the liquids swirled so beautifully together without stirring. Then she took the sugar tongs and plopped in one, then two, cubes and had to stir anyway. I shook my head and insisted that she was "sweet enough already." Margaret made a face at my comment. I suppose it was a silly remark, but I was nervous.

Margaret looked around at the elegant dining room and sank a little deeper into her seat.

"Tell me about your job?" she said.

"I said enough about that at Easter," I replied. "I'd rather hear more about you. Tell me about yourself, Margaret. What do you want to be when you finish school?"

"A teacher," she said.

"Really?"

"Yes," she said. "It's not very exciting like your job, but my father and mother think it's an excellent occupation for a young woman."

"Yes, that's certain, but if it's not something you really want to do, if it's not something you're passionate about, then you really shouldn't do it just for the sake of your parents."

It was Grandma who had told me that. I sat back and thought about her. I thought about how Grandma and I had always celebrated May's birthday every year. Margaret watched me as if waiting for my next words. I weighed them carefully.

"My grandmother was a seamstress," I said. "She made women's gowns and she taught me how to sew as well. That was back in the days when women wore those long, beautiful gowns. Well, you know, but I'm so glad we're free of those things these days. Anyway, I'm losing track of my thoughts." I took another sip of my tea and composed myself. "Grandma loved her job. That's what my mother told me, anyway, though I never saw her work at it. By the time I was born, her eyesight had gotten bad and she couldn't see to do the fine needlework anymore. But my Grandma always said you should find a job you're passionate about and do it passionately. So, Margaret. Do you know what job you would be passionate about?"

"No," she said, "but being a teacher would be a lot better than working for the government and I have no taste for being a nurse. What other jobs are available to women?"

"Indeed," I said. "My mother always said the same thing. She said that it was all very well and good to want a job you have passion for, but you don't always have the opportunity to find and do the work you love, especially if you're a woman. That may be true, but I say, if you don't try to break down barriers, they'll just remain there for you and all the women who come after you."

I felt a little hypocritical saying that. I had done very little to break down barriers, settling for a copyboy's job for so many years.

"But maybe some people, like me, don't ever really have a passion for anything."

"Or maybe you just haven't found it yet. Sometimes it takes a while." I sat back then. "What is your favourite subject at school, if you don't mind my asking?"

"History," she said.

"Mine, too," I said, suddenly remembering my innocent fifteen-year-old self sitting in a desk at school, listening to Mr. Andrews while I dreamed of Arthur.

Meanwhile, Margaret took a scone, smeared it with jelly, then heaped on the Devonshire cream and took a bite.

"So, you might be a history teacher one day," I said, trying to sound enthusiastic. "How exciting for you!"

Then I told her about Mr. Andrews and asked if he was still teaching at Victoria High School. We started talking about our favourite teachers and why we had liked them. By the end of the tea, her enthusiasm had almost totally won me over to her way of thinking and I was genuinely excited about the thought of her becoming a teacher.

That's when the waiter arrived with a cupcake and a pink candle on it. He placed it in front of Margaret May.

"I won't sing," I said. "You'll thank me for that, but I will say 'happy birthday and may you enjoy many more.'" Thinking about school reminded me how we used to sing another song to that same "Happy Birthday to You" tune when I was a little girl. It was "Good Morning to All."

"Thank you," she said.

"Now, blow out the candle, dear. Make a wish first."

While she was blowing out the candle, I took out the little blue box wrapped in newspaper and slipped it across the table to her.

"I have a little gift for you. It isn't much, but it's something meaningful to me. I hope you'll accept it."

She unwrapped the box and opened it. She pulled out the chain with the ring hanging from it. She examined it.

"It's a Vic High school ring," I said by way of explanation. "I thought since you attend Vic High that you might like to have it."

She looked at me. I could tell by her expression that she thought it was a strange gift.

"Did it belong to your high school sweetheart?" she asked.

"Exactly," I replied.

"Then why should I have it?"

"Well, perhaps you could give it to your high school sweetheart when you get one," I said. "Or better still, keep it to remember me by."

"What happened to the boy who gave it to you?" she asked.

I swallowed hard. "He died in the Great War."

She peered at me and swallowed hard. "Then surely you don't want to give it away."

"I want you to have it." I started to tear up. No, this wouldn't do.

"Well, thank you," she said, putting the ring back in the box and the lid on it. Out of sight. Out of mind. She looked at me. "Is everything all right?"

She didn't like the ring. Well, of course she wouldn't. She had no idea what it meant and why I'd given it to her and I could never tell her. I reached into my handbag and took out a handkerchief. I wiped my eyes.

"Why are you crying, Auntie Edith?" That same look of concern. The one I had loved to see in Arthur's face.

"You look so much like him," I blurted out. I was immediately sorry. I almost hoped she hadn't heard or understood.

She looked surprised. "Who?"

"Your father," I replied. It just slipped out. I hoped she would think I meant James.

"I don't look anything like him at all," she said. "And anyway, why would it make you cry if I did?"

"I'm sorry," I said. "It's not my place to tell you."

Margaret's lips grew taut and her eyes flashed. She had his temper too. "Now, you really have to tell me," she insisted.

She was right. Even if it was wrong. I had let the cat out of the bag and I couldn't stuff it back in again, not without the pain of scratches.

"Your parents should have told you that you were adopted."

"I was adopted!" she almost shouted. "How do you know this?"

"I know this because that ring" — I nodded toward the box — "belonged to your father."

She stared at me, some kind of terrifying understanding beginning to bloom in her face.

"What are you saying? My father didn't go to Vic High."

"You're right," I said. "James didn't. But the man who is your real father did."

"How can you know this?"

She was angry, and I wished I hadn't said anything at all. Now I would have to speak the truth.

"Because I'm your mother and your father was my beau who died in the Great War."

"No." She shook her head. "No. Mom was right about you." She stood up, threw her linen napkin on the table and shouted, "You're crazy!"

"Wait, Margaret! Let me explain."

She spun on her heels.

"I'll drive you home and explain everything."

She didn't look back but stormed out of the dining room. I couldn't follow because I had to pay the bill. This was a disaster. I hadn't meant to tell her and, yet, I was glad I had. But I hadn't expected such an emotional response. Silly me! She was fifteen. What other kind of response would there be? And I had just rocked her whole world.

The pink iced cupcake sat untouched beside the box with Arthur's ring in it.

I stared at the box for the longest time. I wept into my hanky. I swallowed the tea that was left in my cup. It was bitter and cold. I picked up the blue box, put it in my pocket and called for the bill.

36

The Daily Colonist   October 24, 1920

Recruiting for the Menagerie

Now that I had a steady job and an apartment and had put some money aside, it was time to indulge my desire to buy a motorcar. I put much thought into the choice. I didn't want a Model T, even though it was what I could afford. I wanted something sleek and classy, like a Roamer roadster, but that was way out of my price range. Finally, I found a slightly used red Chandler Model 19 touring car. The dealer had one of last year's models that had been returned. I had almost enough money saved, but he wouldn't give me credit for the balance. The bank wouldn't give me a loan either, not without my father's co-signature. So, since I had to involve him anyway, I asked him for the loan directly. He was pleased to lend me the money, though I'm not so sure he would have been if he'd known the kind of car I was buying. He owned a Ford Model T himself.

Learning to drive was one of the great pleasures of my life. It stoked my feeling of independence and a good run out in the country always did wonders for my morale. It made me feel alive to press the pedal, fly like the wind and forget all my cares. Some might say I drove too fast, but I was always careful.

In that roadster, I drove all the roads around Victoria. From Sooke Potholes to Sidney Spit, I flew or bounced along with the wind in my face. My world grew from the tiny little town of Victoria to the whole of the Saanich peninsula with its farms and all of the southern tip of Vancouver Island. I never attempted to drive farther north, though. In those days, the Malahat Drive was a treacherous mountain track with a steep cliff on one side in some places, and I would never risk crashing my beautiful red roadster.

The year that I bought my roadster, I was on one of those drives out in the country in Metchosin when I saw a sign at the end of a driveway: 'Free kittens'. I flew on by, but something about that sign spoke to me. A kitten. Wouldn't it be nice to have a kitten to come home to in the evening? Someone to greet me at the door. Someone to talk to when I felt lonely — and I was lonely.

Of course, I did try to have another relationship with a man. I must have dated dozens of eligible gentlemen over the years. Some of them were pleasant enough companions, but I did not 'fall' in love with any of them. In the beginning, none of them measured up to Arthur Brooke, which I think was rather unfair on my part. I was not measuring them against an actual person but against my idealized memory of someone. Then, in later years, as my ideas about a woman's place in society began to grow, I could not find a man able to put aside his inherent feelings of superiority. In retrospect, even Arthur would not have fulfilled my later requirements of a man. It is perhaps even fortunate that I never married him. If I had, I would not be the woman I am now.

I soon found another driveway to turn around in and then I drove my car slowly back to where I'd seen the sign about the kittens and turned into the driveway. It was a much-rutted dirt road that wound for about a hundred feet through the trees. At its end was a house barely worthy of the name, more a shed. A rather fearsome-looking man with a scruffy beard came out of the house. He stared at my car as if it were some kind of mythical beast. I gave him a sort of salute.

"Good morning," I said.

"What do you want?" he said.

"I saw your sign for 'free kittens'," I said. "Could I see them?"

"You can have the whole lot of 'em," he said.

"No," I said, "I just want one."

"I'll bring you one, then," he said, then started to walk away.

"I'd like to choose it, if I may," I called after him.

He shook his head and disappeared into an even meaner building that I took to be his barn. He came out a few minutes later with the cutest little brindle-coloured kitten. She was tawny and blonde and black. He handed it to me.

"A biddy for a biddy," he said.

"I'm not a biddy!" I protested.

"No," the unpleasant man replied, "but you will be."

I turned my attention to the tiny creature that almost fit into the palm of my hand. She meowed pitifully.

"Isn't she too small to leave her mother yet?"

The man shook his head. "Feed it milk with an eyedropper for a few days," he said.

"No," I said, handing the kitten back. "I can't take it from its mother if it's too young."

He didn't take it, but backed away from the car and put his hands up as if to indicate we were done.

"It's yours now," he said, turning around and walking away.

"Biddy," I said, holding her by the scruff of her neck up to my face. She had black stripes above her eyes that gave her a permanent frown. "We're going to be good friends."

She hissed at me.

Well, I must say, we've had a love-hate relationship ever since. She's not much of a conversationalist, except to purr. But she's been great company — far less complicated than people, always willing to listen to me, ready to curl on my lap and purr for the price of some cat food. She's never ever disappointed me.

37

The Daily Colonist   May 14, 1929

Mother's Day Marked Here

Two days later, I wrapped the copy of *To the Lighthouse* and put Arthur's high school ring in my pocket and went to visit James and the two Margarets. It was a Monday evening, Margaret May's actual birthday, so I thought it likely they would be at home.

I didn't know quite what to expect, but I wanted to apologize. I had broken my promise to them, so I knew they would be angry. I braced myself with the thought that it was partly their fault for not telling her that she was adopted.

I walked up the creaky wooden stairs and knocked on the door. A few minutes later, James opened it a sliver. He looked at me and his face soured.

"You have some nerve," he said, peering out.

"Can I come in and apologize?" I asked.

The door flung open and Margaret's mother appeared in my face.

"How dare you tell her!" she screeched.

I stepped back as she flew at me with her hands cupped like claws. James took hold of her and hauled her back.

"She had a right to know," I said.

Margaret seemed to shrink into the doorway. "You've ruined her birthday," she said.

"I've brought her a birthday present," I said. "Can I see her?"

"She doesn't want to see you," James said, his voice like steel.

"Can you give it to her for me?" I asked, holding it out.

Margaret grabbed the book from my hand and flung it down the front stairs.

I turned back, finally understanding this was going nowhere.

"I'm sorry," I said. "Tell Margaret I'm sorry."

I walked down the stairs to retrieve the book and drive back home.

I cried on the drive home. I cried and cried as if Margaret May had died, which in a way, she had, for me. Her parents were the gatekeepers and they said she wouldn't see me. I was sure they would never bring her round to Thanksgiving dinner, or any other dinner, ever again. I wondered if I would ever see her again.

I stopped at the liquor store to buy a bottle of scotch. What was the point of teetotalling if I could never see Margaret May again? Then I drove home, parked the car in the garage behind the apartment building and went inside. I got a clean glass from the cupboard and went into the parlour. I sat down in my armchair and Biddy jumped on top of me. She walked once around in a circle on my lap as if creating her space. Then she lay down and started to purr.

How many nights had she sat like this on my lap while I drank myself into a stupor? It seemed that my life was one tragedy after another and, other than Biddy, I was all alone. I didn't even have Grandma anymore to tell my problems to.

Then followed the worst period of my life. I knew beyond a shadow of a doubt that I would never see Margaret May ever again. I knew her parents would never come to our family gatherings ever again. I knew that I had completely shattered Margaret May's beautiful world and that she would never want to speak to me again.

I chastised myself a thousand times a day for being so selfish. I just had to go and tell Margaret May the truth. I never even thought about how it would hurt her, about how she would react to it. I was so self-absorbed that I thought I could go and talk to her and give her a gift and all would be forgiven.

And, of course, I drank to try and shut up my inner voice of self-condemnation.

I lived in the shadows for months and months. I went about my work as if I were an automaton. Fortunately, it was easy enough to do. I had been doing it for so many years I could probably have done it in my sleep. And so, in a sense, I did.

I kept to myself both at home and at work. I spoke only to Biddy and she answered me with a scowl as she always did. It was, I believed, no more than I deserved.

I'm not even sure how I came through that period of my life without killing myself. I was certainly depressed enough to do so. But I didn't, not even once, consider a swift exit from this world. I was too deeply engaged in a slow self-destruction.

I was drinking myself to death.

38

The Daily Colonist   May 13, 1921
Marriage Laws To Be Explained Here

∼∼ ∼∼ ∼∼ ∼∼ ∼∼ ∼∼ ∼∼ ∼∼ ∼∼ ∼∼ ∼∼ ∼∼ ∼∼ ∼∼ ∼∼ ∼∼

May would have been six years old the day Grandma arrived at my door with a casserole to console me, as she'd done every one of those six years. This time, it was shepherd's pie. We talked as I took out plates to put on the table.

"I'll just have tea, dear. I've already eaten."

She looked tired and frail and I wondered if the walk from Linden Avenue was getting to be too much for her. I determined to drive her home in my motorcar.

As I put the kettle on, Grandma asked me how I was doing.

"Good," I said. "You know May would be in first grade now."

Grandma shook her head. "My! How time flies."

I still thought about May every day. She was out there somewhere knowing no more about me than I knew about her. "I wonder if her parents celebrate her birthday on the day she was born or on the day they brought her home."

"You go ahead and eat," she said.

"Perhaps next year, we could go out for tea. Then you wouldn't need to walk so far to visit."

"Nonsense," she said. "I love to walk and, besides, it's good for you to have a home-cooked meal."

"Yes, but you don't need to bring me meals anymore," I said, "though it looks delicious."

The kettle began to whistle. I poured the boiling water over leaves in the pot.

Grandma looked around my little kitchen. "It's true you've done well for yourself. This is a lovely apartment and you have a good job. I'm proud of you."

"Thank you." I sat down to eat my pie.

"I have some news from home to share." She spoke so quietly it could only be a secret.

"What is it?"

"Your sister Lucinda has gone and gotten herself in the family way."

"Oh goodness! Mum won't be too happy about that."

"Of course not. But fortunately, the young man is going to do right by her. They're to be married next month at First Presbyterian. I expect your invitation is in the mail."

"Oh," I said.

I really didn't know what to say. So many emotions and thoughts were rushing about and through me. Mum would blame me. Mum would be pleased that Lucinda was getting married. And I was jealous, oh so very envious, that Lucinda was able to marry her young man.

"Tell me about the groom, Grandma."

"His name is Lawrence Moore and he's at school with Lucinda. They're both graduating this year, so at least they can finish school. His father owns a business selling men's clothes downtown, a haberdashery, so Larry will have a job right away and eventually inherit the business, so it's a very good match for Lucinda. I only hope they'll be happy together. That's more important than money."

"Yes," I said. Arthur's family had means too, and we would have been happy together. "I'm sure Mum is pleased."

"And what about you? Are you seeing any young man these days?"

"Once in a while, Grandma. But none of them ever measures up to Arthur."

I poured a cup of tea for her.

Grandma sighed. "Perhaps one day," she said, "When you've had more time to heal from your grief."

I knew that Grandma's husband had died when she was young. "You never remarried after your husband died," I said.

"No," she said. "But I was twenty-five when my husband died. That's ten years older than you were when Arthur died. You're too young to grieve the rest of your life."

186

"Perhaps," I said, taking a first tentative sip of hot tea. "But I'm twenty-two now, so I can't see very much difference."

"I suppose you're right." Her hands were wrapped around the fragile teacup. "It is difficult to get over the 'love of your life', isn't it?" She had a faraway look in her eyes as if she could see all the way back into another century, another time.

39

The Daily Colonist   October 19, 1929

Seats for Women in Senate Declared Legal

〰〰 〰〰 〰〰 〰〰 〰〰 〰〰 〰〰 〰〰 〰〰 〰〰 〰〰 〰〰 〰〰 〰〰 〰〰

One of the best things about working at a paper is that you get to hear the news before anyone else.

On Friday, October 18th, a story arrived on the wire from Ottawa that the Privy Council of Great Britain had overturned the Supreme Court of Canada's decision and declared that women were persons under the law. So now, Emily Murphy could become a senator!

I was so excited I was nearly bouncing out of my skin. The only damper was that I had no one to share my joy with. The reporters, copyboys and typesetters were not particularly excited by the news; in fact, some were out-and-out hostile. The few women who worked at the paper — secretaries for the most part — were marginally more interested. I suspect they may have been more excited than they let on, but they didn't want to upset their bosses.

That weekend, I'm ashamed to say, I celebrated in morose solitude with Biddy and the scotch bottle.

Then, scarcely three weeks later, the news took a more sombre turn in keeping with my mood. The newsroom buzzed and hummed with excitement as day after day, stories came in on the wire about stocks falling drastically, banks foreclosing and businessmen throwing themselves from skyscraper windows.

The wall holding up our financial world, which had seemed so solid, was beginning to crumble around us. Soon, that rumbling quake in New York was spreading like a wave across the continent.

It wasn't long before I heard the kind of whispering that I'd heard after the Great War when the men came home, the same kind of snide remarks, like "*Men* are losing their jobs. They can't support their families." The implication was that women shouldn't be working. I was expecting a call into the editor's office any day. I only wondered if I would be demoted or let go. In the meantime, we all received a deduction in pay. I would soon be forced to sell my motorcar. I couldn't afford the upkeep, petrol and rent of the parking garage.

Then, Mum called.

"Why are James and Margaret refusing to come to Thanksgiving dinner this year?" she asked.

"How would I know?" I asked. I knew full well. "What did they say?"

"They said to ask you. They said that you would know why."

How could I explain the whole thing over the telephone? "I told little Margaret that she was adopted."

"What!?" My mother was speechless.

"I told her that she was my daughter."

"How could you, Edith? It wasn't your place to tell her that."

"Maybe not, but I did it. That's why they won't come for Thanksgiving dinner."

"Oh, Edith…" I could tell from her tone of voice that she was going to go on chastising me. I was not in the mood.

"Goodbye," I said, then hung up the phone.

There was not a bottle in the house, so I decided to take the car out for one last run before I sold it. A trip to the liquor store downtown just wouldn't do it, so I decided to drive out to Six Mile House, the scene of my earlier embarrassing date with Kenji.

Ever since I had alienated Margaret May, I had resumed drinking to excess. It was not something I could control anymore. Life was not something I could control. It was one tragedy after another. And why? Because I had been born a woman. Because I had had a child out of wedlock. Because of some stupid war that killed my baby's father.

And I would be expected to give up my job now. Again, because I was born a woman and women's work was to be married and look after children. I had never married and I had lost my child. It was the man's job to provide the family home, so a woman in a man's job was theft. Never mind that every day there were stories in the paper about the first woman in Canada to graduate from medical school or the number of women barristers in Britain. Women were slowly making strides, but the pace was glacially slow. And that glacier would never slide as far as this little backwater town on the edge of the world. Here, I had to fight like a wildcat to hold on to a lowly job writing personals and be vilified for that fight.

I stopped at the Six Mile House, entered the Ladies and Escorts' door and walked to the bar. As many eyes as were in the room turned in my direction. They were equally astonished as they had been when I walked in with Kenji years before. A woman alone in a public house! It wasn't done!

It meant I was loose. It meant I was fair game. But the only men in the room were accompanying other women, so I hoped none of them would be so brazen as to come and talk to me.

The waiter was another problem altogether. If he didn't try to hit on me, he might just throw me out. I remembered why I always drank at home. I should have just gone to the liquor store and bought a bottle as I usually did.

I sat at the bar. The waiter stood in front of me.

"What can I get you?"

"Do you have anything stronger than beer?" I said. "Perhaps under the counter?"

"Sorry," he said, shaking his head. "Would you like a beer?"

I nodded. He filled a glass from the tap and put it down in front of me. I took a long swig and almost downed it in one swallow.

I sensed someone approaching the barstool beside me.

"Can I buy you a drink?"

I looked at him. It was a man in a suit — looked like a businessman — perhaps drowning the sorrow of his financial losses. Men couldn't drink by themselves either, at least not in the Ladies and Escorts' room.

"Where's your lady friend?" I asked.

"She's gone to the toilet."

"Well, I want to be alone."

"It's not a good thing to drink alone," he said.

"Go away."

He sat on the stool beside me and made rude comments that I completely ignored until his lady friend came out of the toilet and glared at him. Then she walked out of the beer parlour.

"Go after her," I said.

"No," he said. "She'd only give me hell."

"You deserve it," I said.

"Pour me another one," I said to the waiter.

After a few more beers, I was finding it harder and harder to ignore the obnoxious businessman and feared I might end up in his car instead of my own. I asked the waiter how much I owed him.

He told me the amount. How reckless of me! I should have stayed home and bought a bottle.

"Let me pay," the businessman said.

I almost considered saying yes. Men had the power and the money and they were supposed to pay. But then, I was sure he would demand services in return. I shook my head.

"No," I said. I put down a large bill and walked away.

"Let me give you a lift," my persistent businessman said.

"I have my own car," I said proudly.

"You shouldn't be driving."

The curses I'd heard at the paper sprang into my mouth and garbled their way out of it. A few more heads turned. The businessman looked disgusted and turned back to his drink.

I slipped into my roadster and rubbed my hand along the leather seat. I felt proud, independent, invincible. I turned the key in the ignition, depressed the clutch and put it in gear. The roadster backed out of the parking lot. I shifted gear again and it slipped forward onto the road. I shifted gears up and up until the engine was roaring. The wind in my hair and on my face felt like the blessing of the gods as I drove home. *Happy. Happy.*

Till I couldn't make the turn at the end of Craigflower and went flying off the road into darkness.

40

The Daily Colonist   June 5, 1921

On the Marriage Day

The organ music blared as Papa and Lucinda came down the aisle. She was wearing a long white dress with a sheer veil as she leaned on Papa's arm. He was smiling, beaming actually, and he didn't even see me when he passed by. Lucinda did not show that she was pregnant at all. I couldn't see clearly through the veil whether she was smiling or not.

Papa placed Lucinda next to a nervous-looking boy who took her arm. My heart stabbed me again when I thought of Arthur. *Don't*, I told myself. *Don't go there.*

At the reception afterwards, everyone asked me when I was going to marry. I had not asked anyone to accompany me to the wedding because I wasn't close enough to any man to ask him to a family occasion. I wished I had, though people would probably have embarrassed the young man as well as me with their questions. Besides, why did I have to marry? And why did I not have the courage to respond to them by asking that question? Did I still harbour hopes in those days that I might still find a man equal to Arthur? Did I not realize that I had put him on such a tall pedestal that no one could ever rise to his height?

Lucinda and her husband Lawrence, who went by Larry, arrived at the reception. She was dressed in full flapper regalia and I smiled. She had escaped the tyranny of our mother but was unaware of the even greater tyranny of motherhood that awaited her. But behind my smile, I hid a terrible jealousy. She would have a baby and I would not.

I nibbled on canapés for as long as I could keep them down. I left as soon as it was respectable to do so and I'm quite sure no one missed me. I kissed Lucinda on the cheek and wished her well. She scarcely acknowledged my presence, but then she was full of the wonder of her marriage and I ought not to have begrudged her a moment of that joy just because fate had deprived me of mine.

Mum and Papa didn't even speak to me at the reception. Grandma at least said goodbye. I went home to my empty apartment. Biddy greeted me at the door and rubbed herself against my silk stockings. Then she bounded off to chase a dust bunny.

I laughed. "Thank you, Biddy," I said. My apartment wasn't entirely empty then. At least I had Biddy.

41

The Daily Colonist   November 7, 1929

Woman Hurt in Crash

~~~ ~~~ ~~~ ~~~ ~~~ ~~~ ~~~ ~~~ ~~~ ~~~ ~~~ ~~~ ~~~ ~~~ ~~~ ~~~

I woke up with that sense of being totally lost, not just in space but in time too. Where was I? When was I? Had some time passed or only the blink of an eye?

A tube attached by a needle to my arm and the stark white walls told me almost immediately that I was in the hospital, but the answer to the second question still eluded me. I looked around for someone to ask. There was a clock on the wall that said twenty-five past eleven, but that was meaningless to me. Was it day or night? The distant window blinds were tightly closed. And how many days or hours or minutes had passed since I flew into darkness? I did not know.

An unknown woman's voice spoke. "So, you're awake."

I turned my head toward the voice and felt a stab of severe pain. The voice belonged to a pretty, dark-haired woman in a well-starched nurse's uniform and an ugly white cap.

"How are you feeling?" she asked.

This, I had not yet fully ascertained in my confusion. I tried to do a quick mental scan but could get no further than my head.

"My head aches," I said, my mouth so dry it came out as a whisper.

"It's not surprising," she said.

She knew my secret shame. "How long have I been here?" I asked.

195

She picked up the chart hanging at the foot of the bed and looked at it. "About twelve hours," she said.

"Is anything broken?" I asked.

"A few cracked ribs, a good knock on the head — hence the headache — and some superficial scratches. All in all, I'd say you got off lucky."

"And my motorcar?" I asked.

"I have no idea," she said. "Do I look like a mechanic?" She laughed a little. "Can I get you anything?"

"Water," I said.

She picked up a glass from the table beside my bed and held it to my lips. I sucked on the paper straw. It felt so good that I kept drinking until I sucked air with a slurp.

"I'll get you some more." She walked toward the door, then turned and looked at me. "It's not visiting hours but your parents have been sitting in the waiting room since the early hours of morning. Are you well enough to see them if I let them in?"

How strange and surprising and good it felt. As if I were a child again and my parents had come to look after me. "Yes," I said softly. "Please send them in."

A few minutes later, my mother appeared at the open door. She looked at me as if she expected to see a corpse. I tried to smile but winced from the effort.

"The nurse gave me this." She held up the refilled glass of water. "Where shall I put it?"

"On the side table," I whispered.

She put it down and sat down on the bedside chair.

"Are you all right?" she asked.

I nodded, but my brain seemed to have turned liquid and sloshed against my skull.

"We were so afraid that you would die," she said.

"Is Papa here?"

"He went to get some coffee in the cafeteria. He'll be back soon." She looked at me. "They said they might have to drill a hole in your skull. I thought you were going to die. Mama always told me that you drove too fast."

They were going to drill a hole in my skull! The nurse hadn't mentioned that.

Mum stood up. She seemed not to know what to do with her hands. Finally, she took hold of my hand lying on the bed.

"I was so afraid, Edith! You gave me quite a turn."

I smiled weakly. The effort hurt.

"I'm sorry, Edith," She dropped my hand and sat down again.

"What for?" I whispered.

"I'm sorry for…" She paused as if searching for words. "For letting you drift away. No." She looked determined. "For pushing you away. Mama always told me I was too hard on you. She was right." Mum put her restless hands on her lap. "I'm sorry," she repeated.

Before I could respond, Papa came in.

"Cheerio," he said, putting on his sparkling voice. "So good to see you're still in the land of the living, Edith dear."

He leaned over to give me a kiss on the forehead. His lips were cool.

"How are you, my dear?" he asked.

"Head aches," I said.

"It would, wouldn't it?"

"Are they going to cut it open?" I asked.

"I shouldn't think so, but then, I'm not a doctor." He chuckled. "Perhaps you should ask one of the blokes in white."

"I shall." I smiled. Again, I felt a stab of pain and winced.

The nurse walked into the room.

"Well," she said, "I think that's enough excitement for our patient this morning. She needs her rest."

I was ever so grateful she'd come at that moment as I didn't feel capable of responding to any more questions. My mother stood up as if to leave. Then I thought of Biddy.

"Mum?"

"Yes, dear?"

"Could you go to my apartment and get my cat? She'll need someone to look after her while I'm here. My keys are in my handbag." I looked around the room for it.

"It's at the nursing station," the nurse said. "I'll go get it for you."

Mum looked back at me. "But your father doesn't like cats," she said.

"I'm sure I can tolerate them for a few days," Papa said. "Edith will be out soon, I'm sure."

"Please, Mum," I said. "I don't know who else to ask."

"Of course, dear," she said, patting my hand.

The nurse came back with my bag.

"It's in the side pocket," I told her.

She pulled out the keys and handed them to my father.

"Edith will be out soon, won't she?" he asked the nurse.

"I can't make such a promise," she said. "That's the doctor's decision. He'll be by to see her soon. Now, follow me."

She walked out, followed by my father.

Mum still stood by my bed. She leaned over and kissed my forehead as she'd seen my father do.

"Get well," she said. Then she turned and left.

I fell asleep again after they left, but it was not a sound sleep. The doctor came by and examined me, shining a light in my eyes, poking and prodding. I heard him say the swelling had gone down and I assumed that meant they were not going to drill any holes. Then he left.

Someone came in with a tray of food, which they placed in front of me. It was broth and jelly. I was not hungry.

They came back and took it away.

The nurse came in and took my temperature.

But in all that coming and going, I stayed in a barely conscious state. My body and brain craved sleep and would not surface fully. The comings and goings diminished as the day wore on. Then I slept the night again.

I woke the next morning, still in my hospital bed. I didn't feel any better even with all the sleep I'd had. I couldn't get up without shooting pains, so I lay there and took stock of myself.

I was weary. I was weary of the grey skies of November, of the constant rain, of the wind that screamed outside the window, of the cold, damp air that reached into my bones.

I was weary already of the pain in my chest whenever I moved, the throbbing pain in my head, my forced inactivity. I felt like an old, old woman and I was weary.

I was weary of grief — of losing Arthur, of losing Grandma, of losing Margaret May. I was weary of worry as well — the worry of losing my job, of not being good enough, of failing again.

I was weary of all that and I realized it was good to feel weary. It was good to feel at all. It was good to lie here in agony, to feel that agony and not to run away.

I chuckled internally. Run away? I could barely walk. I felt as though I'd been run over by a bus. I called the nurse because I needed help to go to the bathroom. The orderly came and helped me through those agonizing steps to the toilet. Then he waited outside till I called him back. I shuffled back to the bed on his arm. I lay down. I was weary.

At breakfast, the nurse brought me a tray. I hadn't eaten in a long time and I was ravenously hungry.

"I heard you're a reporter at the *Colonist*," she said. "I thought you might like this." She handed me a newspaper.

I put it down beside me on the bed.

"Thank you," I said. Then I drank my juice in one gulp and ate my tasteless scrambled egg without toast.

She smiled. "Got your appetite back, I see." She left.

I picked up the paper and perused it. They were able to put together a newspaper quite fine without me. If I were gone, I wouldn't be missed.

Then, I found it — a little story inside about my accident. I saw my name in print and I was described as a reporter. A little thrill went through me. I wasn't completely forgotten. If I had died, it might have been an even bigger story. That is all we are in the end — a story, someone's story, not even our own. Unless we write it first before we die, as I am doing now.

The morning passed with more tests and prodding. The doctor told me that I would be going home the next day.

"Much as I'd like to leave this place," I said, "I don't know how I can. I live alone, but I'll need help for a while."

"Well," he said. "Perhaps you can move in with your parents. At least until you're able to look after yourself."

That was a gruesome thought at first. Then I remembered my parents' visit. My mother had said she was sorry. Perhaps it wouldn't be so bad after all — to get to know her again, to become friends, or at least, mother and daughter.

The doctor left. The day dragged on. My lunch tray was brought. I ate heartily again.

When the nurse came to pick up the tray, she said, "Visiting hours are from one to three. Are you up for visitors this afternoon?"

"Yes," I replied. "Oh, yes." Something to lessen the drag of the hours.

The first visitor to arrive was my mother. She gave me a peck on the cheek and sat down.

"Your father and brother are working," she said. "They both send their regards. And Lucinda says hello. She's busy with the children, of course."

"Aren't they all at school yet?" I asked. To my shame, I had not kept track of their ages, not as I had for Margaret May.

"No, the youngest is still at home."

The nurse came in with a vase containing a spray of yellow mums and put it on my bedside table. "Your mother brought these," she said. "Aren't they lovely?"

"Thanks, Mum," I said.

"We picked up your cat yesterday," Mum said, as if it were a great inconvenience.

"How is Biddy?" I asked.

"She hissed at me when I picked her up."

"She hissed at me the first time I met her, too," I said. "That's just the way she is till she gets to know you better."

"Well, she's gone off to hide. Papa and I can't find her and she hasn't eaten anything."

"Poor Biddy," I said.

We sat in silence for a while till I realized I should broach the subject of moving in sooner rather than later.

"The doctor came to see me this morning."

"Oh?" she sounded interested.

"He says I can go home tomorrow, but I still need nursing care."

"Perhaps they can send a VON," she suggested. The Victorian Order of Nurses made home visits.

"He suggested I move in with you and Papa," I said.

I watched for her reaction. She looked surprised.

"Would you take me in for a few days?" I asked. "Just till I'm up and running."

She stared at me for a heartbeat while I waited to be rejected again.

Her face broke. "Of course," she said. "Of course. You are always welcome at home."

Well, that was not altogether true. After all, she'd kicked me out once. But I took some small comfort from the words. Perhaps it might at least be true now.

"Did you see the newspaper today?" I asked, looking at it on the side table where it lay beside the flowers.

"Yes," she said. "You're quite the celebrity." She seemed pleased.

Then I asked her about my car and she broke the news to me that it was damaged beyond repair. Seeing my misery, she asked if she could get me something at the cafeteria.

"Could you bring me a cup of tea?" I asked.

"Of course. Milk and sugar?"

"Just a little milk."

She was gone no more than five minutes when my second guest appeared. It was my boss at the *Colonist*, Jack Kerne. He had a lovely big bouquet of hothouse flowers with him. I hoped Mum wouldn't be too put out about having hers overshadowed. Jack put the flowers on my bed and sat down on the chair my mother had just vacated.

"How are you?" he asked, looking concerned.

"Broken ribs, concussion, a few scrapes and bruises." I touched the bandage on my forehead. "All in all, not too badly."

"How long before you're back at work?" he asked.

"I don't know," I said. "The doctor says I can go home tomorrow, but I'm going to stay with my parents for a while until I'm able to look after myself."

Jack nodded. "Good," he said.

"Tell me the truth," I said, terrified to ask the question so much on my mind. "Will my job still be there when I get back?"

He looked surprised. "Of course. Why wouldn't it be?"

"I've heard rumours," I said. "With the downturn in the economy, there might be jobs lost. The women always go first."

"Well, I haven't heard any such rumours. You do a fine job, Edith. And we miss you at the paper. Your feminine presence keeps the air from turning blue."

He laughed and I tried not to. I held on to my sides.

"Please," I said. "It hurts when I laugh. Don't make me."

"Oh, I'm sorry." He looked apologetic.

"I really don't believe you," I said. "They couldn't swear any more than they do when I'm there."

"Oh, yes, they can" — he smiled — "and they do."

Just then, Mum came back with a cup of tea balanced on a saucer. She looked askance when she saw a man in her chair. He jumped up.

"Mum," I said. "This is my boss at the *Colonist*, Mr. Kerne."

She looked relieved. He put out his hand to shake hers and noticed the cup.

"Let me take that for you," he said.

Mum handed it to him and he put it on the side table. Then he turned and shook her hand.

"It's a pleasure to meet you, ma'am."

Mum smiled.

"Take my seat," he said. "I have to be going anyway. Must get back to work."

He turned to me as my mum sat down. "And you, get better now. I'll expect you back in a week? Maybe two?"

"I'll ask the doctor and call you when I know for sure," I said. "Thanks for coming and give my regards to everyone at the paper."

"'Bye now." He nodded first at me, then my mother. "Ma'am," he said, then he left us.

"Well," Mum said, her face full of questions. "That's a nice-looking young man."

"He's my boss, Mum," I said. "Nothing more. Besides, he's far too young."

"I didn't suggest he was anything more. Still, it was nice of him to come and bring such lovely flowers." She stood and picked them up. "I'll just go to the nurse's station and get a vase."

"All right, Mum," I said. "But before you go, could you hand me my teacup?"

She passed it to me and I sipped contentedly. As bleak as the morning had seemed, the afternoon was turning pleasant.

42

The Daily Colonist   January 15, 1922

Prodigal Daughters

~~~ ~~~ ~~~ ~~~ ~~~ ~~~ ~~~ ~~~ ~~~ ~~~ ~~~ ~~~ ~~~ ~~~ ~~~

The sky was a blank slate of grey. As I looked out the window, a thin slash of water fell. Rain, but no wind. The trees stood perfectly still. Biddy lay beside me, curled in a tight circle. The phone rang and her ears pricked up, then her head lifted. She knew I would soon stand up and the warmth would leave. She cast a disapproving look my way as I stood up to go and answer the demanding ring.

"Hello." It was Mum. Something in her voice — a little high-pitched and breathless — told me she was happy.

"Hello?" I responded.

"Lucinda's had her baby. It's a girl."

"Oh," I said. *Of course it is.* "Did everything go all right?"

"Yes, yes. She's fine. I'm sure she'd like to see you at the hospital."

"The Royal Jubilee?" I asked.

"Yes. Visiting hours are at two o'clock."

"Okay," I said.

"I'll see you then."

It had only been two weeks since British Columbia had switched from driving on the left side of the road as the British did to driving on the right side of the road the way the rest of North America did. Now, our

American cars with the steering wheel on the left would be easier to drive. At least, they would be once we got used to it.

It was a frightening experience for all of us. It wasn't just that each of us as individuals had to learn — that would have been difficult enough — but everyone on the road was learning at the same time, which meant that we had to watch out for each other. At any moment, one of us might slip up and drive in the wrong lane.

So it was, after leaving the house and driving up Quadra in the right lane that I turned left on Pandora and saw a vehicle coming straight towards me. I could see the bewilderment in the driver's face. He was probably thinking the same thing as I was. Did I make a mistake when I turned or was he in the wrong lane? I quickly ascertained that it was my mistake and swerved into the righthand lane, glancing over my right shoulder to make sure another car wasn't there. As we passed, I noticed the other driver looked relieved. And I was relieved that he hadn't decided to change lanes at the same time.

It was a good thing that I wasn't driving very fast. If I'd been going any faster, I might not have had time to correct myself. The reason I was driving so slowly was that I'd already received two speeding tickets from the Victoria Police Department. They'd been vigilant during this transition period enforcing the speed limit of fifteen miles per hour. So, I continued my slow, dawdling drive to the Royal Jubilee Hospital, thankful there were no more turns to make until I arrived there.

I had plenty of time to think about how unfair the universe was to me. My little sister and I had both conceived babies out of wedlock. We were both prodigal daughters, but the fatted calf had been slaughtered for only one of us and only one of us had been welcomed home. Lucinda could keep her baby, but I would be expected to smile and coo and rejoice as if I'd never seen a baby before. As if this was the greatest event in the history of the world. I would have to put on an act to the best of my ability and keep my grief to myself.

Here was the hospital and I had a left turn to make. So, I put aside my resentful thoughts for the moment and concentrated on turning into the right lane.

I joined my mother looking through the glass window of the nursery at her new grandchild. I could detect no gentleness on her face as she turned to me.

After greeting me and turning back to look through the glass, she said, "These hospital births seem so impersonal. I'm glad I had all my children at home."

"I had my child in the hospital, though."

Mum looked aghast and peered around the hallway to see if anyone had overheard. There was no one in the hallway.

"If you thought them impersonal," I continued, "Why did you arrange a hospital birth for me? I could have had my baby at the Home for Girls."

"I thought it was for the best since you were going to give her up for adoption. I didn't know the home would insist on your nursing it."

"*Her*, Mum. The baby was a girl."

Mum turned back to the glass. "I'd rather not speak of it," she said. "Let's celebrate this birth."

I left to go to my sister's room. If I'd stayed another second in my mother's presence, I would surely have exploded in anger. For her, it seemed to be so simple to distance herself from my child. It was not so easy for me. No matter how much time passed, the slow, dull ache of emptiness was always there.

Lucinda was all smiles and I had to force myself to smile too. After all, she knew nothing of my lost child. None of this was her fault. She might have sinned exactly as I had sinned, but Mum was not about to push her away because she was respectably married. Her hale and healthy baby was just two months premature. It happened all the time.

"What are you going to name her?" I asked.

"We have decided to call her Melissa Rose," Lucinda said.

"How original!" It was a surprising name since in our family it seemed a tradition to name a baby after someone else in the family. I was named for my great-grandmother and Lucinda was named for Grandma. "I approve," I added.

"Isn't she beautiful?" Lucinda enthused.

I hadn't noticed particularly, but I nodded and smiled.

"I'll ask the nurse to bring her in," she said, "if you'd like to hold her."

I wanted nothing of the kind, but I had to be polite. "No, no," I said. "She was sleeping when I saw her. Leave her be. I can wait until you bring her home to hold her."

I dreaded the thought of having to visit her and having to hold the adorable Melissa. How would I be able to hold her in my arms and not think of May, and not remember…? My breasts started to tingle even as I imagined it.

"You must be tired, Lucinda. I really should go and let you rest while your baby is sleeping."

"Oh, no," Lucinda said cheerily. "You might imagine that would be the case, but I have a surprising amount of energy."

"Nevertheless, I should be going."

Mum walked in the room.

"Here's Mum to keep you company," I said.

I walked to the bed and gave Lucinda a peck on the cheek. Then I turned to Mum.

"Goodbye," I said before walking out the door.

43

The Daily Colonist   November 10, 1929

Car Overturns, Woman Injured

~~~ ~~~ ~~~ ~~~ ~~~ ~~~ ~~~ ~~~ ~~~ ~~~ ~~~ ~~~ ~~~ ~~~ ~~~ ~~~

The next day, Mum visited again and chatted until visiting hours were over. I was relieved to finally be alone and wondered how I would survive in her house.

After about forty minutes of fitful napping, the nurse arrived at my bedside.

"Sorry to bother you," she said. "But there's a girl here claiming to be your daughter. I've told her you've had enough visitors today, but she's very persistent."

My daughter! My heart was beating so hard it hurt my ribs.

"Send her in right away!"

The nurse looked skeptical. "Are you sure?"

"Yes, yes."

I patted my hair to make sure it wasn't flying every which way. I wished I had a tube of lipstick. The nurse entered the room with Margaret May behind her.

"No more than fifteen minutes," she said curtly and then left.

Margaret May stared at me without speaking.

"It's not as bad as it looks," I said.

"Oh, you look fine," she said.

"You told her you were my daughter."

"It was the only way I could get in," she said, matter-of-factly. "She insisted visiting hours were over, but it was the only time I could sneak away."

"Is that wise?" I asked, worried that I had turned her into a liar, sneaking around behind her parents' backs. "After all, your parents should know you're here." She said nothing, so I continued. "May I ask why you came to see me at all? I thought you were angry with me."

"I was worried," she said. "I saw the story in the paper. I thought you might be at death's door."

"So you came," I said, revelling in the thought. "I'm sorry that I told you what I did. It wasn't my place to do that," I admitted.

"No," she said.

I didn't know if she was agreeing with me or not.

"But I'm not sorry anymore," she said, "that you told me. Telling the truth is important and I'm angry with my parents for lying to me."

"I shouldn't have come between you and your parents. They love you and they've given you a good home. I hope you'll forgive them for not telling you the truth."

Margaret May sat in silence, seeming to digest my pearls of wisdom. Finally, she said, "It's hard to forgive them. They never even told me I was adopted. And they've known for ages that you were my mother, but they said nothing."

"You're a sensible girl, Margaret May," I said. "You'll come to forgive them in time."

"What did you call me?" She looked alarmed. "That isn't my middle name."

"No, of course not. It's just something I call you to myself and I let it slip. I didn't know your real name so I always called you 'May' because you were born in May. Then, when I met you, I started to call you 'Margaret May'. I'm sorry if I startled you."

"It's all right," she said.

"I won't call you that again if you don't like it."

"It's quite all right," she said. "Besides, I don't know when we might meet again. My parents still won't let me have anything to do with you, but perhaps in a few years, when I can be more independent."

"Oh, don't move out, Margaret May! You'll need your parents' support for Normal School if you want to be a teacher."

"Perhaps I can move in with you," she said.

My heart started to thrum again.

The nurse came in. "It's time to leave," she said.

Margaret May stood up.

"Already?" I said.

She came closer to my bedside, leaned over and kissed my cheek. "Goodbye," she said. "I *will* see you again."

I tried to put my arms around her, to hold her close, but moving my arms up brought on a stab of pain. I gasped. She looked concerned.

"It's all right," I said. "Thank you for coming, Margaret May."

She turned and went out. The nurse followed her.

Tears of joy followed her departure. Bittersweet tears of joy!

I woke up the next morning in a panic. My heart was racing and I was sweating and shivering. It must have been a bad dream that woke me, but I couldn't remember anything about the dream. In fact, I couldn't remember where I was at first. I sat up and that now-familiar pain in my chest laid me back down on the bed. A wave of nausea overcame me but since I couldn't sit up, I turned my head to the side and threw up on my pillow.

It smelled awful. It was so humiliating lying in my vomit. I started to cry.

The woman in the next bed called, "Are you all right?"

"No," I said.

"I'll call the nurse."

I made no response; humiliation or not, I needed help.

A few minutes later, the nurse arrived. She took one look at me and said, "You should have used the bedpan to throw up in."

She picked it up where it lay on the table beside my bed.

"It happened too fast. I'm sorry."

"Well, let's get you cleaned up." She went to work. "Can you turn on your side while I strip the blankets?"

"It's too painful," I said. "I can get up." I slowly and gingerly sat up in the bed.

The nurse put her arm around my shoulders and helped me to the chair.

"You'll need to wash your hair," she said.

I started to shiver and shake.

"Let me get you a blanket." She wrapped it around me. She put her hand on my forehead. "I think you have a fever," she said. "I'll take your temperature once we get the bed changed."

As my contribution to the nurse's 'we', I sat in the chair and watched her in my stinking pain and misery. When the bed was all made and she had helped me back into it, she stuck a thermometer in my mouth and left the room with the dirty bedclothes. I sat there, fighting my gag reflex until there were tears in my eyes. Finally, she returned and took the wretched instrument out of my mouth.

"It's a little high," she said. "I'll have the doctor check on you when he does his rounds. It looks like you won't be going home today."

Later, the doctor came in and looked at my chart. He asked me to hold my arm straight out. I did, and my hand trembled like a leaf in the wind. I tried to master it by tensing my arm muscles, but it only shook more. I relaxed my muscles and the tremor subsided. He put a stethoscope on my wildly beating heart. I saw his eyebrows rise when he heard it.

"What is it, doctor?" I asked.

"Have you had any hallucinations?"

"No," I said. "Only bad dreams."

He stepped away from me and went to speak to the nurse in the doorway. They whispered together for a while. Then he came to my bedside.

"What is it?" I repeated my question though I was terrified of the answer.

"It may be the effects of the trauma to the head," he said. "But it could also be delirium tremens."

I had heard of that before. A long time ago. At the Vancouver Home for Girls. I had almost forgotten the incident, but now it came back to me.

"The emergency medical staff smelled alcohol on you when you were brought in," he said. "Are you, by any chance, a heavy drinker?"

My shame lay there exposed, out in the open. My well-deserved humiliation arrived at last. I didn't answer.

"Be honest with me," he said. "If your symptoms are due to withdrawal from alcohol, we need to know. We can't treat you properly unless we know what we're treating."

"Yes," I said.

"All right." He wrote something down on my chart. Then he looked up. "You'll stay in the hospital for a few more days while we treat you for the delirium tremens."

"Is that absolutely necessary?" I asked.

"No, of course not. You can go home and continue to poison yourself with alcohol and the symptoms will go away. But if you want to stop drinking, it's best that you stay here where we can treat you. The delirium tremens can be life-threatening if not treated."

I thought about that for a moment, but there seemed no way that I could go back and continue my old life. Not now that Margaret May had opened the door to a possible relationship. Not now that my mother had invited me to come home. Not now that I wanted to go home and start over. I would have to go through the symptoms of withdrawal, however bad they might be. I would have to endure them. But at least, a hospital was the best place to be in this situation.

"I'll stay then," I said.

He nodded at me and left, handing the chart to the nurse at the door. He had not expressed any condemnation whatsoever. His personal opinion of my shame was completely hidden behind a mask of professionalism. And yet I sensed it and felt all the more ashamed for it.

The nurse looked at the chart, then at me. She shook her head and tsk-tsked. Then, without a word, she replaced the chart at the foot of the bed and left.

I lay there and remembered that visit in the night — the last night I stayed at the Vancouver Home for Girls. Poor Phyllis! That girl in the throes of delirium tremens. My fear on that night came back to me, fully fledged and even greater now because there was no Miss Havisham to come and rescue me from the alcoholic on the bed. I was the alcoholic and I would have to go through the withdrawal and rescue myself.

44

The Daily Colonist   February 19, 1922

A Page for the Children

~~ ~~ ~~ ~~ ~~ ~~ ~~ ~~ ~~ ~~ ~~ ~~ ~~ ~~ ~~ ~~

Lucinda called in a panic. She couldn't reach Mum but needed a babysitter right away. Larry'd had an automobile accident.

"He's at the hospital," she said. "They say it's not serious, but I need someone to watch the baby while I go to the hospital."

"What about Mum?"

"I told you she's not home."

"I could give you a lift to the hospital."

"I can take a taxi," she said, "but I can't find a babysitter at such short notice."

"All right," I said reluctantly. "I'll be there."

When I arrived at Lucinda's house in Fernwood, she flew out the door. "The cab's here," she called over her shoulder.

She left without giving me any instructions. What did I know about looking after babies? I knew how to breastfeed them. That was the full extent of my knowledge. But I'm quite sure Lucinda would not approve of that even if I had any milk to give her child.

I searched the unfamiliar house to find the nursery. I presumed the silence meant the baby was sleeping. I prayed that she would continue to sleep because I had no idea what to do with her when she woke up. What if she was hungry?

Her mother was gone, but perhaps Lucinda used formula. If that was the case, how did I prepare it?

I found the nursery and looked in. I saw the crib and walked closer. There was Melissa looking up at me. She looked surprised. She was bigger than May had been when I lost her and seemed more aware. When she saw me, she knew immediately that I was not her mother. Her startled look turned to terror and she started to cry.

My worst nightmare!

I picked her up. I patted her on the back and rocked back and forth instinctively. I started to croon a lullaby, but still she cried, a high-pitched unending scream. If I didn't know better, I would have thought she was being murdered.

I walked to the kitchen and looked in the icebox. Halleluiah! There was a bottle with the formula already prepared. I took it out and looked around for a place to sit so I could feed her. I sat on a kitchen chair and lay Melissa on my lap. She didn't like the position and struggled to sit up, all the time crying.

"Hush, Melissa." I tried to soothe her. "Auntie Edith has some milk for you."

I put the nipple of the bottle in her mouth. She started to suck and then immediately sputtered and spit and turned her head away from the nipple. Milk sprayed out all over her face and she winced when some hit her eye, then screamed even louder. Obviously, she didn't like it. I put the bottle on the table and picked her up to pat her back as she was coughing and choking. Lucinda wouldn't be much pleased if I killed her baby. I patted and rubbed Melissa vigorously on the back. The poor baby coughed and coughed. Her face turned bright red, and then after a brief moment of silence, she looked at me accusingly and started to scream again. I stood up and resumed the rocking and patting and singing that had no quieting effect on her.

What now? I walked with her back to the nursery and looked around the room. There was a rocking chair. I sat down and started rocking. I resumed my singing, louder, trying to be heard above the noise she was making.

As I patted her back, I noticed that her diaper was sagging and wet. Of course! That was what the matter was. I looked around and saw the table where Lucinda must have changed her. There was a thick blanket and all kinds of paraphernalia — powders and jars, pins and a pile of cloths that I presumed were for making diapers.

I walked over and lay Lucinda down. She kept up her squealing and started to kick. I tried to unpin the diaper without sticking her, which was no mean feat given her flailing arms and legs. My brain was growing frazzled. I wanted to curse, but I bit my tongue.

Her diaper fell open. It was filled with a yellowish substance that looked like pumpkin pie but smelled outrageous. I gasped and tried not to breathe. I picked up a washcloth and started to wipe, but the cloth was dry and I could tell it irritated her already-red skin. I needed to dampen it, but I also knew I couldn't leave the baby on the table as she would roll off, especially the way she was thrashing about. I couldn't pick her up and carry her without getting smelly pumpkin pie all over my dress, so I pinned the diaper back on. Then, I picked her up, which was a little like wrestling with an octopus, and carried her to the bathroom where I held her in my left arm while I attempted to wet the washcloth and wring it out with my right hand. We went back to the nursery. I put her down, unpinned her diaper again and tried to wipe her bum. Her skin was so red and raw, I almost cried myself, imagining the pain she was feeling.

"Shh! Shh! Poor Smelly," I said, trying to soothe her with my voice while I dabbed at her sensitive skin.

It took a good long time until I'd removed all of the pumpkin pie. It had gotten into every crack and crevice of her bottom and chubby legs. All the time, she kicked and screamed.

Finally, it was done and I looked around for some kind of cream to apply because I knew I couldn't just put a cloth diaper over it. No matter how soft it was, it would feel like sandpaper. There was some petroleum jelly in a jar. I slathered it on her tiny bum and down her legs.

Next, the diaper. I had no idea how to fold it and no time to figure it out. I picked up the square cloth, folded two corners up to make a triangle, put it under Smelly's bum, took a safety pin and pinned the three corners together. At the end of my jangled nerves, I grabbed Smelly and bounced her up and down while I chanted. She stopped crying for about three seconds and then resumed her howling. I walked around the house bouncing and chanting while she wailed.

Perhaps I'd been lucky to lose my baby when I did. I obviously had no idea what I was doing with this child. What a terrible mother I would have been!

I started to cry. I went back to the nursery and rocked baby Smelly. That was my name for her now and it would never change. Melissa, indeed! I rocked, sang lullabies and cried while Smelly wailed. After half an hour or so, she fell asleep. I tried to put her back in the crib, but her eyes popped open as soon as her head fell back. She looked up, saw me and resumed crying. Poor Smelly! She was going to have a sore throat after this. I picked her up, sat back down and resumed rocking.

That's where we were half an hour later when Lucinda came back. She walked across the nursery to the rocker and I handed the crying baby to her. Smelly stopped in mid-scream, heaved a great residual sob and sank into quiet contentment.

I was free!

But I looked at Lucinda and I saw the depth of the bond she shared with this baby who trusted no one else. I knew right then what I had lost. And what a terrible loss it was.

45

The Daily Colonist   November 17, 1929

Roses in Drear November

I spent an extra, excruciatingly awful week in the hospital. By then, finally, the delirium tremens had subsided and I began to feel like a different person. My senses started to wake up again as if they had been sleeping under the deep snow of winter all this time. I could hear, smell, taste and see everything so much more clearly.

I spent the week walking up and down the hospital corridor — slowly, stopping every few minutes to catch my breath and quiet my pain. Breathing did not come easily or naturally, but as time passed and my symptoms subsided, the pain also subsided.

At the end of the week, I was mobile enough to walk out of the hospital and into my father's motorcar — a sensible old Model T similar to the one I had driven in with Cousin John fifteen years prior.

We drove the familiar streets of Victoria, but it was as if I'd never seen them before.

I got out of the car and walked up the path to the stairs. Mother's roses were still in bloom beside the path. I hadn't noticed them in so many years. Their bright colours called to me and I stopped to bring a yellow tea rose to my nose and drink in its intoxicating aroma.

My father came and took my arm. "Come along, dear," he said. "Your mother's waiting."

We walked slowly up the front steps to the house, taking one step at a time and pausing in the middle. I went in the front door and glanced up the formidable stairs to the bedrooms.

Mum arrived at that moment and gave me a peck on the cheek. She noticed my reluctance.

"Don't worry," she said. "We've set up the maid's room so you won't have to deal with stairs." Since my parents had no live-in maid, the room was used as my father's office, but Mum still called it the maid's room.

"What will Papa do?" I asked.

Papa shook his head. "Don't worry about me. I'll make do just fine. You just get better." He looked sympathetic and patted my shoulder. "Let me help you to your room."

"Thanks, but I can manage on my own."

I hobbled to the maid's room beside the kitchen and Papa followed with my suitcase. He put it down beside the cot.

"I hope," he said, "this bed will be comfortable enough."

"I picked up some more clothes from your apartment and put them in this closet," Mum said, entering the room. "But if you need anything else, we can get it for you."

"I'm sure it'll be fine," I said.

"Would you like anything else now?"

"Some tea would be nice," I said.

My parents left and I sat down in my father's comfortable desk chair. No sooner was I sitting than Biddy jumped on my lap. The weight of her made me wince. She walked in her customary circle, lay down and started to purr.

"Where have you been hiding, Biddy?" I asked. It must have been in this very room somewhere. "It's so good to see you." I rubbed her behind the ears.

Mum came back into the room with a plate of cookies. "Tea's almost ready... Oh! Look at you," she said as she noticed the cat.

Biddy glared at my mother in her usual fashion.

"Don't worry," Mum said. "I won't touch you."

She put the cookies on Papa's desk and sat down on the bed. She looked at her hands for a few moments as if she didn't know what to say.

"I hate to bring this up," she said, finally, "but it's been weighing on my mind." She straightened her skirt. "I was very upset when I heard that you told Margaret she was adopted and you were her mother."

I must have tensed my body at that moment because Biddy immediately jumped down and went under the desk.

"I thought she needed to know," I said.

"It was a very selfish act on your part. You were the one who needed her to know."

That was so true and yet I wished she hadn't said it.

"I know. You're right. It was selfish of me. I wanted her — you know that, don't you? — I've always wanted her. And I've always been angry at you for making me give her up."

"You blamed me for that?"

"Of course I did! None of the other girls had to give up their babies. Only me. And I know you were the one who insisted I give her up."

"Do you know what happened to those other girls — the ones who kept their babies? If they didn't go into prostitution, then they went into service." She looked angry. "Did you know that?"

I nodded.

"I wanted better for you. I was a maid for ten years before I married your father."

"I know," I said.

"No. You don't know. I wanted you to come home and finish school. I wanted you to go to Normal School and become a teacher. You still could have, you know. But you were too stubborn. You had to go out on your own and get a menial job."

"You were stifling me, Mum. I just wanted my baby and I wanted Arthur to come home and marry me and we would be a family." I started to cry and it hurt my ribs, so I cried even harder.

Mum jumped up. "I'll go get the tea." Then she left the room.

Biddy immediately jumped back on my lap and curled in it.

"Oh, Biddy," I said. "Oh, Biddy."

I tried to weep without moving — silent, slow tears.

Mum came back and handed me a cup.

"I thought I was doing the right thing," she said. "You were just a child."

"Just like Margaret is now. Perhaps you were doing something selfish too. Perhaps you wanted what was best for you, not me."

Mum sat down. "Perhaps."

"Anyway," I said. "It doesn't matter now. What's done is done."

Mum picked up the plate. "Have a cookie," she said.

I took one and dunked it in my tea.

Margaret May arrived after school the very next day. I was lying in bed, but I could hear Mum at the door trying to persuade her that it wasn't a good idea for her to visit me. Not when her parents didn't know.

I could hear Margaret May being insistent and knew, with my mother's persistence, this was going to be a prolonged argument. But my mother, as usual, had the upper hand. She could close the door at any time.

So, I struggled out of bed to come and lend Margaret May my support.

"No," Mum was saying firmly. "You come back when you have your parents' permission and not before."

"But Grandma," she said.

Oh, good one, I thought. *Go for her sentiment.* How could she deny her granddaughter?

I could see Mum was wavering. Now was the time.

"Let her in, Mum," I said. "She's come all this way."

Mum turned around to look at me and Margaret May slipped in through the open door. I could see her coming toward me and I was afraid she was going to give me a hug. I put up my hands to protect myself. She stopped short, but I did not see kindness in her eyes.

"Do you want to sit in the parlour to talk while I get some tea?" Mum asked. She didn't look happy that she had been bested.

Margaret May looked from me to my mother and then back again. "All right," she said, then went through the glass doors into the parlour.

I followed her slowly and made my way to a tall stuffed chair with a high back that would be easy to get out of. Meanwhile, Margaret May sank into the deep armchair beside me. I could feel her silent anger, but I didn't have to wait long to know what it was about.

"Why did you give me up?" she cried. "Didn't you want me?"

"Oh," I said. "Yes, of course I wanted you. I wanted you very much but I had no say in the matter. Before you were even born, my mother and Cousin John — your grandfather — arranged your adoption."

"Really?" she asked.

"I don't think your parents knew anything about it, though, if that's any consolation."

"So, you didn't want to give me up for adoption?" she asked. "Mom told me I should have nothing to do with you because you didn't love me enough to keep me. You were too selfish."

"I wanted to keep you so much that it hurts even now. Your mom is right, though. I was selfish to tell you when you were better off not knowing."

"Really? You think I was better off not knowing the truth about who I am?"

Just then, Mum came in with the tea tray. Margaret May shot her a look of pure hatred. I wished again that I'd kept my big mouth shut.

Mum put the tray on the coffee table. "How do you like your tea, Margaret?" she asked as she poured a cup.

"Is it true that you and Grandpa arranged my adoption?" Margaret May asked in return.

Mum looked up from the teacup to her granddaughter, startled. The tea spilled over into the saucer. She stopped pouring and put down the pot. She looked at me.

"Why did you tell her that?"

"I was trying to explain that it wasn't my decision to give her up," I said. "You didn't want me to keep Margaret May."

"It's true, I didn't." She cupped one hand in the other and looked at Margaret May. "Edith was the same age as you are now and I wanted what was best for her. She wanted to be a teacher, but that was never going to happen if she had a baby."

"That never happened anyway," Margaret May said.

"That's because Edith was stubborn." Mum glared. "She was so angry with me for making her give you up that she left home and got a job."

Margaret May's expression softened.

"It's true," I said. "In those days, I dreamed that the war would end, that Arthur would come home and then we would look for you together. We would be a family. Instead, Arthur died, the war ended and, by then, you had a family of your own. I could never have broken it up. And I should not have told you now."

Margaret May smiled at me.

Mum looked concerned. "Margaret, you're still a child. For goodness sake, don't be so angry with your parents that you make the same mistake Edith did. They love you very much, you know."

"You didn't call my mom and tell her I was here, did you?" Margaret May asked.

"Of course, I did," Mum answered. "They have every right to know." Mum looked at both of us. "Now let's have tea."

Margaret May jumped up. "I should go," she said.

"Why?" I asked. "You should sit down and have some tea while you wait for your mother to come and get you. We can have a talk and get to know each other better while we wait." I glared at Mum. "After all, it may be the last chance we have to speak for a while."

The doorbell rang and Mum went quickly to answer it. We heard the voice of Margaret's mother and Margaret May trembled.

"Don't worry," I said. "Perhaps it's time to face the…" I was going to say *demon* but I should never speak of her mother that way. "To face the music."

Inside, I was trembling. We were just beginning to get to know each other. Would this be the last time I would speak to Margaret May in a long time? Until she became independent, whenever that would be. For her sake, I hoped it was longer rather than shorter. I didn't want her to make the same mistake I had made and lose her chance to be a teacher, if that's what she wanted.

Mum appeared at the parlour door with a guilty look on her face. "I'm sorry," she said, "but her mother had to be told."

Behind her, Margaret May's mother burst past my mother, pushing her aside.

"Try to be civilized," Mum said.

"What are you doing here?" her mother asked Margaret May.

Margaret May looked at the floor, about to cry. I had to help her out.

"She just wanted to talk to me. She wanted to know why I gave her up."

Margaret's mother turned on me. "You've done enough." There was such fury in her look, as if she were an ensnared animal ready to snap at anyone.

My mother touched Margaret May's shoulder gently. "Come with me," she said. "Let's leave your mothers to work it out."

Mothers. In that moment, I was almost as grateful to my mother as I was angry with her.

"I haven't finished talking to her!" the elder Margaret said.

"Leave her be," I said. "Your argument is with me."

Margaret turned back and looked at me as Mum and Margaret May slipped out the door.

"It sure is!" she shouted.

I was a little afraid to be left alone with her in that moment — afraid she would attack me.

"Why, oh why, did you have to ruin our lives?" She sat down on the armchair her daughter had just left and broke into tears.

I didn't know what to say to her. I looked down at my hands while words passed through my head — useless, unhelpful words. *You ruined mine first. You should have told her yourself.*

Finally, I said, "I was just as sad as you are now the day that I had to give her up." I leaned forward and touched her knee. "But you still have her. What are you crying for?"

"But now I have to share her," she said, giving me a dirty look, "with the likes of you."

"Don't worry about that," I said. "I won't hurt her. Besides you've had her to yourself for fifteen years. You'll always be number one mother.

You've had the greatest influence on her life. I'm just a little blip — a sideshow."

Margaret squinted at me and her sobbing ceased.

"She'll always love you best." I said it to make her feel better, but I knew it was probably true. And perhaps even the way it had to be. I could feel tears welling up in my own eyes. God, I didn't want to cry too. I looked down at my tea and concentrated on the still, calm liquid in the cup.

I looked up at Margaret. "I won't take her from you," I said. "Just let me see her and talk to her once in a while."

"You don't understand. She's at that age when she is always defying me. When we argue, she'll run to you and seek refuge and you'll take her side. I know you will."

"Perhaps," I said.

Margaret glared at me.

"No," I said firmly. "I won't. I want what's best for Margaret too. As much as you do. I don't want her to make the mistakes I made. I'll support you in whatever you decide is best for her even if I disagree — but on one condition — you let me see her once in a while."

"How can I trust you? You've already lied once. You promised you wouldn't tell her and then you did."

"It wasn't a fair promise!" I cried. "I should never have made it. If you let me see Margaret May and let us get to know each other better, I know I can keep this promise."

I stared at Margaret. She looked up.

"I'll do my best."

"What choice do I have?" she asked. "If I say no, Margaret will be even more rebellious."

"It's a deal, then?"

She glared at me again. "If you love her so much and want what's best for her, then why did you give her up for adoption?"

"It was not my choice," I said. "I was the same age as Margaret is now, and my mother and your father-in-law made the decision for me."

"James's father?" she asked, surprised. "He knew about this?"

I nodded.

She looked thoughtful for a moment. "That must be why he didn't want James and I to visit you all," she said. Then she picked up her purse. "That reminds me. I have to call James. He'll be wondering where we are and I haven't put supper on."

She stood up.

"It's a deal then?" I repeated. "We'll shake on it." I put out my hand.

Margaret looked at it as if it were dirty. But then she moved her purse to her left hand and shook mine with the right.

I breathed. For the first time since she'd entered the room, I felt my insides relax enough for my lungs to find space to fill. I wanted to lean over and kiss her cheek, but I felt sure she would slap me if I did. She hated me still. She would probably always hate me. I could live with that as long as I could see Margaret May and get to know her better.

The broken ribs healed, and Biddy and I moved back home. I went back to work.

The first thing I did was walk into Mr. Swayne's office. He looked up from his desk and glared at me. "Who are you and what do you want?"

"I am nobody," I said, "and I want to be somebody."

I let this sink in a moment while he continued staring at me.

"I have been working on this paper for fourteen years, first as a copyboy and then as a writer on the Social and Personal Page." I swallowed hard and looked deep within for my resolve. "I want to be a real reporter and report on the news of the day."

His eyebrows shot up to his hairline. He shook his head.

"I don't think so," he said.

I was outraged. "Are you saying no to me because I'm a woman?"

He nodded. "It's no small impediment to the job of being a reporter."

I took a deep breath before responding, but he interrupted my next words.

"Before you get your knickers in a knot, perhaps we can come to some sort of agreement."

I didn't think so, but I was curious. "Go on," I said.

"Jack Kerne has done a good job as editor of the Social Page. I think it's time he moved on to another section of the paper. If he accepts, which I'm sure he will, we'd be looking for a new Social Page editor. Are you up for the challenge?"

I didn't respond at first. It was not what I wanted. But it was not so bad either. If I said no, what would that get me? I had to accept and to accept graciously.

"I would be honoured," I said.

"There you see," he said. "I knew we could come to an understanding. Now tell Jack to come in here and we'll hash this all out. He'll train you in your new position before he moves on to his." He waved the back of his hand at me. "Now, off you go."

Epilogue

~~~ ~~~ ~~~ ~~~ ~~~ ~~~ ~~~ ~~~ ~~~ ~~~ ~~~ ~~~ ~~~ ~~~ ~~~ ~~~

I was only fifteen and some would say — my mother, for one — that it wasn't a serious affair of the heart, it was only puppy love. But no, I am sure, if things had turned out differently, we would have married. Arthur and Edith would be an old married couple now, sitting together before the fire, reminiscing about our high school days.

Sometimes when I'm alone of an evening, that is a scene I like to imagine. I turn to the chair where Biddy's grandkitten, Virago, is curled up asleep and I talk to her as if she were Arthur.

"Remember the time when we first heard about the war being declared? We were practising for a play. What was the play, Arthur? Was it *The Importance of Being Earnest*? No, nothing so grand as that. *The Playboy of the Western World*, perhaps?"

Virago looks up at me, stares for a long moment as if settling into Arthur's role, blinks, then puts her head back down.

"No, you're right, Arthur. It was nothing that famous. Probably something called *Blue Stocking* by a nobody named Mrs. Peabody. Totally forgotten now." Then I break into song: "I've got her on my list — the lady novelist — she never will be missed."

And Arthur says something like "You shouldn't be bitter" and my dander gets up.

Tea at the Empress

"Why shouldn't I be bitter? We were talking about the war and you know what came of that."

"No," he says. "No, we were imagining that the war never happened and that I'm here with you and that we're happy."

"And you would be here, Arthur, and we *would* be happy if you hadn't been so gung-ho, so ready and willing to rush off to fight for king and country."

And the old man Arthur, whose face I can't really imagine anyway, disappears to be replaced by that eighteen-year-old boy, whose face is lit by the fires of patriotism and the thought of going off to fight the Hun. I want to reach out to him and tell him, "No, don't be foolish," but this is a memory and instead I see my fifteen-year-old self, foolish and giddy and impressed with the enthusiasm of the time.

Is it the warmth of the fire that makes me flush so? Or is it remembering your earnest face imploring me to have carnal knowledge with you before you embark on your perilous journey across the sea?

I would, you know. Even now, I would.

226

Also by Edeana Malcolm

House of Crows

"Written from seeds scattered through archival sources, the women's voices in this novel have an authenticity seldom seen in historical fiction. They say that crows speak a specific dialect unique to the West Coast, and this novel captures that language from the vantage point of the newcomer."

SHERI-D WILSON, D. Litt, C.M., Member of the Order of Canada, Poet Laureate Emeritus of Calgary (2018–2020) and author of *Open Letter: Woman against Violence against Women*

EDEANA MALCOLM

THREE GENERATIONS OF WOMEN struggle and toil against harsh realities and constant challenges to better their lot in life and build a future for their family, from a work camp to their shared home with a view of the posh residences along the water's edge. With two dressed in widow's weeds and one in a maid's uniform, their home gains the nickname 'the House of Crows'.

Edie journeys across oceans, searching for the place where she can build a home.

Lucy readies herself for the challenges of a new world, only to suffer loss after loss.

Maggie slaves away her days in service to the rich, never losing hope that more awaits.

Interwoven timelines explore the earliest days of Victoria, illuminating the oft-forgotten histories of the women who laid the groundwork for the world we know today.

299 pages · 6×9" · ISBN 978-1-988915-26-5
threeoceanpress.com/authors/edeana-malcolm

About the Author

Edeana Malcolm loves a good cup of tea and conversation with friends and family. She's a history nerd, a mother of three and a grandmother of four.

She lives with her husband, David Bray, across from the Gorge Park, an important location in *Tea at the Empress*. The Japanese gardens that were destroyed during the Second World War have been restored, but sadly, there is no tea house on the site as yet.

Edeana is the current president of the Victoria Writers' Society and also the chair of the Board of First Metropolitan United Church, formerly First Presbyterian, Edith's family's church in *Tea at the Empress*.

CPSIA information can be obtained
at www.ICGtesting.com
Printed in the USA
LVHW030214200323
741981LV00008B/529